RED

SNIPER

RED

SNIPER

A THRILLER

DAVID HEALEY

INTRACOASTAL

Intracoastal Media digital edition published 2017. Print edition published 2017.

This book is a work of fiction. Names, characters, places and incidents are products of the author's imagination or are used fictitiously. Any resemblance to actual events or locales or persons, living or dead, is entirely coincidental.

Cover art by Streetlight Graphics.

BISAC Subject Headings:
FIC014000 FICTION/Historical
FIC032000 FICTION/War & Military

ISBN: 0692847952
ISBN: 978-0692847954

Let us learn to appreciate that there will be times when the trees will be bare, and look forward to the time when we may pick the fruit..
—Anton Chekhov (1860-1904)

This one's for mom and all the encouragement she gave her family over the years. We love you and miss you.

PROLOGUE

Standing in the Oval Office, President Harrison Whitlock IV reached out and took down the brutal horse whip that hung on the wall just to the left of the most famous desk in the world.

Technically, this was a Cossack whip or *nagyka,* once used by Russian teamsters to control their massive draft horses. It also happened to make a cruel weapon. The whip consisted of a wooden handle that measured eighteen inches in length, covered in braided horsehide that elongated into the whip itself. The *nagyka* was just about three feet long.

The leather was starting to dry rot and the battered *nagyka* looked out of place in the formal presidential surroundings that included portraits of George Washington and Abraham Lincoln. In truth, the whip held nothing but bad memories. The president kept it there, however, as a reminder of a time when he had lived in fear of that lash.

More and more these days, Harry Whitlock's thoughts seemed to return to those times. Just getting old, he thought. Given that the war had ended fifty years before, it was likely that he would be the last president to have served in World War II. Back then, as a very young pilot, his B-17 had been shot down over Germany. One could still catch a glimpse of that young man in the president's bright blue eyes.

"Sir?" his chief of staff had materialized and caught him reminiscing.

"It's all right, Bob," the president said, turning to face his chief of staff and the business of the day, but not before returning the whip to its place on the wall.

The whip served as a reminder that freedom must be defended, and that it comes with a price.

CHAPTER 1

Micajah "Caje" Cole squinted through the eight power telescopic sight of his Springfield rifle, looking for a target. Somewhere in the ruins of a barn high above the road, a German sniper was dug in like a tick on the back of a coonhound. That one enemy soldier had managed to pin down an entire squad that was an element of the advance toward Berlin.

Cole considered his options, none of which were good.

Too far away to get a grenade in there. They had an M1919 machine gun, which might make the sniper keep his head down, but it was ineffectual against the thick stone walls. What they needed was a battering ram. Maybe a tank.

All Cole had was a bullet.

Vaccaro crouched beside Cole, his head well below the stone wall that bordered the road. "Punch his ticket, Hillbilly, and let's get the hell out of here," he muttered.

"Ain't that easy," Cole replied, his eye playing over the ancient stones of the barn, the empty gaping windows, the slate roof. *Where you at?* The enemy sniper may as well have been hunkered down inside a fortress. The sniper had chosen his hiding place well, Cole conceded, because the barn had a commanding view of the road below.

Keeping his eye pressed to the telescopic sight, Cole puzzled it out.

So much of surviving as a sniper was about getting inside the other guy's head. Cole thought about what he would have done in the German's shoes. He would be back from a window, shooting from deep inside the barn in order to be less of a target. The squad had already poured bullets into the windows until Lieutenant Mulholland called a ceasefire. The only real possibility for the German's hiding place was the window in the loft, from which the sniper could shoot anything that moved on the road.

But how experienced was this sniper? He doubted that the German pinning them down was much more than a boy with a rifle. In these last weeks of the war, it was considered good enough to give a soldier a week of training, along with a rifle that had a telescopic sight, and call him a sniper. Cole damn well knew it took more than that, especially if the sniper expected to outlast his first day on the job.

Unfortunately, these Germans had the advantage of knowing the ground, and they also had desperation on their side. Making it worse was the fact that the young ones tended to be fanatics. Although the enemy snipers the Americans had been encountering were barely more than teenagers, they were all too deadly.

This sniper had waited until the squad was directly below, and then had picked off two men. Their bodies lay in the muddy road where no one could reach them now.

To Cole, it seemed like a waste, dying so close to the end of the war. Everybody talked about that, how they didn't want to get killed when the war was sure to end any week now. Nobody wanted to stick his neck out. For the two dead guys, walking down a road in Germany had been their final act of the war.

"This guy is acting like it's the last stand of the Reich," Vaccaro muttered.

"I reckon for him, that's just what it is," Cole said.

The Germans were done. It didn't take a

general to see that. Germany's looming defeat was obvious to the lowliest private. At the sight of approaching troops, German civilians came out of their houses, grim faced, waving white handkerchiefs. Since D-Day in June 1944, the Allied troops had pushed steadily across France and Belgium. Cole and Vaccaro had walked nearly every step of the way since June, and for most of those months all they had done was fight. The Germans' final attempt to turn the tide of the war had come in December 1944 at the Ardennes Forest during what the Americans had labeled The Battle of the Bulge. They had been in the thick of the German breakout attempt in the Ardennes, where their sniper skills had been put to the test again and again.

Now it was April 1945 and it was only a matter of time before Germany was defeated. The Americans were on German soil. Rumors flew about what Hitler was up to, but it was likely that Der Fuhrer and his minions were holed up like rats somewhere in Berlin, probably deep in a bunker with lots of champagne and plenty to eat, hoping for a miracle.

Cole glanced up at the contrails in the sky, wispy fingers of white dragging across the blue dome above as Allied bombers made their way to the next target. The war was happening on the ground, as well as in the sky.

While the Third Reich, for all practical

purposes, was over—*kaput*—not everyone had gotten the message or wanted to believe it. Germans were still being urged to fight to the bitter end, hence the last stands like the one taking place in this barn. Cole had been a hunter and trapper long before he was a soldier, and he knew too well that a cornered and wounded animal was the most dangerous kind.

Cole turned to Vaccaro. "You still got that tent?" he asked.

Vaccaro groaned. "You think he's dumb enough to fall for that?"

"Unless you got a better idea."

Vaccaro sighed and dug around in his pack for the tent. In fact, it was a canvas shelter half, or half a tent. It could be buttoned together with another shelter half to form an actual tent. Cole carried the other half strapped to the top of his pack.

"I suppose you want me to use my helmet, too."

"Mine's already got one bullet hole in it," Cole pointed out. A German sniper named Kurt Von Stenger had put it there.

With a dramatic sigh, Vaccaro whipped off his helmet and jammed it onto the sausaged canvas. Through trial and error, the two snipers had found that a helmet on the end of a shelter half, raised above a wall or poked around a tree, looked convincingly like an actual GI's head. The grungy canvas resembled a grimy face just enough to fool a distant sniper. They had tried using a helmet on a stick in the past, but it wobbled too much. A helmet held in one's hands had the problem of there being nothing beneath it—and besides that, it wasn't a good idea to have actual body parts anywhere near a high velocity Mauser round.

"Ready?" Vaccaro asked.

"Yep." He drew in a breath, held it. Kept the rifle scope focused on the barn window.

The rifle was a Springfield Model M1903A4 in .30/06 caliber. Cole knew its lines and curves intimately, and the stock fit against his shoulder and jawline like a part of his own body.

He sensed the movement in his peripheral vision as Vaccaro slithered a few feet away and popped the helmet above the wall. The trick was to do it fast, before the sniper had time to think. You just wanted him to react and shoot before he figured out that he was firing at a decoy. Along with very little experience, the sniper in the barn was bound to have an itchy trigger finger.

"Here goes nothin'," Vaccaro muttered, and popped the helmet above the wall.

Right on cue, the German in the barn fired, his bullet smacking into the helmet and shelter half with enough force to knock it out of Vaccaro's grip. Vaccaro muttered a curse.

There. Deep back in the darkness of the barn,

Cole spotted the enemy sniper's muzzle flash, no brighter than a firefly on a July night. Locking his crosshairs on the spot where he had seen the flash, he touched the trigger at the same instant and the rifle pounded into his shoulder.

He slid down behind the stone wall next to Vaccaro. "Got him," he said.

Cole could not say exactly how he knew that. It was as if he could feel the bullet hitting home.

Vaccaro was more cautious. He insisted on giving the helmet-above-the-wall trick one more try, although it would be a sorry sniper who fell for the same trick twice. Maybe a kid with a rifle would. This time, no shot came.

Vaccaro looked at him.

"When you're right, you're right," Cole said.

"In that case, you go first."

"On three." With Vaccaro covering him, Cole slid over the wall and ran in a crouch toward the barn. Vaccaro came right behind him. Cole poked the muzzle of the rifle into the barn and held his breath, listening for some sign that the sniper might still be alive. Most of the time, he could sense a person hiding in a building. It was like their body gave off vibrations.

Now, there was only a deathly stillness. He went on in, rifle at the ready.

They found the sniper on the floor of the hay loft. He lay with the slack pose of the dead. Cole's bullet had hit him in the chest. The sniper's face was untouched, the blue eyes gazing sightlessly out from the rim of his *Stahlhelm*. This sniper couldn't have been much more than seventeen or eighteen. Blond peach fuzz on his upper lip.

"I am so sick of this shit," Vaccaro muttered, looking down at the dead boy's face. Vaccaro was always playing the smart aleck when he wasn't playing the macho Italian guy from Brooklyn, but there was nothing macho about his expression at that moment. He looked deflated, like someone had punched him in the gut.

Cole grunted. He didn't like killing kids, either. But the fact remained that this young sniper had shot two Americans on the road below. Cole thought it was a lousy place to die— not that he had seen many good places, come to think of it.

This kid had killed them, and there was a price to pay for that.

Maybe you couldn't entirely blame this dead kid, considering that he'd been brainwashed since childhood, having come of age in Nazi Germany. That didn't change the fact that were now three dead men on this nameless stretch of road.

Some dust had stuck to his rifle barrel, just in front of the action. Cole rubbed it away with his thumb. There was something reassuring about the tangible feel of the metal, still warm from the bullet he had fired a minute before. The smell of gunpowder filled his nostrils. He hefted the familiar weight of the rifle in his hands. He pushed whatever regrets he had about killing the young enemy sniper to the back of his mind and locked them away.

He would never have told this to Vaccaro or to anyone else, but he was not sick of this at all. He dreaded seeing it end. It was not because he enjoyed the killing, but he *did* like the way that being on the hunt—even being hunted—made him feel so alive.

There wasn't a damned thing he could do after the war that would come close. Other men had lives and families to go back to. What did he have but a crowded shack in the mountains and a few dozen rusty beaver traps to set in Gashey's Creek? Was he going to set up a still and drink most of what he made, like his pa had?

It wasn't a whole hell of a lot to look forward to. Cole wondered if maybe there was something wrong with him, because he wouldn't mind if the war went on a while longer.

"Come on," he said gruffly to Vaccaro, turning away from the young sniper's body. "We've still got a few hours of daylight. Let's see if we can make it to the next town before dark."

CHAPTER 2

Yegor Barkov had seen his share of bad situations, and he didn't like this one at all. He stood on the marshy plain just west of the Oder River, looking up at the high ground beyond, where masses of German troops were dug in to make their last stand on what was known as the Sellow Heights.

His commander had once pointed out that Barkov was an imaginative man, so it was not surprising that when studying the German fortifications before him, he had the passing thought that this was how the hammer must look to the nail.

He clutched his Mosin-Nagant sniper's rifle in his big, rough hands and tried instinctively to get the lay of the land so that he could put that rifle to use.

"At least it isn't Stalingrad," said Oleg Tarasyuk beside him. The little man hawked and spat to further illustrate his opinion of Stalingrad. He was also a sniper, and the two had been together through thick and thin during these long years of the war. Where Barkov was massive as a bull, Tarasyuk gave the impression of some small, quick animal that was fond of baring its sharp teeth. He had earned the nickname *norka*, which was Russian for *mink*, a furbearer often made into sleek coats but that had a nasty disposition in the wild.

"What do you want to bet that these stupid generals want us to march right into those German guns?"

"Yegor," the Mink cautioned, ever mindful that one of the political officers might overhear. Like a mink, he lived by his wits.

Barkov hadn't needed to say it; they both knew well enough that marching right into the guns was just what was going to happen. Marshal Zhukov had lined up his army across from the Germans entrenched on Seelow Heights. It was the nature of the Soviet army that generals were expected to out-do one another, and Zhukov could sense the other generals snapping at his heels. Stalin encouraged competition over cooperation. It was better to have the generals at each other's throats, after all, than at his own.

Stalin wanted Berlin so badly that he could taste it, and he did not care how many men it took to overwhelm the German defenses. Lives meant nothing to him. By default, Marshal Zukov could place no value on the lives needed to sweep aside the Germans. The problem was that the Germans did not want to be swept.

Barkov and Oleg had been fighting Germans nearly every inch of the way from Stalingrad, pushing the Germans back, again and again. It was clear by now that the Germans were not simply giving up, so now here they were at Seelow Heights.

Marshal Zhukov had Stalin himself breathing down his neck to make some progress. Hourly telephone calls from Stalin were not unusual. Stalin wanted immediate results, so Marshal Zhukov had developed a brilliant strategy for a full-on frontal assault. If this was going to fail, in Zhukov's eyes it was best to do so spectacularly. Artillery was being moved in to soften up the German positions first.

From somewhere in front of the Russian lines, a rifle shot rang out. An officer a hundred meters away crumpled and fell. It was the second officer that the German sniper had shot in the last thirty minutes.

The sound of the German sniper at work was like music to Barkov's ears. With any luck, he and the Mink could get themselves assigned to picking off the sniper, which would help them avoid the suicidal slaughter that Marshal Zhukov clearly had planned.

Barkov was no coward, but he was a survivor. One did not last long as a sniper without being wily. What was the point in dying stupidly?

Barkov thought about his options. The political officers to the rear would shoot any man who turned back from the front lines. In the Russian army, courage was strictly enforced at gunpoint. The sniper's rifle was something of a talisman enabling him to move more freely than the average soldier.

"Come on, Oleg. Let us see if we can put our talents to use."

The Mink understood Barkov's meaning at once. The two of them headed toward the rear, with the thought that they could move off to the flank in pursuit of the German sniper. Their chances of survival would be marginally better once the assault began.

They hadn't gone far when a commissar appeared, pointing a pistol at them. There was a dead boy at the commissar's feet, presumably a young soldier whose nerves had failed him and who had been stopped from fleeing with a bullet from the pistol. Only the fact that Barkov and Oleg were calmly walking, rather than running for the rear, kept the commissar from shooting them outright.

"Get back to your positions!"

"Comrade, we have been ordered to move to the flank to engage the German sniper," Barkov said.

The commissar did not lower his weapon. Barkov felt his mouth go dry. It was just like a commissar not to have any appreciation for military strategy. Political officers tended to fall into two categories. There were the ones who were too smart for their own good, and the ones who were too stupid for anyone's good. This one had a lumpy face like a potato and eyes too small for his head, which seemed to put him into the second category.

In addition to being stupid, the commissar was a scrawny man, and if he had not been holding a pistol—and particularly if he had not been a commissar—Barkov would have taken two steps forward and snapped his neck like kindling.

The political officer nodded and waved them on with the pistol. That was the Soviet army for you, Barkov thought. The generals and the political officers were all eager to kill you before the Germans even had their chance.

"That one was a real shit for brains," Barkov muttered.

The Mink replied, "One of these days you're going to say that too loud, and it's then it's off to the Gulag for you."

Barkov shrugged, and then he and Oleg trudged on toward the flank, where they set up hides for themselves.

Barkov got behind a dead horse, which was starting to stink, but was good for stopping bullets. On the ground, he appeared heavy and shapeless, like a big sack of grain dumped there. The Mink, who was a much smaller man, got into position beside him and scanned the marshland beyond through his telescopic sight. It was their habit when they worked together that the Mink served as the spotter.

"See anything?" Barkov asked.

"No sign of the sniper. But you could probably hit one of those machine gunners from here."

"Good idea."

"Try the one at two o'clock."

Through his scope, Barkov saw a couple of square helmets peeking from above the rim of a trench. They probably thought they were safe— the distance was at the more extreme range for the Mosin Nagant sniper rifle. Meanwhile, the Germans were really chewing things up with an MG 42, spitting twelve hundred rounds per minute toward the Russian lines. The gun fired so fast that it made a sound like tearing paper.

Someone had nicknamed it "Hitler's bone saw."

As a sniper, Barkov knew his trade after long years of war. He had been born in a remote commune on the edge of Siberia, which was, as an American might say, on the wrong side of the tracks. No one of consequence came from Siberia; it was where Russians were sent to be punished or re-educated. But a Siberian knew how to hunt, and Barkov had moved easily from stalking wolves to stalking men. Barkov also possessed a kind of animal cunning for survival that served him well as a sniper. Like any predator, he possessed a ruthless streak. There was no sentiment in Barkov. He did not sing along when the other Russians sang their ballads, but drank his vodka in silence. He did not write letters home. He did not have faith in Stalin or his commissars. He found his satisfaction in being a good hunter.

He put the post sight of his reticle a foot above the helmet and a little to the right to account for the wind. There was no formula for this—Barkov simply used the experience of a hundred other shots just like this one to aim. He squeezed the trigger. *Pop*. Down went the German. Barkov lowered his head behind the dead horse's belly, but no one shot back at him.

"You want to move?" the Mink asked.

"I don't think anyone spotted us," Barkov said. "We'll take at least one more shot from here before it gets dark, and then we can find another position."

They still couldn't locate the sniper, so Barkov picked off another German machine gunner. Enough of the man was exposed that this time he took a belly shot, so that the German would scream for a while in agony, discouraging his fellow soldiers. The noise carried on well after dark. Barkov lay there listening the way that some listened to birds singing, a faint smile on his lips.

He and the Mink were just getting ready to move when the Soviet artillery opened up. The ground beneath them rumbled and they both covered their ears. It sounded like the end of the world, and for the Germans on Seelow Heights, it was exactly that.

• • •

Unfortunately for his troops, Marshal Zhukov would discover that the Germans defending Seelow Heights were not fools. They could see the Russian artillery moving in, so under cover of darkness the Germans withdrew their forces from the first defensive line and deployed them in the secondary defenses instead. The Russian shells rained down on empty fortifications.

Zhukov had an innovation planned for his nighttime assault. Giant searchlights were maneuvered into place, and switched on as the order to attack was given. Instead of providing illumination as intended, the lights created chaos. The bombardment had filled the humid marsh air with smoke from the exploding shells, along with dust and bits of vegetation that swirled like confetti, all of it mixing together to create a low haze that hung over the ground. The searchlights reaching into this haze created a blinding mist, leaving the Russian army to stumble forward, much like an automobile trying to drive into a wall of fog with its bright beams on.

The Russians couldn't see a thing. Many troops were under the false impression that Zhukov had brought into play some sort of super weapon to turn the tide of battle. How wrong they were.

On their heights, where the shelling hadn't reached them, the Germans could see the advancing Russians backlit in the fog. The enemy was silhouetted like so many paper targets. Fire from machine guns and small arms poured into the Russian ranks, cutting them to ribbons. Fresh troops pressed forward from the rear.

Barkov and the Mink crept forward, taking their time, yet not so slow that they would earn a bullet in the back from one of the commissars. Thirty minutes passed, then an hour.

The whine and whisper of bullets still filled the glowing darkness. They started stumbling over the bodies of the first ranks of Russian soldiers, mixed here and there were a few dead Germans.

"It looks like our boys caught a German sniper," the Mink announced.

He was standing over a body in the bottom of a shell hole. The man was nearly naked, his trousers down to his knees and his shirt gone, and his torso was covered in cuts. But these were not shrapnel wounds—on closer inspection, it was apparent that he had been sliced and stabbed multiple times by bayonets—no single one of which would have been a killing wound. In the Soviet army, snipers were celebrated as specialized soldiers and heroes. However, German snipers were seen as sneaky, inhuman scum, and treated accordingly. The fast-moving Russians wouldn't have bothered to torture just any soldier, and the fact that he was a sniper was evidenced by the scoped rifle, the muzzle of which had been jammed far up the German's rectum.

"One less for us to worry about," Barkov said.

The Mink knelt down beside the body. "Hey, this one is still alive, poor bastard. We should finish him off." The Mink moved to shoot the German, but Barkov reached out to stop him.

"Death would be a mercy," he said. "Let him suffer a while."

The Mink grinned. "Of course. What was I

thinking?"

They stayed in the shell hole for a few minutes, getting their bearings. The Mink went through the bloody rags that remained of the helpless sniper's clothes and found some chocolate, which he shared with Barkov. They munched while the man lay there moaning.

From the sounds ahead, it was clear that the attack on Seelow Heights pressed forward. Some military genius had finally figured out that the searchlights were causing more harm than good, and one by one they blinked off, leaving the battlefield illuminated only by small burning fires. By then the damage was already done, however. Bodies blanketed the marshes and hills. Barkov couldn't have known it then, but decades later, the skeletons of the dead would still be turning up whenever there was a heavy rain or a construction project in the vicinity.

The Russian strategy had been to overwhelm the Germans with sheer numerical superiority. For every two Russian soldiers mowed down, another one or two had gotten through the killing fields to make a direct attack on the German positions. Those numbers had been enough. Inexorably, foxhole by foxhole, the defenders of Seelow Heights were being defeated.

"Come on, we don't want to miss any of the fun," Barkov said, and the two snipers trotted in the direction of Berlin, still many miles away.

CHAPTER 3

High above Germany, the B-17 Flying Fortress left behind a white contrail as if someone had dragged a piece of chalk across the slate blue sky. The plane was just one of a squadron flying in formation. At the controls of the lead bomber was Harrison Whitlock IV, a 22-year-old first lieutenant who had left Harvard University in his junior year to join the Army Air Corps.

This was his fourteenth mission with the *Lucky Girl*, as the crew had decided to call the plane. It had cost Whitlock twenty bucks to get a private who had been an art student at Columbia to decorate the fuselage with a portrait of a buxom young woman with flowing red hair. She wasn't based on anyone Whitlock or the other young crewmen had known outside of their fantasies, but she was just their sort of ideal girl —that is, all tits and ass and gratitude—that they wouldn't have minded coming back to at the end of a mission. They liked to joke that they would make her one Lucky Girl, all right.

Maybe it was silly to be motivated by a girl straight out of a fantasy, but 27,000 feet up with German flak coming at you, you held on to what you could.

"Smooth air so far today," said Chip Bronson, the co-pilot.

"Don't jinx us," said Whitlock, who was known for being easygoing, except when he took command of the *Lucky Girl*, at which time he became a hard ass. That was just fine with the nine other crew members aboard the *Lucky Girl* who put their faith in Whitlock to get them back home in one piece. Whitlock had done just that so far, but they were all well aware that sometimes a plane and its crew just drew the short straw when it came to luck, regardless of the girl on the fuselage.

They had seen it happen on their third mission, when the tail gunner shot a German fighter practically right out of the sky. They had all cheered on the intercom, but then watched in horror as the cartwheeling fighter slammed into another B-17. Silence had fallen as the B-17 plummeted to earth, too quickly for any parachutes to get out. Back on the ground, they never had talked about it.

"Not a bandit in sight," Bronson said.

"What did I just say about jinxing us?"

Bronson smirked, clearly busting the pilot's chops, and they flew on in silence. Whitlock had to admit that the job had gotten a little easier over the last few weeks. The Luftwaffe was mostly gone from the skies. Earlier in the air war, that had not been the case at all, and the German fighters had devastated the B-17 bombers.

For defensive purposes, it was critical to stay in formation. The fighter escorts did not have the range of the bombers, and so had to turn back as the bombers pressed deeper and deeper into German territory as the weeks progressed. That left the B-17s unprotected from the Messerschmitt fighters. However, it wasn't for nothing that the American bombers were called Flying Fortresses. With an array of heavy machine guns, a B-17 created a defensive perimeter around itself. The Germans nicknamed the B-17s "Flying Porcupines" for good reason. There were weak points and blind spots, however, which was why it was critical to stay in position. The squadron's formation enabled the planes to cover one another, thus creating a zone of defense around their bombers.

That was the theory, anyhow, and it all sounded good in flight school. Reality was a bit different. A German Me109 moved at more than four hundred miles per hour, fired 20 mm cannon rounds that left holes the size of a softball in a bomber's thin skin, and flew circles around the lumbering B-17. In close air combat, it tested the limits of human reflexes to be able to swivel and fire at a target moving at that speed. To be sure, it took a young man's reflexes. Whitlock used to do some trapshooting with his grandfather, Senator Harrison Whitlock II, and it had been hard enough to hit a clay pigeon with a 12-gauge shotgun. Compared to a German fighter, a clay pigeon now seemed like a slow, lumbering target. And the clay pigeon wasn't shooting back.

It took a lot of firing, and a lot of luck, to knock a German fighter out of the sky. Fortunately, the B-17 made up for being slow by being tough. *Lucky Girl* could take an awful lot of abuse of the flying lead variety.

As they neared the target, bursts of flak began to claw the sky. *Lucky Girl* danced in the turbulence from the explosions. Whitlock tried not to think too much about what it would mean to take a direct hit. Until a few months ago, he had never heard of the word "flak," which was a British interpretation of what the Germans called *Flug Abarhr Kanone*—anti-aircraft ordnance. Now he was all too aware of the word. Call it whatever you wanted—by any name it was nerve-wracking as hell.

The intercom crackled, and the navigator came on to give him an update.

"Hey Cap, we're getting close."

Whitlock glanced at his own map, which was more rudimentary than the navigator's. He could see they were near the drop zone. He got the bombardier on the intercom.

"I'll hold her steady," Whitlock said. "You send the presents down the chimney."

On this plane, there were several jobs going on at once. The navigator. The bombardier. The flight engineer. The radio operator. Four separate gunners, including the Sperry ball turret gunner, provided defense. And there was a co-pilot, in case Whitlock caught a piece of that flak, or became otherwise incapacitated. His own job was to get them to the target and back in one piece.

Every crew member could hear the mechanical whirring as the bomb bay doors opened. *Lucky Girl* shuddered and a different pitch or sound filled the plane, which was now exposed to the terrible cold of high altitude Germany.

"We are on target," announced the bombardier, his voice made crackly by the intercom. Whitlock could imagine him hunched over the Norden bombsight in the nose of the aircraft. "Bombs away!"

The bomber's payload dropped, whistling toward the earth far below. A single pound of high explosive contained enough energy to turn an object the size of a pickup truck into scrap metal. By comparison, each bomb carried by *Lucky Girl* contained up to 500 pounds of high explosive, enough to level a factory—and then some. The squadron had just dropped several dozen such bombs.

Whitlock tried not to think too much about the people far below. They were only bombing military targets, but that definition had become broader with each passing month. These were not the front lines. There were schools, churches, and homes down there. Death from above did not always discriminate. And Whitlock was the courier.

Far below, they watched the impact of the bombs pucker the German landscape.

With the bombs dropped, it was now Whitlock's job as pilot to get them home. In a long, graceful maneuver in the thin air, the squadron turned together, and started back.

They flew through another curtain of flak. Hot metal splinters raked the air.

The co-pilot leaned forward, peering into the sky ahead. The lumpy patches of cloud provided good cover for enemy fighters waiting to pounce.

Whitlock gave his co-pilot a nervous sideways

look. They all knew that the Luftwaffe was down, but not out. Even at this late stage of the war, the enemy managed to scramble a few fighters.

"You see something?" Whitlock asked.

"Nah, there's nothing." Then Bronson bolted in his chair. "Wait! We've got a bandit at three o'clock!"

"I see him!"

"What the hell?" Bronson's voice was shrill. "That guy came out of nowhere!"

Whitlock shouted a warning over the intercom, but it was too late. The Messerschmitt gave them a good raking before they could get off a shot or take any defensive measures.

The big holes in the thin aluminum skin appeared almost instantly, where there had been metal before. The 20 mm cannons of the German fighter had taken a big bite out of them. In places, *Lucky Girl*'s fuselage now resembled a colander. He looked over at Bronson, who was slumped in his chair, head lolling on his chest. He reached over to help the unconscious co-pilot, then saw the gaping wound in his neck. *Jesus. He's a goner.*

"Bronson's been hit," Whitlock announced over the intercom. "Everybody else OK? Stay awake back there. You know that bandit is going to come around again."

"How bad is Bronson?" the bombardier asked. "You need some help up there?"

"He's dead," Whitlock said flatly. He was too shocked by Bronson's death for it to even register. And there would be no time for it to sink in. He looked out the cockpit window at the rapidly approaching German fighter. "Here he comes again!"

The German made a second pass. This time, the crew of *Lucky Girl* was ready and opened fire with everything they had. The German plane flashed past, seemingly unharmed. *Lucky Girl* hadn't gotten off nearly so easy. Smoke began pouring from one of the port engines, smearing the sky with a greasy black stain. Seconds later, bright orange flames licked at the wing.

Through the intercom, he could hear shouts of panic and alarm. Had anyone else been hit? He glanced out the window to his left. The engine was now engulfed in flames. Reluctantly, he gave the order to abandon the aircraft.

"We are on fire," Whitlock said into the intercom. He dispensed with any sort of formal orders. "Everybody out!"

The crew was well drilled in the procedure, but drills were one thing, and reality was another. In a drill, there was no smell of blood and leaking fuel, no crackle of flames or whistle of cold air through the bullet holes in the fuselage. As the pilot, Whitlock would be the last to leave, much as the captain was the last one to abandon a sinking ship. Whitlock wrestled with the controls, trying to keep the plane steady so that the others could evacuate. His stomach lurched as the plane dropped altitude at a sickening pace.

The bombardier and navigator exited through the bomb bay area. The two waist gunners and tail gunner had an escape hatch at the rear of the plane. It would take the ball turret gunner some time to extricate himself from the transparent globe suspended from the belly of the plane. One by one, parachutes bloomed. Whitlock kept count. When he got to eight, meaning that the other crew had evacuated, he unbuckled his safety belt and made his way to the hatch.

He paused for a moment and looked around at the aircraft, which shuddered now as she began to go into her death throes. Goodbye, *Lucky Girl*. It felt like he was abandoning a living, breathing creature instead of a fragile structure of metal supports and aluminum skin.

Below him, the German countryside reminded him of a green, checkered tablecloth that his mother used to bring on picnics. He gulped, not really wanting to jump. It was a long, long way down, and while he had practiced parachuting, he had never actually jumped.

The plane shivered, and snapped him back to reality. There really wasn't any other choice.

He leaped.

One of the most dangerous moments in parachuting was getting past the tail structure, which could club a man fatally. Whitlock spun, free falling, and then he was relieved to hear the sound of the chute opening above him. Almost instantaneously, he felt the sharp tug of the parachute itself.

Beneath his dangling feet, he could see enemy territory rushing up at him.

• • •

Whitlock found that descending by parachute was both thrilling and terrifying. On the one hand, Whitlock felt glad to have made it out of the doomed plane. He could see it breaking up, leaving a trail of smoke and flame across the blue sky. Other chutes floated down in the distance. Below him, he felt a sense of awe while watching the patchwork quilt of fields getting larger, and then there was a particular field below him.

His heart hammered in his chest because he seemed to be coming in too fast. He hit the ground and rolled, just as he had been trained to do. A few moments later he was back on his feet, assessing how he felt. Aside from a twinge in his ankle, he seemed to have landed unscathed.

He looked around. The sky was devoid of planes or parachutes. He had no idea where the other *Lucky Girl* crew members had landed.

Now he was totally alone in enemy territory. He had landed in *Germany*. That thought overwhelmed his sense of relief at being back on the ground.

Unfortunately for Whitlock, his descent had not gone unnoticed. As he wrestled with the chute, trying to get out of the harness, he saw a truck with bluish-gray paint drive up at the edge of the field. Three figures started running toward him. Soldiers.

Whitlock looked around him. The field was large, and there was absolutely no cover. He was having a hard time getting out of the harness. By the time he did, the soldiers were close enough that he could make out the details of their faces under the square helmets. Damn, but two of them were fast. He soon saw why. The quick soldiers were just teenagers, skinny and rangy. The third soldier, who was running more slowly, bringing up the rear, was practically an old man, closer to sixty than forty. The trio was some sort of home guard, then, not regular Wehrmacht. That did not change the fact that all three had rifles. Pointing at him.

When he raised his arms in surrender, he realized that he was shaking.

• • •

The two younger Germans looked excited about having captured an American. Wearing giddy smiles, the boys herded Whitlock toward the truck at gunpoint. It was as if they had just won a game of Capture the Flag, and he was the prize.

The older man looked grim, evidently more aware than the boys of the seriousness of the situation. He did not seem to outrank the boys, at least not by any rank visible on his uniform, but was their de facto commander due to his age. In civilian life, he could have been their schoolteacher or perhaps a successful village merchant. He had that softness about him of an indoors man, but also an air of casual authority.

The boys certainly shaped up when he barked something at them in German. The older man used his rifle to point Whitlock toward the truck, and then climbed in after him with the boys. An even older man was behind the wheel. He hadn't bothered to get out.

They all rode together in the back of the truck. Nobody bothered to tie his hands—he was unarmed, and where could he go? These young guys had already shown that they could run like rabbits, and the older one looked like he wouldn't mind using that rifle of his. Unlike the boys, he did not appear excited, but world weary and distracted, as if he missed his classroom or his shop.

One of the young ones offered him a drink from a canteen, which Whitlock accepted gratefully. He drank and drank, having been unaware of how thirsty he was. He supposed it was fear that had turned his mouth to cotton.

He finally remembered to think of Bronson. They had waited together in the chow line this morning. Now Bronson was dead. *Lucky Girl* was gone. He glanced at his Timex watch and realized that from the time the German fighter had attacked until he had touched down in the field, just fifteen minutes had elapsed. It seemed like hours. The whole thing felt unreal, like a bad dream.

Whitlock sat in the battered truck, aware that the three German soldiers were staring at him. Nobody attempted conversation. They drove out of the countryside, and into a town. In the distance, Whitlock could see heavy smoke rising, presumably from where the squadron had delivered its payload.

At least one of the bombs had gone off target and struck the town. The truck slowed, and then stopped as they passed a smoking crater, beside a building that was now largely rubble. A crowd of people, mainly civilians, was attempting to put out several small fires with buckets. Whitlock realized that there wasn't much to burn—mostly there were just piles of rubble. Other villagers stood nearby, weeping.

"Get out, American," the middle-aged soldier said in English. "I want to show you something."

Whitlock did as he was told, surprised that

the man spoke English, though it was heavily accented. *I vant to show you sum-tink.*

On the ground, the two young guards gestured at Whitlock, and then seemed to make an appeal to the older man. He held out his hand to Whitlock. "These boys want your coat."

Whitlock shrugged out of the heavy leather jacket with its warm sheepskin lining. He felt exposed without it—and cold. The boys flipped a coin, and the winner slipped on the coat, which was too big for him. Searching the pockets, the kid found a packet of Beeman's gum, which he gave to the other boy as a consolation prize.

The older man pointed the way, and they walked a short distance to the ruined building. Whitlock had no idea what the German wanted him to see. Maybe it was a portrait of Hitler or some other symbol of the Third Reich? The walls of this building still stood, and Whitlock noticed a smear of red. It looked exactly as if someone had dipped a large paintbrush in crimson paint and swiped it on the wall.

Then Whitlock saw. Nearby on the ground were the bodies of two girls in school uniforms, partially covered with a blanket. He was horrified to realize that it wasn't paint that he saw on the wall, but blood.

A handful of townspeople began to shout angrily at him. Some shook their fists. Whitlock had no idea what they were saying, but he could guess.

The German soldier pushed Whitlock roughly toward the bodies. Then he bent down and pulled back the blanket. Whitlock guessed that they were twelve or thirteen years old. He had a kid sister that age. Both of the girls' faces looked angelic in death, pale and peaceful, like in an old painting. But their bodies were torn and burned, resembling a raw steak that had made contact with a red-hot grill before being yanked off. The sight made him physically wince away. *They're just kids. School girls.* He realized that the devastation to the village could have been from the bombs dropped by *Lucky Girl.* It didn't matter if it was Whitlock's plane or another, especially not to the dead girls or these villagers.

Whitlock tried to turn away, but the older German caught him and forced him closer to the bodies. He said something low and angry.

Whitlock had seen enough. He shoved the German away, which caused the two boyish soldiers to point their rifles nervously in his direction.

But Whitlock wasn't interested in escape just then. He bent over and vomited with such force that he sagged to his knees. He was sick repeatedly until nothing came up but thin, ropy spittle.

The older German took hold of him again, but this time he did it almost gently, helping

Whitlock to his feet. He even handed him a handkerchief to wipe his mouth.

"I'm so sorry. Whose children are they?" Whitlock asked, looking around at the crowd, which had fallen silent. They would not meet his eyes. Something about Whitlock's reaction had clearly left them embarrassed. They were expecting a monster; what they got was a scared-looking young American who appeared just as horrified as they were at the carnage.

"They are God's children, as are we all," the German soldier said in clear but halting English. "Get in the truck. We will take you to the prison camp now."

CHAPTER 4

For Cole and the rest of the squad, the next
town that came into view around a bend in the
road was Arnouthbourg.

"At least, that's what the map says," Lt.
Mulholland explained. "I don't know how to
pronounce it. I also don't know how the good
people of this particular town feel about
American GIs, so keep your eyes peeled."

The squad approached cautiously, with the
snipers leading the way. Since early April their
squad had not encountered any serious resistance
from German units. Most German soldiers with a

lick of sense had tossed aside their weapons, changed out of their Wehrmacht uniforms, and tried to get home. As an organized fighting force, the Wehrmacht had essentially fallen apart.

The trouble was that there remained battle groups cobbled together out of a few die-hard soldiers from different units, or who served under the command of a particularly patriotic officer. As a result, the German military still had strong pockets of resistance even as the odds mounted against any outcome but defeat.

Then there were the lone sniper to worry about, like that kid in the barn.

"I wish these bastards would just give up," Vaccaro said, keeping to the edges of the macadam road leading into Arnouthbourg. "All that they're doing is prolonging the inevitable."

"If the Germans were marching into Brooklyn, would you give up?" Cole asked.

"Damn it, Hillbilly. Why did you have to go and put it that way? I'd fight with sticks and stones if I had to, so thinking about some Kraut with an MP-40 and the same attitude is not reassuring."

"Just keeping you on your toes."

"Yeah, thanks a million."

Cole saw movement on the road ahead. He put his rifle to his eye to get a better view. He blinked once or twice to make sure that he wasn't seeing things. A white-haired man wearing a suit stood waiting for them. In one hand, the old man held a stick with a strip of white cloth tied to one end.

"You see that?"

"Yeah."

"What do you think?"

"Somehow, I doubt that old man has a machine gun up his sleeve. It's a better welcoming committee than a panzer and a battalion of SS stormtroopers."

Cole raised a fist to signal a halt. The lieutenant came running up. Like any experienced soldier, he barely made a sound as he moved, even though he was loaded down with his pack and gear. Strips of cloth and string secured anything that might rattle as he ran and give him away. You could always tell green troops because when they ran anywhere, they made a racket. Vaccaro liked to say that that green troops sounded like Mama Leoni carrying the trash can out to the curb.

Mulholland studied the older man through binoculars, then swept his eyes over the windows of the houses facing the road. He didn't see any soldiers, but in several windows the concerned faces of women or elderly residents peered out.

"Nothing but civilians, as far as I can tell," he said. "Maybe that guy is the local burgermeister."

"The what?" Vaccaro asked.

"The mayor, or whatever you want to call him.

Cole, Vaccaro, you two check it out. The rest of us will cover you."

Vaccaro looked at Cole. "I was afraid he'd say something like that."

"Shut up, Vaccaro," said the lieutenant. "Now get a move on."

The lieutenant hurried back to join the rest of the squad. Cole thought that Mulholland wasn't a bad guy, except for the fact that if there was an i to dot, he had to dot it. He was a rule follower. If somebody like General Patton was full of piss and vinegar, Lieutenant Mulholland was maybe full of Coca Cola and sweet tea. He was just a little too damned decent to be a soldier.

Maybe that was a good thing, considering that he and Mulholland had had something of a falling out over Jolie Molyneaux, the French resistance fighter who had been their guide in the days after D-Day. Jolie had taken up with Cole, despite the lieutenant's efforts otherwise. If Mulholland harbored a grudge, his Boy Scout nature wouldn't let him act on it.

By now, Jolie was back in France, trying to help piece together a country—and a life—that had been wrecked by the Nazis.

In the end, Mulholland was typical of many officers—they were all trying to look good for the boss. Meanwhile, soldiers like Cole and Vaccaro were mostly trying not to get killed. Being the first Americans to march into a German town was not a good way of improving their odds of getting home, but orders were orders.

"You first," Vaccaro said. "I'll cover you."

"We need to have us a united front," Cole said. "Get your ass up here."

They advanced toward the white-haired German. As they approached, they could see that he held himself ramrod straight, maintaining a dignified pose. He raised his arms to show that they were empty. While his body language indicated neutrality, his deeply line face showed the strain of having to welcome the enemy.

After the long winter, and the scarcity of good food, he looked pale and unwell. He was a tall man, towering several inches above them. Given his fine suit and height, he could have been intimidating in other circumstances, if his eyes had not expressed uncertainly. Even terror.

"What can we do you for, pops?" Vaccaro wanted to know. "*Sprechten zie* English?"

"Welcome," the man said in heavily accented English. "I wish to surrender the town peacefully to you. I have gathered the town fathers so that we can do that officially. It is our wish to avoid any violence." He paused. "There has been enough of that already."

Vaccaro looked at Cole. "Well, there you go. Should we head back and get Mulholland?"

Cole thought about it. He glanced toward the windows overlooking the road into town, but still could see no dangers there. For all he knew, this was some sort of trick and there was a tank hiding just around the bend, but it seemed unlikely. "Let's see what he has to say before we bring up the others."

Vaccaro nodded. "Lead on, Herr Burgermeister."

They followed the tall man toward the Rathaus, or town hall. The town was small enough, and far enough from Berlin, to have avoided the wrath of the high-altitude bombers that had devastated so much of the country. Arnouthbourg remained downright picturesque.

A few spring flowers poked through the soil. The bright yellow daffodils punctuated the tiny front yards with bursts of color. The air smelled pleasantly of damp stones and vegetable soup.

None of the buildings was more than three stories high. The streets were macadam, except for directly in front of the town hall, which was paved in cobblestones. Warming to his task, the tall gentleman attempted a smile and waved them inside. Cole unsnapped the holster of his Browning and kept a good grip on his rifle, just in case.

The interior of the Rathaus was freshly painted and neatly kept. Paintings of local scenes lined the walls. The dark and somber paintings looked as if they were maybe a couple hundred years old. Floor-to-ceiling bookcases contained leather-bound volumes of what Cole assumed were local records. It reminded him of the courthouse back home, where he and his pa had once gone to pay a fine to get his uncle out of jail after he had gotten drunk and smashed up a roadhouse. This room represented order and civility. He became acutely aware of his own muddy clothes that stank of sweaty wool and wood smoke. It was as if they had brought the war in with them.

With a final gesture and urging, "Come, come," the white-haired man brought them into what appeared to be the burgermeister's office. As promised, the town fathers had assembled. There was also what Cole supposed was a town mother, a well-dressed grandmotherly woman. Her eyes widened at the sight of Cole and Vaccaro. The burgermeister joined them, and the group of elderly, dignified town officials stood solemnly around the mayor's desk, which seemed to be covered with the inventory of a pawn shop.

He spotted binoculars, wristwatches, cameras, hunting shotguns, and even an antique brass telescope.

He could see at once that it was an offering or a kind of ransom. It was payment in advance for not destroying the town, even though that was the last thing that the Americans had on their minds.

Cole looked over the loot that the

townspeople had gathered, and he felt embarrassed. Not for himself. Instead, he felt ashamed for these people. He could tell they were a proud bunch. They wanted to be in control, even here at what to them must be the end of the world. They had tried to organize their defeat and package it up neatly to avoid anything messy.

He didn't give a damn about these valuables. It was true that Mulholland's squad had "liberated" some things along the way, but you couldn't call it actual looting. Did these people really think that the Americans were here to pillage?

Beside him, Vaccaro's eyes lit up at the collection of watches. He'd always had a hard time saying no to another watch. He grabbed a nice gold model, worth twenty dollars at least, and prepared to shove it into his pocket. The townspeople simply watched, their faces stoic.

This was just what they expected from the barbarians, Cole thought. Greedy for the spoils of war. He reckoned that he would disappoint them.

"Jesus, Vaccaro, how many watches do you need? You still ain't been on time yet. Put it back."

"Hillbilly, are you nuts?"

Cole picked up a delicate teapot and handed it to the elderly woman. Then he turned to the burgermeister. "We ain't here to steal your teapots and cameras. You can tell your friends that you are now officially surrendered. Deutschland kaput."

Grasping the teapot, the old woman nodded at Cole in understanding, while tears flooded her eyes.

Sheepishly, Vaccaro put the watch back on the desk.

• • •

They didn't take any valuables from the good people of Arnouthbourg, although they did accept some cheeses, sausages, and whatever bottles of liquor the townspeople pressed upon them. It was a whole lot better than C rations and canteen water.

Cole and Vaccaro continued scouting ahead of the squad.

They were just leaving the town when a young woman came running toward them. Like most of the other women they had seen, she had on a patterned dress that had been washed to the point where the fabric was wearing thin. Over the dress, she wore a drab-colored button-down sweater and heavy black shoes. She also wore eyeglasses. The clothes were more suitable for an old lady and made her seem older than she actually was, but she was not what the boys would have called a looker. A couple of young girls trailed in her wake.

She was in tears, and at first, Cole thought that maybe she was just overcome by the sight of Americans marching through good ol' Deutchsland. The woman seemed to have noticed his sniper rifle, and came right for him. She reached out and grabbed the weapon, babbling hysterically in German.

Cole wrenched the rifle away.

"Nein," he said, using just about the only German he knew.

The woman took a deep breath and seemed to compose herself. The next words she spoke were in halting English.

"Please," she said. "You must help me stop them. They are just boys!"

Now Cole was even more confused, not the least by the fact that the woman spoke English. He found it surprising that so many Germans seemed to know the language. There weren't nearly as many Americans who spoke German.

He turned to Vaccaro for help. "What is she jabberin' about?"

"I dunno. Why don't you ask her?" Vaccaro said, looking amused. "She sprechen ze English real goot."

Cole turned back to the woman, who grabbed for his rifle again. He pulled it away. "What is it, miss?" he demanded.

"I am their teacher," she said. "Some of the boys are in a house beyond town, and they plan to shoot at your men."

"They'll be sorry if they do."

"They are just children!" she pleaded. "One of their sisters told me that they think they are going to be heroes. They are foolish boys. Please!"

Beside him, Vaccaro said, "I don't like the sound of this."

"Me neither," he agreed.

The most dangerous soldiers they had met with so far in Germany were not hardened SS troops, but kids just fourteen or fifteen years old. Most of them had been brainwashed from growing up under Hitler. They also didn't have a grasp yet of adult behavior. Half the time when they surrendered, the next thing you knew they were pulling a grenade out of their pocket. Crazy kids.

Now here was their teacher, in tears. Cole didn't smell any sort of trap or deceit. The strange thing was that she looked just like a spinster schoolteacher would back home. The girls with her were no more than twelve or thirteen. He reckoned one of them must be the sister that the schoolteacher had mentioned.

He sighed. "Show me."

They started up the road, letting the schoolteacher lead the way. When he saw the girls run to join her, Cole called a halt. "Go on back to town," he said to the girls, not sure if they could understand English. "This ain't a good place for you to be."

The girls looked puzzled, but the teacher spoke to them in German and they nodded and started toward Arnouthbourg. He and Vaccaro walked on with the schoolteacher. They soon came to a bend in the road, presided over by a neatly whitewashed house.

He spotted movement in one of the windows. A rifle appeared in an open window upstairs.

"Sniper!" he shouted.

Vaccaro scrambled for cover, diving into some bushes at the side of the road.

Cole raised his own rifle and would have fired, but the teacher stepped in front of him, shielding him. Facing the house, she raised her arms and shouted in German. Cole couldn't understand her, but she sounded almost hysterical. She kept herself in front of Cole, preventing whoever was in the house from shooting.

"Aw, hell." Cole put down his rifle and pulled out a white handkerchief.

"Cole, what the hell are you doing?" Vaccaro shouted from the side of the road.

"Something goddamn stupid, that's what," he replied.

Holding the white handkerchief high, he moved forward alongside the schoolteacher.

"You reckon they'll shoot me?" he asked her.

The teacher stepped closer to Cole and hooked her arm through his so that they were walking hip to hip. "Not if I can help it."

The door of the white house was locked, but the teacher pounded on it and shouted in German. Cole couldn't understand the words, but it was unmistakably the stern tone of a schoolmarm. He heard movement inside, and put his hand on the pistol. Wouldn't do him a damn bit of good if those German schoolboys shot through the door.

He heard some arguing on the other side of the locked door, but finally the door opened. Four boys stood just inside, crowded into the doorway. One boy had an old hunting rifle that had a stock wrapped with twine, and a second boy held a rusty shotgun. The third kid didn't have a weapon and seemed to be there for moral support. The fourth boy held a standard issue Mauser K98 military rifle. The sight of it made Cole's spine tingle. Given half a chance, the fourth kid wouldn't have had any trouble picking off American GIs passing on the road.

The teacher seemed to be scolding the boys. When she finished, she turned to Cole expectantly. "What should they do now?"

"Tell them to put their guns down on the floor, miss. Tell them there ain't no shame in it. The war is over. It ain't their fault. And one of you has got a sister back in town who is awfully worried about you."

The boy holding the Mauser started crying. Cole kept one hand on his pistol until, one by one, the boys put down their guns and filed out of the house. Cole didn't realize until then that he had been holding his breath. The schoolteacher herded her students back toward town like a mother hen, looking back over her shoulder to give Cole a grateful nod.

Cole gathered up the weapons and unloaded them. The ancient shotgun didn't even lock up tight—it likely would have blinded whoever had fired it. He pulled the bolts from the rifles and hurled them into the weeds. Then he tossed the ammunition in another direction. One by one, he took the rifles by their muzzles and swung them as far into the surrounding fields as he could.

Vaccaro walked up. He was holding the rifle that Cole had left on the road. "That's it? We just let them go?"

"You got a better idea?" Cole grunted as he hurled the shotgun into some bushes. "Maybe you want to line 'em up and shoot these kids?"

"I guess not." Vaccaro handed Cole his rifle. He looked shaken. "Those kids could have killed us both. I can't believe you walked right up to that house and got them to surrender. Cole, you are one crazy son of a bitch. It's not like I haven't said that before."

"Yep, but that's the first time today. I reckon I must be getting worried about living until the war's over."

CHAPTER 5

With the victory at Seelow Heights, won by grinding thousands of Russians to a bloody pulp until the Germans were simply overwhelmed, all roads were now leading to Berlin.

On one of these roads, a very drunken Yegor Barkov was riding in the back of a Studebaker truck emblazoned with a Soviet star. He had a bottle of liquor in one hand and his prized Mosin-Nagant rifle with its telescopic sight in the other. Balanced in the bed of the slow-moving truck, he looked like he was posing for a photograph.

The advance toward Berlin resembled a victory parade after so many months upon months of slogging through snow and mud and blood. The truck slowed yet more to move around a trio of German women who struggled to push a wheelbarrow piled high with their possessions. The women appeared hunched and beaten, not even bothering to look up. *These damn Germans,* he thought. *They deserved this defeat. Now they were reaping what they had sown.*

Barkov took one last swig of alcohol and hurled the empty bottle at the women. The bottle struck one of them in the head with such force that it knocked her down. Barkov laughed. He'd always had good aim.

"What else is there to drink, Oleg?" Barkov wanted to know.

"We are dry as the dessert," the Mink said, his eyes glassy with booze.

"Not for long," Barkov said. He staggered across the bed of the truck and banged a big fist on the roof, shouting, "Pull over, if you know what's good for you!"

The truck slowed. They had reached the outskirts of Berlin. Beyond, they could see the city—or what was left of it. Soviet troops now encircled the German capital. Earlier, they had opened fire with an artillery barrage that went on and on, punishing the city with nearly two million pounds of high explosive. Berlin no longer had any fight and there was no military purpose to the bombardment; it was a beating, pure and simple.

When the Studebaker stopped, Barkov and the Mink jumped off, along with several other men in their squad. They were mostly snipers, but there was little need anymore for their services, not when the artillery and tanks were busily at work on what little remained of German resistance.

The road around them was filled with advancing masses of Soviet troops. The scene was chaotic—there was very little order among the men. The officers and even the dreaded commissars kept their heads down, letting the men enjoy the fruits of victory after long months of war.

To the Germans peering from whatever shelter they could find, it looked like a horde of barbarians had arrived. Some of the enemy troops had the facial features of Mongols, as if Genghis Khan's soldiers had arrived. Others wore sheepskin caps and bandoliers of brass-jacketed bullets draped across their shoulders. If the frightened Germans looked closely, they would have noticed an especially large, drunken barbarian, trailed by a much smaller man, step off the road. A handful of soldiers followed them.

Barkov and his men spread out through the ruins, searching for anything of value. Many of the Russian soldiers were simple peasants, and the richness and plenty of the plunder they found was overwhelming. Some wore several layers of captured clothing—sweaters, suit jackets, raincoats, even women's fur stoles—it was all too good to pass up. They stuffed their pockets with bottles of perfume, silver combs, and costume jewelry, so that each man seemed to be carrying the contents of a shop wherever he went. Along with the churning of muddy tires could be heard the clink of bottles and the rattle of beads.

By Stalin's order, every Russian was entitled to ship home a five-kilo parcel. Officers were allowed even more. In this way, many a Russian sister or wife received an expensive German dress or new silverware. The higher-ranking officers took their pick of the plunder, which included expensive hunting rifles, radios, or even artwork.

The Germans saw them as barbarians, so why disappoint?

Mainly, what the soldiers wanted was booze. They ransacked houses and shops, grabbing anything that looked remotely like alcohol. Already, there had been several incidents of soldiers fatally poisoned by drinking industrial solvents at one of several factories the Russians had overrun. It turned out that the Russians could not believe their good luck in discovering the huge vats and tanks of intoxicating liquid. All that booze for the taking! There had been quite a party as a result. As many as several hundred soldiers had died, or were in the process of dying horribly. The Russians were convinced that the Germans had deliberately poisoned them—never mind the fact that the vats and holding tanks clearly stated that the contents were not for human consumption. It was not the way of the Russian soldier to bother with the fine print, even when he had some knowledge of the German language.

"Spread out," Barkov ordered his squad. "Look at these *bomzhi*, getting all the good stuff! See what you can find us to drink."

"I only drink red wine," the Mink said. He was so intoxicated that he reeled; Barkov reached out a hand to steady him.

"Look at you, Oleg, drunk as a lord! Ha, ha! That's the spirit." He looked around at the men. "Don't listen to him. He's drunk. Bring back anything you can find, just as long as it's not that poisoned shit the Germans have been leaving for us."

"What about women?" one of the men asked, grinning.

"If you find any German women who don't look like hags, you let me know," Barkov said. He had already seen plenty of ugly ones, like the women he had thrown a bottle at.

The men fanned out. They had their orders, and when Barkov gave orders, they listened. His men ran from house to house like dogs chasing rabbits. Barkov sat on the fender of the Studebaker and smoked a cigarette, waiting to see what they would find.

• • •

In a cellar nearby, a dozen people were hiding from the Russians and the shelling. So far, they had been lucky. The Russian shells had spared them while knocking down other houses and burying the occupants alive. None of the marauding Russians had bothered with the cellar. There was more than enough bounty in the rooms above.

The knot of frightened people hiding in the dark included a mother, her eighteen-year-old daughter, and thirteen-year-old son—the last they had heard from the father was two weeks ago when he was being rushed to defend Seelow Heights, and they did not know if they would ever hear from him again. There was an elderly neighbor and his wife, both of them frail old people. There was also a woman whose husband had died serving in the Luftwaffe, and she had managed her grief by eating—even in these lean times she looked fat as a sausage. In comparison to the other three women, the girl stood out like a diamond among lumps of coal. The girl's mother was acutely aware of this fact, which was why they had gone into hiding.

The cellar hideaway had been spared so far, but the men of Barkov's squad were more enterprising than most. Snipers were used to ferreting out hiding places; it was how their minds worked. Under Barkov's direction, they had also become skilled looters since crossing over into Germany.

One of the men, whose name was Murushko, entered the house and made a quick circuit of the rooms. Clearly, the place had been picked over. He did, however, notice a door in the kitchen that appeared to lead to a cellar. When he tried the door, it was locked. *Ah.* Who bothered to lock the cellar door and left the front door open? He took a step back and kicked it open with a muddy boot.

He stood at the top of the stairs and sniffed. The smell alone told him that Germans were hiding down there. He caught the smell of boiled potatoes and cabbage, along with a whiff of the bucket in the corner that served as a makeshift latrine.

Someone, probably several someones, was hiding in the cellar.

Keeping his gun ready, he descended several steps and flicked on a flashlight. Playing the beam over the floor, he picked out several Germans, all huddled together, as if hoping he wouldn't see them.

One of the Germans looked up. His flashlight beam fell upon a pretty young face. The first one he had seen in weeks.

He turned on his heel to fetch Barkov.

• • •

Barkov was smoking another cigarette when Murushko came running up. Before he could explain the situation to Barkov, an old German man materialized out of nowhere and began berating the Russians. He seemed very excited and angry, to the point that he waved his arms about. He looked silly, like a mad babbling puppet. Barkov was not sure what the old man was yelling about, so with a sigh he drew his Nagant M1895 Revolver and shot the old man.

A lead bullet weighing 9.5 grams and traveling at just over 1,000 feet per second entered the skull and tunneled through the gray matter, immediately putting an end to the old man's protest. Barkov watched with half-hearted interest as the body collapsed into the mud. Now the old man was a puppet whose strings had been cut.

He turned to Murushko. "What?"

"I found something in that cellar over there."

"Booze?"

"Better."

"Show me." Barkov tossed away his cigarette.

The Mink wobbled nearby in an alcoholic haze, so Barkov grabbed him by the shirtfront and dragged him along like a bewildered child.

It wasn't far. This time, it was Barkov who went down the stairs with the flashlight, keeping his pistol ready. A cornered animal was a dangerous one. Murushko and the Mink were right behind him, the later having sobered up quickly enough. Barkov always felt better with the Mink watching his back—drunk or not.

In the flashlight beam, the people huddled in the corner stared with frightened eyes in the direction of the light. They were a pathetic, harmless bunch. An old man who would break like a stick. Three ugly women dry as an old boot. The boy might be trouble if he showed a little bravery. Barkov's light picked out the face of the girl.

"What have we here?" he growled.

He approached the group. Barkov's German was limited, but in this case it was enough. Only an imbecile would not understand what the men wanted.

"Fräulein," he said. *"Lestnitsa."* Upstairs. He pointed at the girl, and then pointed at the steps.

When the girl did not move, Barkov waded into the little group, kicking them aside like dogs, and grabbed the girl by the arm. *"Poyekhali!"*

The mother had the good sense to know that there was no point in protesting, considering that they were staring down the barrels of three Russian rifles. Cooperation was the only hope they had of survival.

The brother couldn't know that, or didn't care. He decided to be brave. He launched himself at Barkov, shouting something in German and swinging bony fists. Barkov simply reversed his rifle and smashed the boy's face. He went down on the dirt floor and curled up into a ball. The girl tried to help him, but Barkov dragged her away and shoved her toward the stairs.

They forced her at gunpoint through the house and to an upstairs bedroom. Barkov pointed at the bed. She sat down on it. Barkov sighed and made motions like he was pulling a shirt up over his head. Were German girls so dense? The girl stared at him, horrified, and he reached over to slap her to get her attention, and then repeated the motion of pulling his shirt over his head. This time, the girl complied and took off her dress. Barkov nodded and gave her a push so that she fell back on the bed.

By now, the rest of the squad had crowded into the bedroom. Six men. All in various states of intoxication. Staring at the girl on the bed. Barkov unbuckled his trousers, his intent all too obvious, and the girl started to wail.

They were all so intent on the scene on the bed that the younger brother slipped in unnoticed and leaped onto Barkov's back like he was climbing a mountain, shouting and pounding his fists. Cursing, Barkov shrugged him off, dumping the boy to the floor in a heap. Murushko kicked him, and the Mink raised his pistol to shoot him. The girl wailed even louder, sounding like an air raid siren to Barkov's ears.

This was not going as he had planned, not at all. He slapped the girl and shouted at the Mink, *"Nyet!"*

Drunk as he was, Barkov quickly explained his plan. The Mink hauled the boy to his feet, wrapped an arm around his throat, and put a revolver to his head. Barkov pointed at the boy and then at the girl. Unless she was a complete *Oyabuk,* she ought to understand the situation, and what Barkov wanted.

Horribly, the crime that was taking place in that bedroom was being perpetrated all across Berlin. Rape was being used by the invading Russians as both a form of punishment against the German people and as a grotesque spoil of war. It was as if the medieval era had returned to the 20th century.

• • •

When Barkov finished with the girl, he took another big swig from some bottle they had found, and then Murushko took his turn. The brother was sobbing, unable to take his eyes off the nightmare scene in front of him because the Mink was holding him so that he was forced to watch. Still, the boy strained against the Mink's grip. Barkov absently punched him in the belly.

It turned out that the girl's initial screaming had not been for nothing. Murushko was busy humping away, his pale ass bobbling up and down, when a commissar appeared in the doorway. He was young and looked startled by the scene he had walked into. These hardened soldiers all resembled drunken thugs, and he looked from one to the other uncertainly, despite his commissar's uniform.

"What is going on here?" he demanded.

"What do you think?" Barkov said. "Go away."

The young commissar did not seem sure what to do about the rape, but he did know one thing: "You cannot speak to me that way." His hand fumbled at his holster.

Barkov gave him a shove that sent the officer crashing against the wall. Then the sniper reached down with a hand the size of a bear paw and took away the officer's gun. It was a Tokarev TT-33 Service Pistol in 7.62 mm, ugly but reliable as a hammer. "This does not concern you, Comrade Commissar. That is, unless you want a turn."

Barkov gestured at the bed. The young officer blushed, and averted his eyes. He darted from the room, chased down the narrow hall by the laughter of the soldiers.

Only the Mink wasn't laughing. "Yegor, what have you done?"

"That little runt won't be back, not if he knows what's good for him," Barkov said. "You worry too much."

They all had a go at the girl. Murushko went twice. To take his turn, the Mink released the brother, who sank to his knees, blubbering. Barkov considered killing him anyhow, but that seemed too kind. The boy would be having nightmares about this day for years to come—it would serve the little Nazi bastard right. The boy would always be reminded of the day when he had been too weak to defend his sister.

Finished, Barkov and his men stumped loudly down the stairs of the neat German house and out the front door—where he saw the young commissar approaching again. This time, he was not alone.

An older political officer flanked him, and if the young commissar had the look of a puppy, this one had the appearance of a watchdog who enjoyed biting. Barkov recognized him vaguely as having been one the senior commissars to give speeches before the attack on Seelow Heights. He had then gone to the rear to shoot those for whom the speech had not been sufficient motivation for advancing toward the German lines. As if the appearance of the commissar wasn't bad enough, a couple of NKVD guards marched along, submachine guns casually aimed in Barkov's direction.

"You," the older commissar said to Barkov. "I know you. You are the sniper. Your name is Barkov."

"Yes, Comrade Commissar."

"Why do you think I am here, Barkov?"

"The girl—"

"Girl? Do you think I give a shit if you screw some German girl? No, I might give you a medal for that. No, Barkov, you stupid *Oyabuk*, your crime is that you dared to put a hand on this officer here, who hesitated in shooting you because he still believes in the milk of human kindness. I have no such frailties."

Barkov started to speak, but thought better of it.

The commissar went on, "The only reason I am not going to shoot you right now is because of your service. I know who you are, Barkov. In your drunkenness, you have made a serious error in judgment that will require some reeducation." He made an expression that he must have thought was a smile, but the sight of his perfectly square teeth gave even Barkov a shiver. "I have new duties for you now that the fighting is over."

"Yes, Comrade Commissar." Barkov felt a sinking feeling. Whatever a commissar had in mind couldn't be good. "What about my men?"

The commissar nodded at Murushko and the Mink. "You can bring those two along. They look dependable. Now, give the commissar his pistol back."

Barkov did as he was told, handing back the Tokarev TT-33.

Then the commissar turned to the younger officer. "Make yourself useful, Comrade. Shoot these others."

CHAPTER 6

Whitlock's first impression of the POW camp was not what he had expected. In his mind's eye, he had pictured something with tall barbed wire fences and guard towers, a muddy yard, snarling Rottweilers on short leashes, and starving prisoners—like those old Civil War photos you sometimes saw of a hell on earth like Andersonville.

Instead of horrors, he found bored prisoners and equally bored guards. The sewage plant back home had a taller chain link fence, with more barbed wire on top. Instead of drab buildings, the prison barracks were neatly whitewashed. Concrete walkways crisscrossed the grassy yard. It wasn't exactly cheerful, but it could have been a lot worse.

"Is this a prison camp?" Whitlock wondered out loud. "There's not a guard tower was in sight."

The older guard riding with him in the back of the truck gave him what might have been a look of pity. Whitlock had almost forgotten that he spoke English.

"Where would you go?" the guard asked. "You are in the middle of Germany!"

So many Allied airmen had been taken prisoner by this late hour of the war that no one even bothered to interrogate him beyond a few rudimentary questions. The processing of a new prisoner was brief and Whitlock found that he was treated diffidently enough by the prison guards, most of whom were either young enough to be in junior high school or old enough to be the same age as Whitlock's father, or possibly his grandfather. The fittest soldiers were likely off at the front, rather than guarding POWs.

Whitlock was submitted to a brief questioning by an officer who was going through the motions. The officer concluded by giving him some advice: "Don't do anything stupid, and you'll be home again soon."

If the camp had been south of the Elbe River,

the officer would have been right. As it turned out, he couldn't have been more wrong.

After that initial interrogation, an officious sergeant took his name and compared it to the list presented to him by the guard from the truck. Once the sergeant was satisfied that all prisoners were accounted for, they were each given a bowl, a spoon, and a blanket—which, judging from the moth-eaten holes and the smell, was used.

There were no prison uniforms anymore, so Whitlock kept his grungy uniform. He didn't mind the lack of prison uniforms, but there were also no coats, despite the fact that the air was chilly. He had lost his leather bomber to the young soldiers. To stay warm, Whitlock draped his thin blanket across his shoulders.

The sergeant had the new POWs line up and all the prisoners received a cursory search. They submitted silently to being patted down. The sergeant even made Whitlock take off his boots, and he worried for a moment that he would be left barefoot. The German was only interested in seeing if Whitlock was smuggling anything. Satisfied, the sergeant nodded and moved on.

He was led to one of the barracks by a guard who was clearly not yet old enough to shave or even to get a pimple, and pointed to the door. The boy carried an old rifle slung on his bony shoulder and Whitlock realized it would be a simple matter to overpower him and take away the weapon. But then what? As the guard on the truck had pointed out, Whitlock was in the middle of Germany.

Whitlock slipped the blanket off his shoulders in an attempt to look more presentable. Carrying his newly issued bowl and spoon bundled up in the blanket, he crossed the threshold into the dark interior of the barracks.

The prison barracks smelled like a locker room, or just about any barracks that he had ever been in—the atmosphere was thick with the odor of stale sweat and old farts. He blinked as his eyes adjusted to the gloom. He could begin to see that several heads had turned his way, watching him curiously. Most of the men lay on bunks, but a few huddled around a stove in the corner, sitting on upturned crates.

One of the men approached. "Aren't you a sorry bastard," the man said, and Whitlock's guard went up at the words, although the man's tone was friendly enough. "It looks like you had the bad luck to be one of the last prisoners taken in this war."

For the first time since those terrifying moments when his plane had begun to disintegrate around him, Whitlock had to smile. "I've been thinking the same thing ever since I found myself staring into the barrel of a Mauser held by some kid."

The man extended a hand, and Whitlock juggled his bundle to take it. "Max Macdonald," the prisoner said. "Captain in the Army Air Corps. I've been here, fifteen months and twelve days, which makes me the ranking officer."

"Good to meet you, sir," Whitlock said.

"Oh, none of that." MacDonald said jovially. He had a British air about him, as if he had been spending a lot of time with the Englishmen in the barracks next door. Whitlock half expected the man to click his heels together. "What I mean to say is that it is good to meet you, too, but we don't stand much on formality around here. We leave that to the Krauts."

Another man came up. "Bill Ramsey. Lieutenant, Army Air Corps. Here, let me help you with that," he said, taking the bundle from Whitlock. "You can have Hinson's bunk."

"Won't Hinson be needing it?"

"It's not likely, considering that he went to the Great Beyond last week." Ramsey looked him up and down. "How are you feeling? Any injuries we should tend to?"

"No, I'm fine." Whitlock wanted to add, *unlike my crew*. He had no idea whether or not they had made it. None of the Germans had been able to tell him. He felt bad about it. A thought occurred to him. "Was Hinson sick?"

MacDonald's face clouded. "Well, in a way he was," MacDonald said. "He tried to climb the fence, and the Germans shot him."

"He was trying to escape?"

"Something like that." MacDonald sighed. "You might say he committed suicide. The poor bastard had had enough."

Ramsey put Whitlock's bundle down on the hard planks of the bunk. "Home sweet home," he said. "Welcome to Stalag Twenty-Two B. That's the Germans for you, giving their prison camps such efficient names. Unofficially, we like to call it the Hotel Hitler. Just don't let the guards hear you say it."

"That sounds like a good name for it." Whitlock smirked. "So, how long have you been in this place?"

"Since last summer," Ramsey said. "Too long."

"One day seems too long right now."

"I wish I could say the time passes quickly, but that would be a lie." They talked for a while, with the POWs eager for any news from the war. Once Whitlock had filled them in, Ramsey clapped him on the shoulder. "Well, now that we've got you settled in, get some rest."

Whitlock wouldn't have believed it was possible, but as soon as he stretched out on the bunk with his tattered blanket, he fell fast asleep.

• • •

Ramsey's question about how Whitlock was

feeling proved to be prophetic. By the next morning, he was shaking with fever. It had been a long time since Whitlock was sick, and the flu or whatever it was hit him like a windshield hitting a bug. His throat burned. His bones ached. He felt miserable.

Fever made him dizzy. When he got up to relieve himself, he staggered drunkenly. The room spun. He could barely keep any food down. Ramsey nursed him through it. He sat him up in the bunk and fed him spoonfuls of watery cabbage soup. He could barely gag down more than a few sips. Whitlock felt embarrassed to be so helpless, but Ramsey was having none of it.

"You're not the first one," Ramsey explained. "I'm no doctor, but I've got this theory that sometimes the shock of going through being shot down amplifies whatever illness you've got. Your immune system is a ninety-eight pound weakling right now, getting sand kicked in its face."

"And you're supposed to be Charles Atlas?"

Ramsey snorted. "It used to be that the Germans would put a guy in the infirmary if he got this sick, but there's not so much as a nurse or an aspirin there anymore. All the medical staff and supplies are at the front. So it's up to me, good ol' Nurse Ramsey."

Ramsey arranged for Whitlock to sleep closer to the stove, which struggled to heat the barracks. He brought Whitlock an extra blanket, and that helped with the shivering. At some point he became delirious, shouting warnings that the Germans were about to march down Main Street during the Fourth of July parade.

Two nights later, Whitlock woke up, knowing at once that he was better. The fever was gone. The room no longer spun, but he felt weak as a kitten. Ramsey was sitting almost within reach on a crate pulled up next to the stove. He brought Whitlock a mug of warm water, since there wasn't anything resembling tea.

"You're awake," Ramsey said. "Goddamn, but you had it bad. I wasn't sure you were going to pull through."

"I guess I was out of it for a couple of days."

"Yeah, you were. The good news is that it looks like you're going to live. The bad news is that you're still a prisoner in the Hotel Hitler, and the war is still going on." Ramsey grinned. "Feeling better now?"

CHAPTER 7

Even as the war ended in fitful gasps, winter seemed to cling to the land in those early days of spring. Leaden skies overhung the brown landscape. The air still held an icy chill, no matter what the calendar said.

Vaccaro developed a cold that he couldn't seem to shake. He sneezed and coughed so much that if they had still been facing German snipers on a regular basis, it would have been one sneeze too many.

Cole offered to shoot him to put him out of his misery.

"Fortunately, I know you're just kidding, Hillbilly," Vaccaro said, swiping at his nose with a grayish hankie that he had found somewhere in Belgium.

"If you was back home, my ma would dose you with a big spoonful of whiskey and kerosene."

"Jesus, it's a wonder you survived."

"I reckon there is some truth in the remedy being worse than the sickness." Cole studied Vaccaro with those unsettling eyes of his.

Crazy eyes, Vaccaro thought of them—just not out loud. He sneezed.

"You know what you need, Vaccaro? You need about two weeks in some sunshine with nothin' to do."

"Sounds about right," Vaccaro said wistfully.

"Ain't gonna happen, though," Cole said. He handed Vaccaro a flask of some unidentifiable booze that they had liberated from one of the towns en route to Berlin. "Try some of this. It's the next best thing."

Vaccaro took a drink and grimaced. "What is this? Paint thinner?"

"Could be, for all I know."

Vaccaro took another swig. "Well, if it is paint thinner, at least it will put me out of my misery."

"That's the spirit. Have another drink."

Vaccaro did.

Cole and Vaccaro, along with the bulk of American forces, had washed up against the southern shore of the Elbe River, roughly thirty miles from Berlin. And there they all sat. Hostilities with the Germans had effectively ended. All that the Germans seemed to want to do was to get away from the Russians. One might have thought that what remained of Germany was being invaded by demons, not the Soviet army. Entire families could be seen fleeing with everything they owned on their backs and a glint of fear in their eyes. The Germans were eager to put as much distance between themselves and the Russians as possible.

Maybe the Germans had good reason to be afraid. Rumors had reached the GIs of atrocities being committed by the Russians. Wholesale looting. Murder. The rape of any female they could find. By comparison, the Americans looked like saints.

Vaccaro gazed across the river. "It's a cryin' shame that we won't be going all the way to Berlin."

"That's the brass for you. Just like Ellie Mae Smith used to do to me out back of the county fair. She got you all worked up, and then she told you to put it back in your pants."

"This Ellie Mae, did she have two legs or four?" That set Vaccaro to laughing, which fizzled out into a coughing fit.

"Keep it up, Vaccaro. With any luck, you'll laugh yourself to death."

The fact that the Americans were not rushing toward Berlin was a source of keen disappointment, not to mention more than a little confusion. Berlin had been the Allies' Holy Grail since the D-Day landing. Now that they were so close, that grail had been snatched away.

Just days ago, Eisenhower had an encounter with one of his generals, making an offhand remark that the troops should push on to Berlin. After months spent fighting their way across Europe, there wasn't a soldier who didn't want to get to the German capital. Ike's words had seemed like encouragement.

Then the Supreme Allied commander had reversed his orders, so that all forward motion had come to a grinding halt for reasons that nobody could see. The rumor was that it had everything to do with the Russians—and a simple desire to save American lives. Berlin had no real strategic value, but was more of a symbolic goal. Most of German territory was under Allied control west of the Elbe. If the diehard Nazis wanted to make a last stand in Berlin, it might cost a lot of lives—but to what end? Better to let the Russians fight it out and take the losses. That also meant they would get all the glory.

It had been ingrained in the GIs to see the Germans as enemies, but that perception faded at the sight of the desperate women and children and middle-aged fathers—along with more than a few men who had likely been German soldiers until very recently, but had returned home to help their families escape ahead of the Russian hordes. Another uncomfortable fact was that the Germans looked so much like the Americans themselves. Hardly a man could watch a German family struggling along with small children and a few possessions, without thinking of his own family back home.

Cole and Vaccaro found themselves stationed near the twisted ruins of a railroad bridge spanning the Elbe at a town called Tangermunde. The SS had blown up the bridge in an attempt to slow the American advance toward Berlin. As it turned out, politics had done a better job of that than TNT. Much of the bridge still stood, knitted together by twisted irons rails and girders. The tangled wreckage dipped down into the water in places. Crossing it was so precarious that a knot of refugees had formed on the other bank, uncertain of their chances. A few strong swimmers took directly to the turbulent water, while others were attempting to build makeshift rafts.

"Looks more like a roller coaster ride than a railroad bridge," Vaccaro remarked.

"There sure as hell won't be any tanks getting across," Cole said.

Cole had never been to an amusement park or seen a roller coaster. He had gone straight from the mountains where he had grown up near Gashey's Creek to basic training, and then on to England and Normandy. He thought that the bridge looked much like the ruins of the old trestle bridge across Gashey's Creek that the Union army had dynamited during the Civil War. Things being as they were back home, the bridge hadn't been rebuilt even eighty years later.

Ostensibly, Cole and Vaccaro were helping to guard the bridge against SS units using it for a final dash to the defense of Berlin. That seemed unlikely at this late stage of the war. Now, there were rumors going around that there would be trouble if the Russians tried to cross into American-held territory. The jury was still out on that possibility.

Cole was waiting to see his first Russian, but there were plenty of German refugees. They watched a father wearing a suit and an overcoat, holding a suitcase in one hand and his daughter's hand in the other. The girl was six or seven. Slowly, they picked their way across the bridge. At one point, they had to wade where the iron rails disappeared below the river's surface. The little girl lost her footing and was almost swept away by the current. The man dropped the suitcase and grabbed the girl with both hands, struggling to keep her from going under.

Cole, who had faced some of the Germans' deadliest snipers and dodged bullets and bombs for the last few months, found that his heart was pounding from watching the two try to make it across. He had almost drowned once as a teenager, running a trapline in an icy creek. That experience had left him leery of any kind of water.

He breathed again when the father and daughter made it out of the water. The suitcase had drifted out of reach and was beginning to sink. Their next leg of the bridge was dry, but just as treacherous where missing sections of ties left gaping holes high above the river.

"To hell with this," Cole said. He handed his rifle to Vaccaro.

"You've got that look, Hillbilly. I don't like it when you get that look."

"I ain't gonna stand here and watch, no matter what our orders say."

"The lieutenant won't like it."

"Tell him I went to take a leak and got lost."

"Cole, what the hell are you up to?"

"You'll see."

Cole started down the bank. There were several rowboats down there, battered things, but they had made it across the expanse of river. Refugees had rowed them across, but then abandoned the boats on the bank. Nobody wanted to row back across once they had made it to safety. Meanwhile, desperate refugees crowded the river banks without any way to get across.

The boats were all on the wrong side.

Official military policy was that the refugees would not be stopped—not unless they appeared to be Germany military. At the same time, U.S. troops were not to give any active assistance to refugees.

Cole was about to break that rule.

He tied three boats together and clambered into the one that seemed the most seaworthy. There were a couple of oars lying in the bottom, and he took hold of them, trying to figure out what to do next. What Cole knew about boats could fit into his back pocket.

The sound of someone coming down the bank made him look up.

"Those are called oars," Vaccaro said. "You have to put those in the oarlocks in order to row. Also, it helps if you keep your back toward the bow."

"The what?"

Vaccaro sighed. "Move over. My uncle has a place at the Jersey shore, so I've been in a boat at least once in my life, Hillbilly. I don't suppose you have much use for boats up there in the mountains."

"I reckon not."

With Cole gripping the sides of the rowboat, Vaccaro fitted the oars to the locks, and started rowing, pulling the two other boats in their wake. On the opposite bank, the German refugees saw them coming across and shouted encouragement. "You do know that once some officer spots us doing this, there's gonna be hell to pay."

"You think I give a damn?"

"The good news is that all this rowing will get us into shape for breaking rocks at Fort Leavenworth."

The trip across took just a couple of minutes. Cole had worried that there would be a ruckus over who got into the boats, but to his surprise, the refugees were very orderly.

A couple of men had taken charge and were forming people into lines, keeping families together. Cole thought that the organizers, with their military bearing and close-cropped hair, looked suspiciously like German officers, but they wore civilian clothes. They seemed used to giving orders.

The boats filled quickly. Suitcases were abandoned in favor of fitting more people—the refugees carried only what they could hold in their arms. Cole got into the second rowboat, noticing that a few inches of river water sloshed in the bottom from some unseen leak. He just hoped the damn thing didn't sink on him.

He counted eighteen Germans spread across the three boats. Cole didn't like the fact that with so many passengers, his rowboat now sat low in the water, but fortunately the river was smooth and calm. He put his back into pulling the oars, eager to cross the expanse of river. However, the trip back to the western shore took longer because of the weight.

On the American side of the Elbe, the passengers disembarked in orderly fashion. A handful still had relatives on the opposite bank. They looked imploringly at the two GIs.

Cole settled back down and took up the oars. "If I keep this up long enough, maybe they'll let me join the navy."

"We're going back?" With a sigh, Vaccaro reached for his own set of oars. "I guess we can't leave the job half done."

They rowed to the other side and loaded the boats again. The Germans jabbered at them, and although neither man spoke the language, it was plain that the refugees were thankful. Someone tried to give Cole a roll of money, but he shook his head and muttered, *"Nein."*

On their fourth trip across, he did accept a bottle of schnapps from an old man, mainly because the poor codger seemed so excited to give it to him. Cole nodded his thanks and tucked the bottle into what he had learned from Vaccaro was called the bow.

The water was getting deeper in the belly of his rowboat. One of the German organizers on the bank noticed and produced an empty tin can. He jumped in and started scooping out water.

Cole was built lean and rangy, which was good

for covering ground, but not for rowing heavy boats back and forth across the muddy Elbe. His hands were far from soft, but he didn't have the leathery skin of a farmer. By the fifth trip he had blisters. By the eighth trip his hands were bloody. On the tenth trip, a beautiful blond woman, dressed in fashionable clothes, noticed the blood where he gripped the oars. She took his hands, making *tsk, tsk* sounds of sympathy. She had eyes the color of a blue sky and looked as if she had just stepped off a movie screen. She tore strips from the hem of her dress and then gently wrapped his hands. He went back to the oars.

Now the number of Germans waiting to cross was not diminishing, but growing. Where the situation had been almost hopeless before, now Germans were being drawn to possibility of escape. Previously, the Germans had been calm, but there was a new urgency in those waiting for the boats. He overheard the words *die Russen* repeated again and again, clearly in an apprehensive tone. Did that mean the Russians were closer?

There seemed to be some confusion about who was getting into which boat, and what they were taking with them.

"Hurry up," Cole said, hoping they understood.

One of the men who might have been a German officer got what he was saying and nodded. Turning to the crowd, he started counting off people and pushing them toward the boats, shouting, *"Hop, hop, hop!"*

On that trip across, a major Cole didn't recognize came down the bank to watch them. He just shook his head and walked away. Some other GIs came down the bank to help people off the boats, but it was only Cole and Vaccaro rowing the boats. A couple of younger Germans started going back and forth with two more boats.

They made their fifteenth trip across. That was damn near two hundred Germans that they had ferried across the Elbe.

The major Cole had seen earlier reappeared as they reached the American side. "All right, you two. That was your last trip."

Vaccaro started to protest. "But sir—"

The major jerked his chin toward the opposite bank. There were still just as many refugees waiting to cross, if not more. Now there was another presence visible. Several military trucks had appeared, along with a squad of soldiers. They spread out in what appeared to be a loose battle formation. However, they were not Germans. They ignored the refugees, but their eyes were on the GIs on the western bank of the Elbe.

The Russians had arrived.

"Soldier, you did what you could for these

people," the major said. "Now put down those oars and go find your rifle. These Russians are supposed to be on our side, but I don't like the looks of 'em."

CHAPTER 8

Whitlock's days at the Hotel Hitler fell into a mind-numbing routine. First there was the morning *Apfel*, or head count. The officers moved out into the chill morning and literally counted off. Whitlock soon learned there were eighty-seven American officers at Stalag Twenty-Two B. The number had not changed since Whitlock's arrival. Then there was breakfast, which consisted of a hunk of bread and ersatz coffee.

"They used to serve real coffee, but not even the Germans have that luxury anymore," Ramsey said.

Following breakfast, they were allowed an hour of exercise in the yard. Some of the more energetic men played baseball or football with a makeshift pigskin. No one was allowed within ten feet of the chain link perimeter fence. If a ball went out of bounds into this dead man's land, the prisoners asked a guard to retrieve it.

"Don't let the propaganda fool you," Ramsey said. "The Germans are decent enough, considering that we *are* in a prisoner of war camp. They are more indifferent than cruel. Of course, these Kraut bastards know that soon enough the tables will be turned and *they* will be the ones who are held prisoner. But for now, don't push your luck by getting too close to that fence. Those bastards with the guns mean business."

Almost every day now when out in the exercise yard, they could see the contrails high above of bombers going to drop their payload on Berlin. Scarcely a Luftwaffe fighter was ever seen anymore, which meant that the Allied B-17s went about their business of destruction nearly unmolested, except for the flak guns that still peppered the skies.

"Give 'em hell, boys!" someone shouted up at the sky. Several others whooped at the sight of the bombers.

Whitlock recalled the dead girls he had seen as the result of the bombing. The thought still made him sick.

He noticed that Ramsey hadn't joined in the cheering, although he was watching the planes.

"It's an ugly business," Ramsey said, as if he had read Whitlock's mind. "The sooner this war is over, the better."

After the morning exercise, it was back into the barracks to pass the interminable hours until dinner. There was little reading material and nothing to do.

Ramsey looked out the window wistfully as the men in the enlisted barracks next door trooped out to work. Most of their day was spent in manual labor; lately, they had been spending time repairing damage from the Allied bombing raids, which was ironic.

"According to the Geneva Convention, officers aren't to be made to work, but I've got to tell you, what I wouldn't do to get outside in the fresh air with a shovel in my hands or maybe a pick," Ramsey said. "Anything for something to do. That's what got to poor Hinson in the end, you know. He got too much inside his own head and couldn't get back out, poor bastard."

The grounds of the camp were roughly divided into four quadrants, according to the nationalities of the prisoners. Opposite their own barracks were those of the English prisoners of war. The consensus was that they were uptight bastards, particularly the officers. Military decorum was strictly adhered to in their barracks, and the men were made to drill and sing patriotic songs. The approach was supposed to keep up their spirits. It all seemed forced to Whitlock's eyes.

"There they go again, marching for King and Country," Ramsey remarked. "Those damn Brits have the attitude that the beatings will continue until morale improves."

In another corner of the camp were the French prisoners. They were considered to be disorganized and hot-tempered, with shouting at all hours of the day and night. It was no wonder that they might be a little crazy and lacking in discipline—some of the French had been prisoners there since 1940.

Finally, there was the Russian section, which occupied nearly half the camp. If the Germans treated the Americans, British, and even the crazed French with some degree of civility, this was not the case with how they treated the Russians. The Russians were made to work constantly, sometimes just moving piles of rocks from one end of the camp to the next. Those who slacked off earned a rifle butt to the head. There was even the occasional gunshot.

"The closest I can explain it is that the Germans view Russians in the way that some Americans view negroes, if not worse," Ramsey said. "The Russians don't have any love for the Germans, either."

"The last I heard before I ended up here was that the Russians were pressing in on Germany from the Eastern Front," Whitlock said. "Some of the worst fighting is taking place there."

"When it comes time to surrender, you can bet the Krauts are going to go looking for the nearest American," Ramsey said.

To pass the time, the officers discussed the end game of the war, debating how it would play out. When they weren't talking strategy, they told the same stories involving either women or copious amounts of alcohol—sometimes both— over and over again.

Whitlock became so bored after a few days that he couldn't imagine the plight of those who had been held for months and months.

Fortunately for him, the war was progressing at a faster pace. They soon heard artillery in the distance. Because the sound was coming from the east, they assumed it must be the Russians. The German guards began to look nervous.

Two weeks after Whitlock's arrival in the camp, they woke up to find that the Germans had fled. Sometime during the night, their captors had quietly unlocked the doors of the barracks, which were normally barred. The gates of the Stalag were open. One by one, the POWs wandered into the empty silent yard, feeling a little dazed.

The Germans had not freed the Russian

prisoners, however. They were left to kick out the windows and crawl from the barracks once they had figured out that the Germans were gone.

Some of the prisoners of all nationalities immediately fled. Whitlock wasn't so sure that was the best option. This part of Germany was about to become a battleground between whatever Wehrmacht forces remained and the oncoming Russians. Caught in the middle, unarmed prisoners wouldn't stand a chance. Also, the Germans had left behind food and water, so there was no real reason to leave the Stalag. By mid-day, the prisoners sat around in quiet groups, trying to figure out their situation. Some thought it best to wait for Allied troops to appear.

Their decision was soon made for them. Like a sight out of another time and place, a horde of Russian Cossacks came into view. To the Americans' amazement, they rode horses. The Russians wore wool hats and had machine guns slung over their shoulders. For the most part, they seemed a jovial bunch. They rode into the camp, horses and all, greeting the prisoners with cheerful shouts.

Then the rest of the Russian army arrived. Whitlock thought that the word "rabble" was the best way to describe them. They were a motley bunch, wearing bits and pieces of uniforms mixed with captured civilian clothes. Outlandishly, some wore silk evening jackets. Only the officers wore real uniforms, though theirs were disheveled from long months of living rough in the field. Whitlock was not particularly worried because the Russians were their Allies. They greeted the prisoners pleasantly and offered them food from their captured stocks.

The mood changed quickly, however, when a trio of trucks and Jeeps arrived. Oddly enough, these were American vehicles, but with Russian markings. The Russians who got out wore neat uniforms, some of which even looked tailored. The other Russians eyes them anxiously. As Whitlock was soon to find out, these were the dreaded NKVD political officers, come to make sure that good Soviet values were upheld. At gunpoint, they herded the Americans back into the barracks.

"For your own protection," said one of the Soviet officers, who spoke English.

Then he locked the doors.

CHAPTER 9

For the next three days, Whitlock and the other Americans were in a kind of limbo. The Russians kept them locked inside the barracks. At first, it was possible to believe that the Russians were simply trying to maintain some order. It made sense that they did not want or need former POWs wandering around a combat zone. But what Whitlock and the others witnessed began to change their minds.

Through the window of the barracks, they saw the Russians let all the French go. The French marched out like a kind of rabble, still squabbling among themselves, but at least they were free. Whitlock began to regret not getting out of the camp at the first opportunity, as some of the other officers had done. There hadn't been much concern then about the Russians, who were supposed to be their allies, after all.

Next, they saw the enlisted Americans and British being released. It was only the officers who were still being held.

"What I would like to know, is what the hell is going on?" Ramsey asked, giving voice to the question that was on everyone's mind.

"I studied French in high school, but a fat lot of good it did me," MacDonald said. "What I should have studied was Russian."

In part because of that language barrier, there was little interaction with the Russians, except when they brought the Americans water and food. When questioned, their new captors simply shrugged, or muttered meaningless responses in broken English about "security."

In the end, it was what they saw the Russians doing to their own kind that made them most anxious. The former Russian POWs were not greeted with open arms by their liberators. Instead, they were contained in their old prison quarters. Then, on the morning of the third day, individual Russian officers who had been the prisoners of the Germans were led out and lined up in the prison yard.

"I believe they're going to shoot them," MacDonald said in disbelief.

From inside the barracks, they watched as a handful of Russian soldiers with machine guns faced the line of officers, who stood glumly, knowing full well what was coming next. One of the NKVD officers, in his tailored uniform, read some kind of pronouncement from a sheet of paper that threatened to fly away in the breeze. Then he stepped back behind the line of machine gunners, raised his arm, and brought it down in a chopping motion.

Whitlock jerked back from the window, both horrified and fascinated by what he saw. As the guns opened fire, the bodies jumped as if on puppet strings as the bullets pumped into them. In moments, there was only a heap of bodies on the ground. The NKVD officer moved forward with a pistol, and shot the ones who showed any sign of life.

"I hate to say it, but things are about to get ugly around here," Ramsey said.

They had a glimmer of hope the next day, when the Russians rousted them from the barracks and marched them out of the camp itself. They could only think that the Russians were marching them to rejoin the American forces.

Whitlock looked around at the German countryside and marveled at what he saw.

Everywhere he looked, German civilians seemed to be on the move, carrying whatever they owned. Some pushed handcarts loaded with suitcases, pots and pans, and small children. One burly man carried an elderly woman on his back, in the same way one might give a child a ride. All the Germans were headed to the east in a slow, steady tide. The Russians showed little interest in the refugees, unless any of them looked like they might be former German soldiers. Anyone seen wearing even part of a German uniform was doomed.

"Where are they going?" Whitlock wondered.

"They're getting the hell out of Dodge," Ramsey said. "If what we've seen so far from the Russians is any indication, I'd say these people have the right idea."

There were now sixty-three American officers remaining. Some still held out hope that they were being marched to be turned over to an American unit, but instead, they reached a railroad siding. On the rails was a battered troop train, pocked with bullets where it had been strafed by Luftwaffe planes that were now just a bad memory. The locomotive faced east—toward Poland and then Russia beyond.

From the sounds within the other cars, it was clear that the train was loaded with human freight. Any mystery about who might be inside was settled when a detachment of German

POWs marched up and was herded into a car. The entire train seemed to be filled with POWs. Whitlock thought there must be hundreds of men jammed into the cars.

Then it was the Americans' turn. This time, there was nothing jovial or subtle about their captors' intentions. The Americans were forced aboard the train at gunpoint, crowded in like sardines. Then the doors rolled shut with a thunderous clang.

The POWs were now enclosed in what was essentially meant to be a rolling prison. Inside, it was nearly dark, with the only light coming from rectangular, uncovered openings high above their heads. To call these windows wasn't quite right, considering that there was no glass, and they were not wide enough for anyone to crawl through. The latrine facilities consisted of a hole cut into the floor, about one foot square. It was enough to step into and break a leg, but not large enough to escape. The floor beneath them lurched, causing the men to sway and grab one another for balance. Then they could feel the train begin to move.

Toward the east. Toward Russia.

• • •

The atmosphere inside the rail car could be described as one of indignant anger mixed with disappointment. After months of German captivity, the Americans had expected freedom. It had been stolen away by the Soviets.

"That does it," MacDonald announced. "We have to get out of here. Ramsey, you and Whitlock stand under that opening."

MacDonald found the smallest man there, a skinny lieutenant who could have been a jockey, and had him clamber onto their shoulders. The idea was for him to squeeze through the opening.

"If he gets out, what is he supposed to do?" Ramsey wondered, grunting with the effort of holding up the lieutenant. "Run around and unlock the doors?"

"He can let someone know we're here," MacDonald said. "The American lines can't be all that far away."

What MacDonald said made sense. Of course, how the lieutenant was supposed to get off the moving train unharmed was anybody's guess.

But escape was a moot point. Not even the skinny lieutenant was small enough to fit through the ventilation opening.

"Does anyone have a paper and pencil? We can toss out a note!"

That seemed desperate to Whitlock, considering that they would need to have the good fortune of some American stumbling across the note beside the railroad tracks. The nearest

Allied troops were close—but by anyone's best guess the American lines were twenty or thirty miles away. Soon, even the effort to write a note proved futile, considering that no one had so much as a scrap of paper, let alone a pencil.

As the miles rolled on, their will to escape lessened as reality settled in. Now, the focus turned to surviving these miserable conditions. From time to time, one of the officers crawled up on someone's shoulders and reported what they had seen. The train crossed a river that they guessed was the Oder; soon they would be in Poland. The smell of woodsmoke filled the air from burned villages and blackened forests. The ravaged countryside was punctuated with the empty husks of tanks, both Russian and German.

At nightfall the train stopped, and all up and down the tracks they could hear the sounds of car doors being opened and Russians shouting. When their turn came, a few men prepared to rush the doors.

The sight that greeted them quickly changed their minds about that tactic. Standing well back from the car were several Soviet soldiers with machine pistols, pointed into the packed Americans. If one of the Russians touched a trigger, it would be a massacre. Another Russian brought a bucket of water, and another tossed in a sack of bread. *Dinner*. Then the door rolled shut again.

MacDonald organized the rationing of the bread before it could become a free for all, seeing that each man received an equal-sized hunk. The water was more problematic because there was nothing to drink it with. Nobody had so much as a cup or spoon. They resorted to each man having to kneel and scoop up water in his hands.

The water was barely enough to sustain them, considering that in the heat of the day the cramped interior of the rail car grew to be as sweltering as an oven. Nightfall brought little relief, because by the chill hours before dawn they were all shivering. No one had so much as a blanket or a spare coat.

Ramsey developed a hacking cough that wracked his whole body. Though he was a tough and wiry man, he was a good deal older than Whitlock, and the poor diet and conditions were taking their toll on him. He had been a prisoner for several months, subsisting on lousy food.

The car rolled on and on. If life in the barracks had been dull, the passage of time was now stultifying. Whitlock found a crack to peer through for a glimpse of the countryside. They passed through cities and towns. He saw tall buildings topped by exotic minarets that must be Russian. It sure as hell wasn't Boston. Whitlock had only a dim grasp of the geography beyond Germany, so he had no idea exactly where they were.

The steel wheels ground on. Once they reached Russia, the train began to make stops to disgorge POWs. In some places, load after load of Germans from the neighboring cars were marched away at gunpoint.

No one came for the Americans until days later, when the train lurched to a stop after midnight. Whitlock peered through the crack but could see only inky darkness—there was no sign of civilization. Without warning, the car door opened and the Soviets began pulling prisoners roughly out, simply grabbing the ones nearest the opening. But when others got the idea to leave, they were stopped at gunpoint. The door rolled shut again.

That routine continued for the next few days. The train would stop, and the Russians grabbed a few of the Americans. Some men positioned themselves near the doors, just for a chance to get off the endless train.

Almost by instinct, Whitlock shrank away from the doors, ensconcing himself in a corner.

MacDonald and Ramsey joined him. "The three of us need to stick together. I don't know what these Ruskie bastards have planned for us, but it can't be good. Let's see how long we can ride it out."

The train rolled on, stopping every now and then for the Russians to unload more Americans. Whitlock tried to make some sense of it, or to find a pattern. When he mentioned it to Ramsey, he said that it seemed obvious to him: "They're splitting us up, don't you see? A few here, a few there—they don't want us all in one place."

"Why the hell would they do that?"

"If you've got a lot of something to hide, what do you do? Spread it out in different hiding places."

Finally, it was just half a dozen men left in the car. The empty car grew cold and echoed with every clank and creak. Ramsey's cough had grown worse. At night, they had to huddle together for warmth. MacDonald took to calling their trio The Three Musketeers. A couple of days sometimes passed before someone thought to bring them food, although now there would be a pail of cabbage soup or even some kind of meat—there were now only three of them to feed so the Russians didn't have to be so stingy.

One night, Whitlock thought he heard a wolf howling. When he persuaded MacDonald and Ramsey to put him up on their shoulders, all he could see was darkness uninterrupted by a speck of light. He thought at first that they were passing through a tunnel until he looked up and saw stars. When he stared out between the cracks in the slats by day, he saw vast empty plains, rolling hills, and thick, wild forests. Where on God's green earth were they being taken?

Two nights later, MacDonald made the

mistake of sleeping too close to the door, and got rounded up with three others. He tried to crawl back into the car, but the Russians dragged him out.

"I'll see you back home or in hell, fellas!" he shouted before the door slammed shut. Now it was just Whitlock and Ramsey. MacDonald was gone. The train started rolling again, with both men too heartsick to even attempt conversation.

Then one morning, the train finally stopped for good. The door of the car was opened, and Russians on the ground gestured for them to come out. The soldiers were already wearing winter coats. They carried rifles slung over their shoulders, but didn't bother to point them at the Americans.

Whitlock soon saw why. They were in the midst of a desolate landscape. If Whitlock started to run, the guards could go get coffee and by the time they came back, he would still be in rifle range on that vast landscape.

The only structure visible was a prison camp. Unlike Stalag Twenty-two B, this Soviet camp looked exactly like the prison that Whitlock had imagined and feared. Guard towers stood at each corner. High barb wire fences stretched in between. The barracks were squat, rusting hulks set into muddy prison yard. The impression it made was of a medieval castle, but one built out of barbed wire.

Ramsey said, "Say what you want about the Russians, but they really know how to build the hell out of a prison camp."

"Where are we?" Whitlock wondered.

"I'd say that we're in hell, but the sort that freezes over," Ramsey said, then doubled over with a wracking cough as the cold air hit his lungs. When he coughed lately, his chest sounded like an empty paper bag. "We're stuck so deep in Russia that it's going to take a corkscrew to get us out. God help us."

CHAPTER 10

Vaccaro looked at the Mosin-Nagant rifle in Cole's hands.

"You're really going to do it, aren't you?" he asked.

"I'd like to see someone try to stop me. You comin' or not?"

"Hell yeah," Vaccaro said. "What's the worst that could happen? It's not like they can send us to the front. The war's over."

Cole was feeling itchy, or maybe just plain ornery—there wasn't any other way to describe it. It all came down to there being nothing to do.

He did not mind sitting for hours on end, staring through a rifle scope—but this business of having nothing to do jangled his nerves. Some men passed the time drinking and playing cards, or chasing the local *fräuleins*. Fraternization with the enemy was officially forbidden, but there wasn't much the hungry local girls wouldn't do, being so desperate for food from the well-supplied Americans.

The women didn't much interest Cole. If he longed for anything, it was the sense of power that being a sniper had given him. Now he was just a nobody. He missed the biting smell of cordite. He spent hours cleaning his rifle, and then cleaning it all over again.

The war had just plain petered out. For the Americans, there had been no final, climactic battle. The fighting at the end had been in fits and starts, with brief but vicious skirmishes in a final bloodletting. Then the Germans surrendered. Spring became summer and now there was talk of starting to send everyone home. Guys were talking about the first thing that they were going to do once they got home.

From their side of the Elbe River, the Americans kept a nervous eye on the Russians, who, in turn, kept watch on them.

They had gone through the motions of seeming like Allies and old friends, but the actions rang hollow. The Russians had sent over some emissaries to meet the Americans, and there had been much swapping of cigarettes, toasts with vodka, and many photographs taken. Everyone kept their guns handy, just in case.

The news came and went that President Roosevelt had died. Nobody had known what to make of that, or what to make of this new president, Truman. He seemed to be a steady and reliable man. The Russians and even the Germans had speculated on what the news meant, considering that FDR had been president for sixteen years—in fact, he had been in power longer than Stalin or Hitler. But the transfer of power turned out to be uneventful. Democracy's institutions made for a smooth transition. The Soviets could scarcely believe that there had been no coup attempts or secret plots to seize power.

The grand events taking place on the world stage gave the average soldier something to think about as he contemplated his place in these events. Cole, however, was mostly bored.

Today, he finally planned to have a little fun.

He looked pointedly at Vaccaro. "Come on, then, if you're comin'."

"Wouldn't miss it for the world."

Cole and Vaccaro struck out for the countryside. It felt strange to walk along the roads without having to worry about meeting an enemy patrol. Cole carried a pack, but along with ammunition, it held four bottles of beer wrapped in damp rags to keep them cool, and some ham sandwiches.

They walked through woods and pastures, until they came to a large, level field. "This here spot will do," Cole said.

Strictly speaking, what Cole had in mind was against regulations. It was a funny thing, but in the Army, you weren't allowed to shoot your rifle whenever you wanted. Especially now that the war was over, there was not much call for shooting.

When the Russians had paid them a visit, Cole had sought out one of the Russian drivers who was not part of the festivities or photo shoots. The driver happened to have an almost brand new Mosin-Nagant rifle. The Russian had been glad to trade it for a carton of cigarettes.

Since then, Cole had been eager to shoot it. He knew this was the rifle that the Ghost Sniper had used with deadly effect in Normandy, and then in the Ardennes Forest. What was so damn special about it?

Cole walked out and used four sticks, like giant pushpins, to secure a target to a haymow two hundred yards away. The target in this case happened to be the front cover of Life magazine, featuring a picture of a Buddha statue in Japan. Then he walked back and picked up the rifle.

It was a heavy beast, weighing much more than his Springfield. There was nothing graceful about the Mosin-Nagant. The Russians had manufactured a blunt instrument in the plainest way possible, almost like a shovel or a hammer that happened to shoot.

This rifle had open sights rather than a telescope, so he would not be able to use it for real distance shooting. However, the target in the field would give him an idea of what this weapon was like.

The driver had thrown in a few rounds of 7.62 mm ammunition. Cole inserted the five-round magazine.

He put the rifle to his shoulder, lined up the rear sight with the front sight so that they both hovered over the paper target. He took a deep breath, held it, let the ball of his finger gently take up the pressure on the trigger. Almost by surprise, the butt slammed into his shoulder.

"Damn thing kicks like a mule," he said. "How did I do?"

Vaccaro had brought along Zeiss binoculars that he had liberated from one of the small towns they had passed through early that spring.

"Looks like you nicked old Buddha's ear. See if you can do any better."

Cole fired four more shots, two from a standing position, doing yet more damage to Buddha. He passed the rifle to Vaccaro, who also fired it five times. That used up the ammo he had gotten from the Russian.

Cole decided the Mosin-Nagant wasn't any better than the Springfield or a Mauser. In his assessment, the rifle was too heavy and kicked too much. He had no doubt, though, that in the right hands it was a deadly sniper weapon.

"Ready to trade up?" Vaccaro asked.

"I think I'll keep ol' Betsy," Cole said. "The thing about shooting is that it's like an apple pie. There's different recipes, but it all comes down to the apples."

Vaccaro looked at him. "Now that was hillbilly wisdom if ever I've heard it."

Cole set aside the Russian rifle and reached for his Springfield. Everything about it, right down to how it fit his left hand and the pocket made by his shoulder, felt so familiar. "Let's see how rusty I've gotten with this thing. You ready? Call the targets."

They started with the paper target. With the four-power scope on the Springfield, Cole was able to put a bullet square in the Buddha's forehead. Vaccaro said the magazine cover was too easy, and picked out a tree on the other side of the field where a huge branch had sheared off, leaving a blank patch on the trunk.

Cole fired. Wood chips flew.

Next was a stone that someone had set on top of the wall in the next field over.

Cole's bullet knocked it flying.

A hawk soared far in the distance, drifting on

the air currents as if in slow motion. Vaccaro called it, but added, "Cole, if you hit that bird I'll name my first born after you."

Seconds later, the hawk tumbled from the sky.

Vaccaro said nothing for a while, which was unusual for him. Then he gave a low whistle. "I'll be damned. You are scary with that rifle. I'm not sure that even I could have hit that hawk."

"Vaccaro, you can barely hit that paper target. Who are you kidding? Here, take the rifle."

Vaccaro shook his head. "That's the difference between you and me, Hillbilly. I don't care if I ever shoot a rifle again. What would I do with a rifle in Brooklyn? Nah, once every summer I can go out to the shooting gallery at Coney Island, and that will be plenty for me."

"Well, City Boy, let me just say it straight. You done earned yourself that trip to Coney Island. Now, you want a ham sandwich?"

Vaccaro took the sandwich, then glanced over a Cole. Most soldiers talked about home, how good they'd had it with mom's cooking or maybe how lucky they'd been with the local girls, and how they couldn't wait to get back there. Vaccaro understood that distance put things in soft focus and that home was never as good as anyone remembered it.

Cole, however, hardly ever talked about growing up. In fact, it was hard to think of Cole as a kid—except maybe a smaller version that was just as lean and rangy, with the same serious expression on his face. He did know that Cole's daddy had been a mean drunk. He knew that Cole had never really gone to school. Beyond that, Vaccaro knew better than to ask.

Cole handed him another sandwich. "Just like a Sunday School picnic," he said.

"Did your Sunday School teacher bring beer along, too?" Vaccaro wondered. "That's my kind of religion."

They sat in the grass and ate the sandwiches and drank the beer, soaking up sunshine. It was the best that Cole had felt in a long time, but he realized it wasn't because they were playing hooky from the Army. It was because he had finally gotten a chance to do some shooting.

The beer made them both lazy in the warm afternoon. They shared the knapsack as a pillow, both of them stretched out in opposite directions. They had done this by necessity in the war; now it just felt companionable. Cole was starting to drift off when he heard the whine of an approaching Jeep. He sat up.

"Aw, hell. We done made somebody nervous."

The Jeep was being driven by a couple of MPs, distinguishable by their white armbands and the white bands on their helmets.

Cole and Vaccaro weren't making any particular effort to hide, but the road was far from the edge of the field. One of the MPs stood up in the Jeep and waved at them.

"If we run, they're not gonna catch us," Vaccaro said.

"Shut up, Vaccaro. You ever try to outrun a Jeep?"

Instead, they packed up and headed toward the Jeep, fully expecting to be get in hot water for disturbing the peace.

The MP was a big, thick-necked fellow.

"Are you Cole?"

"Well, I reckon I am."

"You are wanted at HQ, sir. You're late for a meeting. We've been looking for you since this morning. One of your buddies said you might be out here testing a rifle. We heard the shooting and figured it might be you."

"A couple of regular detectives," Vaccaro said.

"Who are you?" the MP asked.

"My name's Vaccaro."

"Nobody said anything about you, Vaccaro. But we'll give you a ride back, if you want."

They got in the back of the Jeep.

"What's this about?"

"Nobody told me, sir."

Cole was getting confused about this "sir" business from the MPs. "Listen, I'm only a corporal."

"That's not what I was told. I was ordered to find Sergeant Cole. Apparently, you've been promoted."

"That's news to me. How can I get promoted and be late for a meeting I didn't know about in the first place?"

The MP grinned. "That's the Army for you. You're always the last to know."

CHAPTER 11

Somehow, despite the fact that the war was ending—or maybe because of it—new uniforms were in short supply. The replacement troops sent to occupy Germany were the only men with new uniforms, and as a result, they stood out in stark contrast to the combat veterans.

Cole had to make do with the fatigues he'd been wearing since before the Battle of the Bulge. They had been washed, but the uniform was badly worn and patched in places. He did take some time to give his boots a quick polish and to comb his hair.

Cole glanced at himself in a mirror. *That's the story of my life. Always trying to make do with worn-out clothes and a sliver of soap.* After living on C rations and cigarettes for months in the field, he had put on some weight during their occupation duty, and filled out the uniform better. Nobody would describe him as beefy.

"How do I look?" he asked Vaccaro.

"Just about right for a court martial."

Vaccaro wished him luck. The MPs had waited outside for Cole to get cleaned up, and they gave him a ride to HQ. Cole couldn't tell if they had been sent to keep in an eye on him, or to actually assist him.

A dozen thoughts ran through his mind, the chief one being why he had been summoned to HQ. Vaccaro's comment about a court martial scratched at the back of his mind. Had disobeying orders back at the Elbe by ferrying refugees across finally caught up with him? Was there some other infraction he could only guess at? It would be just like the Army to promote him just in time to bust him down to private.

Headquarters was located in a grand old mansion. You could count on the generals to find the fanciest digs around. The MPs had to stop for yet more MPs at the gate, who reviewed their orders before letting them through. The entry gates were topped by a couple of hideous-looking beasts straight out of some story intended to scare children. Gargoyles, he'd learned that they were called. Judging by how many he had seen, Europeans seemed to be fond of them. You just didn't see that kind of thing in the States. It was a reminder that there was something dark and ancient running through the heart of Europe.

Inside, it looked to Cole like the mansion had been stripped of anything valuable, like a house gone up for auction by the bank. He was brought through a set of tall carved doors into an office the size of his squad's entire barracks. A small fire burned in the fireplace. It might be warm outside, but the mansion's stone walls felt cool and chill.

Three men stood around the fire. Two wore uniforms, but the third man did not. He was an older, snowy haired man, with high cheekbones and a sharp nose that made him look like a hawk. All three looked up as he walked in. To Cole's astonishment, one of the officers wore general's stars.

"Sergeant Cole," said the general. "Glad you could make it."

"Yes, sir." Cole did his best to come to attention. He saluted. Military pomp and circumstance never had been his strong point, but you were never wrong to salute a general.

The older man spoke up. "No need for all that, Sergeant. We are an informal bunch here today." He stuck out a hand. Cole stared at it for a moment before it registered that he was supposed to shake.

"Yes, sir. The MPs told me I was a sergeant now."

"Yes, well, we needed someone with some rank for what we have in mind," the older man said.

"I don't want to be in charge of nobody," Cole said defiantly. Like most mountain people, Cole didn't like anyone telling him what to do. At the same time, mountain people had no interest in giving orders to anyone else.

The older man gave him what Cole could only think of as a kindly look. "Why don't we sit down and discuss it? Major, pour us all a drink."

He seemed to have taken charge, never mind the fact that there was a general and a major in the room. Who the hell was he?

They went over to a massive carved desk that must have belonged to some German millionaire, or maybe to a baron. The general took a seat behind the desk. The major was busy at a sideboard, filling glasses. The older man pulled his chair closer to Cole, so that they were almost knee to knee. He smelled of good cigars and aftershave.

"You're probably wondering who I am. My name is Harrison Whitlock. You can see that I'm not a military man. However, I am a United States Senator, for whatever that's worth." The way Whitlock put weight on the word "senator" made it plain that it was worth a great deal.

"All right." Cole took the crystal glass that the major handed him. Sipped. The liquor went down as fiery and smooth as lava, and seemed to go straight to his head. Cole already felt a little dizzy. He was out of his element here among these men, and none of it made any sense.

"Now you know who I am, and let me share what I know about you. The general here tells me that you grew up hunting and trapping, and that you know just about everything there is to know about surviving in the woods. You are one of the best snipers in the United States Army." The senator paused. "Word has it that you are also one tough son of a bitch when the need arises."

Cole had no idea how the general could know any of that about him. The general seemed content to sit quietly while the senator talked. Now that the drinks were served, there was no chair for the major, who found a place to stand near the fireplace.

"Yes, sir." It was all Cole could think to say.

"That said, you are probably wondering why you are here," Whitlock said. "Major, let me see that intelligence report."

"Sir, may I remind you this is top secret information and the sergeant here—"

Senator Whitlock waved a hand dismissively. "It's all right, major."

The major handed a sheet of paper to the senator, who then gave it to Cole.

Cole scanned the pages. He could pick out words here and there, like landmarks in a landscape, but that was all. The general and the major didn't pick up on it, but when Cole looked up, he saw that the senator was watching him with new understanding. He was relieved to see that the glance held no judgment in it. Then the man blinked, and absorbed Cole's secret without saying a word.

"Well, you can see from this report that it's clear the Russians have some of our men. When the Russians took over former German POW camps, they did not let all of our boys go."

The thought made Cole angry. "Why the hell not?"

"Stalin wants them for poker chips, that's why. He wants to make sure we don't put up a fuss about the Russians grabbing all this territory for themselves. What the Russians have done is wrong, plain and simple. Our government is afraid to act officially, because we're walking on eggshells here in Europe. Everyone is so damned scared of upsetting the Russians."

The general interrupted. "The president ought to do something about this. It's not right."

Senator Whitlock waved a hand. "Truman is all right, but he's a weakling where the Russians are concerned. He doesn't want to start another war. To be honest, nobody in America wants another war. So the president is just going to roll over and do what Uncle Joe tells him."

Cole was a little shocked to hear the senator talk about the president that way, and the way he said it made it clear that he knew Truman personally. "Sir, what's this got to do with me?"

Senator Whitlock smiled. "Gentlemen, why don't you leave me alone with the sergeant for a few minutes?"

The general and major looked at one another. It was the major who spoke up. "Senator, I don't know if—"

"Go on," Senator Whitlock said, waving a hand again like he was shooing flies. "The sergeant and I need to get to know one another."

Whitlock waited until the two officers left, and then closed the massive doors behind them. Then he went over to the sideboard and brought back the decanter to refill their glasses.

"This is fifty-year-old cognac. Wonderful stuff. Why should we let the general have it all to himself, ha, ha! Now let's get to brass tacks, Sergeant Cole. Any American would be indignant to learn that the Russians are holding our soldiers hostage. It's only natural. I'm as mad about it as you are. But let me be frank. You see, I have a personal interest in this as well. The Russians have my grandson. His B-17 was shot down in April, at which point in time he was captured by the Germans. I have confirmation that he was taken to a stalag in a part of Germany now held by the Russians. He has since been taken by the Russians and transferred to a remote Gulag—that's a Russian prison camp, by the way—in northern Russia. Fortunately, it is within a few day's walk of the Finnish border."

The senator stopped short of explaining that Gulag was not a proper name, but an acronym for the Russian words for Main Administration of Camps. The Soviets had made their harsh system of more than one hundred forced labor camps sound as innocuous as possible.

"How do you know all this, sir?"

"We have our spies, just as the Russians do."

Suddenly, Cole understood where the conversation was going.

"You want to get him out of there," he said. "Why me?"

The senator looked him over. "You know, it's kind of interesting. Here's a young man from Appalachia who can't read, who probably grew up without shoes on his feet, a real nobody. Does that sound like you?" In what was becoming a familiar gesture, the old man raised a hand to wave off the angry response on Cole's lips. "I don't say this to insult you, Sergeant. Quite the opposite."

"I ain't so sure about that."

Whitlock went on, "You know what else is

interesting? When I had my people ask around to find someone capable for this sort of mission, your name came up. More than once. Here's a nobody who lands at Normandy and a year later he's not a nobody at all. I would call that sort of person a somebody. Somebody who is respected. Does that sound better to you?"

Cole didn't have an answer to that.

"I have to say, it wasn't always in a good way that you were mentioned," Whitlock added. "People are a little scared of you. They say you're a killer."

Cole had heard enough.

"Why should I do this?" he asked sharply. "Go all the way to Russia to rescue some rich guy's grandson? It's crazy."

Whitlock nodded. He leaned back in the chair and studied Cole, as if reconsidering him. "I can't order you, simply put. This wouldn't even be a military mission. It can't be, not officially. I am asking you because you are the best we've got. That, and the fact that the goddamn Russians have taken our soldiers hostage, including my grandson." The senator pounded the desk so hard that the general stuck his head in for a second to make sure everything was all right, then retreated. "My question for you, Mr. Cole, is what kind of man are you?"

"I reckon I don't understand the question."

"Oh, I *reckon* you do." The senator locked

eyes with Cole. There was nothing soft there—they were as flinty as his own. Then Whitlock nodded. "You don't need to answer the question, Mr. Cole. I can see it in your eyes."

"So what kind of man are you, Senator?"

Whitlock spread his hands as if the answer was obvious. "I am a man who gets things done. I would consider this a personal favor to me, one that I could repay someday."

"There ain't nothin' I need."

Whitlock laughed. "I'm not talking about getting you a carton of cigarettes and a week's furlough, Cole. I am talking about a personal favor from a United States senator, the sort who pulls ropes, by the way, not strings. That favor is the kind of thing you bury in the Mason jar out back for a rainy day."

"Like I said—"

Whitlock touched Cole's knee. "I know that you are a proud man, Cole. I wouldn't expect anything less. We can all use a favor now and then. Even you. However, here's the real reason that you'll take on this mission."

"And what's that, Senator?"

The senator leaned in close and spoke quietly. "You'll do this because you're bored now that there's no one left to fight. You miss it. Are you going to argue with that?"

Cole said nothing.

Senator Whitlock nodded. "Now, let's get the

general and the major back in here and talk details, shall we?"

CHAPTER 12

Two days later, the mission briefing was held at the Munchshofen Air Base in Germany, where the Army Air Corps had taken over the former Luftwaffe hanger and the surrounding airfield. Senator Whitlock wasn't there, but the briefing was run by Major Leon Dickey, who had been present at the initial meeting between Cole and the senator.

During that meeting, a couple of other understandings had been reached between the senator and Cole. The first was that Cole would not be in charge. Senator Whitlock explained that while the mission was off the books, it was still a quasi-military operation, and Major Dickey wanted someone he already knew and trusted in charge of the team. That was all right with Cole, who preferred to be the lone wolf. The second accommodation was that Cole managed to get Vaccaro added to the team.

The major met Cole outside the door of the briefing room, and gave him a hearty handshake. "Good to see you again, Sergeant." Then he turned to Vaccaro with an uncertain expression. "Who's this?"

"This here is Corporal Vaccaro," Cole explained to Major Dickey. "Second-best shot in the Twenty-ninth Division. I reckoned we could use another man."

Dickey shook his head. "Maybe you talked the senator into it, but I've already assembled a team. We need to keep this small and tight."

"The way I see it, major, is that you got your team, and I got mine."

"Like I said, Cole. We've got everyone we need."

"There's two in this here poke. You want me, you got to take him."

"Poke?"

"That's what I said, ain't it? Now, do we go in or do we leave?"

The major looked from Cole, then to Vaccaro. "It's your funeral, soldier. Go on in, the two of you."

They entered the cramped, windowless room. The air was thick with cigarette smoke and smelled strongly of aftershave. Cole could smell someone's spearmint gum. Two men already sat in folding chairs around a battered table. They looked up with interest as the door opened.

Cole's impression of the man on the left was that he was a big son of a bitch. The furniture looked too small for him, like maybe he was sitting in a chair meant for a kindergartner. He had shoulders the width of a fireplace mantel. The big hands on the table in front of him nearly smothered a coffee mug. Despite his intimidating size, his face was placid and almost simple—a gentle giant.

The second man took longer to notice, but he was just as hard to forget. At first, it was almost as if Cole was looking in a mirror. The second man had the same lean build and appeared to be of similar height. That was where the similarity ended. This man had dirty blond hair that was a little too long for a soldier's. He had dark eyes rather than Cole's cut-glass ones. The contrast between his light-colored hair and dark eyes was disconcerting, like wearing a striped tie with a plaid shirt. A twin set of scars ran along his cheeks. They were not fresh war wounds, however, but long faded—scars from some childhood injury perhaps. The man seemed to struggle to contain either nervousness or energy —one foot was tapping away when Cole and Vaccaro walked in, and never stopped during the briefing.

"Gentlemen, here's the rest of our team. This is Cole. And this is, uh—"

"Vaccaro."

The major nodded at the big man. "The big guy here is Samson. And that's Honaker. He's our team leader."

The big man smiled agreeably. He heartily shook hands with Cole and Vaccaro.

"Samson, huh?" Cole asked.

The big guy nodded. "Uh, huh. You know, like in the Bible."

Honaker nodded in their direction and offered a forced smile as an afterthought.

"Like you guys, Samson here landed at D-Day," Dickey said. "Since the war ended he has done some work for the OSS."

"OSS?" Cole asked.

"Office of Strategic Services."

"Never heard of it."

"You aren't supposed to," Dickey said. "That's the whole idea. Honaker here was recommended for this mission based on his reputation, just like you. He's also done a little work for the OSS. He speaks some Russian, which might come in handy where you're going. We served together for a while in Italy, so Honaker and I go way back."

Cole cocked his head; he was getting a vibe off Honaker that he couldn't quite make out, like the dying vibration of a banjo chord. The man's dark eyes were inscrutable as they flicked from Cole to Vaccaro.

"Is this the whole team, Major?" Cole asked.

"You're looking at it." Dickey held up a hand as if he had a question. "Just so you know, we're not going to use military ranks from here on out. Technically, this is not a military operation. It's also hush, hush. Nobody outside of this room is to know about it. Agreed?"

"Sure."

Major Dickey handed out some sort of report. To Cole's eyes, the words marched meaninglessly across the page, and he handed the pages on to the next man without comment. The last thing he wanted was for the team to realize that he couldn't read.

Dickey spread a map on the table and the four men bent over it. Cole felt more confident— you didn't have to read to understand a map.

Dickey remained standing as he began to lay out the mission. "Gentlemen, as you know, our mission is to rescue Senator Whitlock's grandson from a Soviet Gulag where he is being held captive. It took a while to determine where he was located—believe it or not, there are more than fifty of these camps across Russia."

Samson let out a low whistle. "That many?"

"These are re-education camps for the most part," Dickey said. He said it in such an earnest way that it almost sounded as if he were defending the Gulag system. "These are people who have spoken out against the government in some way, so they have been sent to the Gulag to be re-trained through hard labor to be better Soviets."

"Hell of a country," Samson said.

"The American POWs have been divided among several such camps," Colonel Dickey continued. "I'm not going to lie and tell you that getting Lieutenant Whitlock out is going to be easy. We don't know what condition he's in, or all of the challenges you may face. I do know one thing, which is that we have a very limited window of operations due to the weather. The Gulag camp is located in a region known as Vologoda, which is closer to the Arctic Ocean than Philadelphia is to New York."

"So what you're saying is that it's cold," Honaker said.

Dickey nodded. "There is a short autumn in this area of the Soviet Union. Basically, winter sets in once the first storm hits in October. We're talking about snow, maybe even blizzard conditions, long before the kids back home are trick or treating. Given our current date, we are looking at maybe a two-week window to complete our mission before the weather starts to get dicey."

"Not much time," Honaker said.

"Then there is the political situation to consider. You are going to be flying out of Finland, which borders the Soviet Union. It's a big border, more than eight hundred miles long. The Finns don't necessarily love the Soviets, but they need to make nice with them because they're neighbors. Any cooperation they extend will be very limited."

"What you're trying to say is that Finland is another limited window of opportunity," Honaker said.

"The senator is pulling some strings and working the back channels. He's setting it up to look like an official diplomatic visit. Mending fences after the war, or something like that. It appears that the Finns will let us fly out of there, and look the other way when we walk back in. After that so-called diplomatic visit ends, all bets are off. So, you're really gonna have to hoof it to get back across the border in time."

Cole spoke up. "It's Russia that I'm concerned about. What kind of countryside can we expect?"

Dickey sighed. "In a word, inhospitable. There's a whole lot of nothing. There are some villages, but essentially it's a wilderness full of swamps and forests. The Russians call those forests *taiga*. I understand it's mostly evergreen forest like you see up in Maine and Canada.

There aren't any particularly large rivers that you'll need to cross so long as you play things right, but you will have to ford some smaller waterways."

Cole thought that Dickey sounded as if he had memorized some sort of encyclopedia entry, fancy words and all.

"Don't forget the wolves," Honaker said.

"Right. Vologda, and the region next to it, Kirov, has a wolf problem. Two winters ago, wolves killed something like sixty people across the region when the game became scarce. But you won't be sticking around there long enough to encounter any wolves."

"Wolves?" Vaccaro looked pale. "Any other wildlife we have to worry about?"

"If the weather was going to be warmer, I would warn you about the asiatic pit vipers. They should be hibernating by now. There are some bears around, mostly up in the higher country, so they shouldn't be a problem." Dickey clapped his hands, which made Vaccaro jump. "Anyhow, your main problem is going to be the two-legged kind of animal. Once the Soviets figure out that their precious American prisoners have escaped, they will give chase. The good news is that they won't have much of an advantage because there are almost zero roads. Anyone who comes after you is going to have to do so on foot."

"What if there's more than one American?"

Cole wanted to know.

Dickey held up one finger. "You need to concern yourself about one man. Lieutenant Whitlock. We don't know how many other Americans the Russians are holding there, but trying to liberate any others is just a recipe for failure."

"That don't seem right to me," Cole said. "We're goin' all the way to Russia and then we just leave any other poor bastards behind?"

"That's the mission, Cole. You get Lieutenant Whitlock and get to Finland. Nobody else."

"I don't like it."

"That's the way it is." Dickey shrugged, and looked around. "You will have some help on the ground. There is a local who will be your guide."

"Can we trust him?" Cole asked.

"Believe it or not, not every Russian loves Stalin," Dickey said, giving him a look usually reserved for schoolchildren who asked too many annoying questions. "Also, money can be a great motivator. You're from hillbilly country, right, Cole? Did anybody ever make any moonshine even though it was illegal? They sure as hell did. It's no different in Russia. Money is money. This guide will put you in touch with a contact who lives in the village near the Gulag compound. The contact is your best shot at getting access to the camp itself."

"So we'll need to wing some parts of this once

we get there," Honaker said, sounding annoyed.

"This is a Gulag in a remote part of Russia that we're talking about here," Dickey said. "There is no other way than to wing it."

• • •

Dickey led them out of the briefing room and into the cavernous hangar. Although the American forces had moved in and made the space their own, there was still a strange feel about being in the old Luftwaffe lair. It was as if there was still a palpable smell of Nazis in the air, like a whiff of rotten hamburger.

Spread out on worktables and on the floor itself was a variety of gear: clothing, weapons, packs, rations.

A young officer saw their group and approached. "What's all this for?" he asked.

"Don't worry about it," Dickey said.

The officer glanced at the group, then at the weaponry, and went on about his business without another word.

They turned their attention to the gear. Most of it was distinctly non-military, the kind of stuff one might expect for a trip to someplace cold. This was gear that you might take mountain climbing, or maybe on a hunting trip to the north woods of Maine. Dickey handed Cole a sheepskin coat with a fur-trimmed hood. "That ought to keep you warm," he said. "Grab a pair of boots, mittens, long underwear—the works. I can guarantee you that it's going to get goddamn cold at night where you're going."

Cole and the others sorted through the gear and stuffed it into packs. There were rations as well, but they took only the bare minimum, figuring it would take them no more than a week to hike out of Russia.

Cole was impressed by the sleeping bags, which were stuffed with goose down and mummy-shaped to minimize heat loss. These had been issued to some of the commando units in the war. However, he opted for a thick wool blanket.

"Old school, huh?" Vaccaro wondered.

"Let me tell you, if them feathers get wet that fancy sleeping bag won't keep a badger warm."

"A badger? Where do you come up with this stuff?" Vaccaro thought it over, put down the mummy bag, and grabbed a blanket instead.

Once he finished packing for himself, Cole went through the pile again.

"Cole, does this look like a garage sale to you?" Dickey wanted to know.

"No, but I reckon Whitlock is gonna need a coat and a blanket and some decent boots if we don't want him freezin' to death."

Dickey nodded. "Good point. Better bring along some extra rations, too."

But it was the weapons that the team was really interested in. Again, most of it was not military issue in order to avoid the appearance of this being a military mission. Dickey had procured quite an assortment, leaving the team feeling like boys turned loose in a candy store.

"Look at this," Vaccaro said, hefting a beautifully made Krieghoff double rifle, elegant down to its scrollwork and walnut stock. A Zeiss four-power scope was offset over the right barrel. "A double-barreled shotgun!"

"That's a big game rifle," Dickey said. "Some rich German probably took it on safari before the war. Maybe shot a lion with it. You could buy a Cadillac for what that rifle is worth."

Vaccaro grinned. "I'll take it. It's just the thing if I run into a wolf."

Cole looked over the rifles. In the end, he decided to hang onto the 1903 Springfield back in the barracks. He couldn't ask for a better blade than the Bowie knife he'd been carrying for months. Hand-forged and wickedly sharp, it had got him out of more than one tight spot.

"Don't you want something new?" Dickey wondered.

"I reckon I'll stick with what I know," he said. "A man don't go on a mission with a rifle he don't know."

Honaker chose a German Mauser hunting rifle with a beautifully carved stock. Samson selected a brutal-looking pump action 12-gauge shotgun.

"That's a good choice for you, big guy," Vaccaro told him. "Let the bad guys get nice and close, and any that you miss, you can beat them to death with that thing."

Samson just grinned. He handled the heavy shotgun effortlessly.

"If you gentlemen are finished with your shopping spree, then I would advise you to make your goodbyes here in Germany. I'm sure I don't have to remind you not to be too specific about your plans," Dickey said. "We leave for Finland in the morning."

CHAPTER 13

The Russians were building a railroad to
nowhere. At least, that's what it looked like to
Whitlock, even if the railroad was officially
known as the Vologda-Kotlas-Ukhta Railroad
Line. That first day after their arrival, Whitlock
and Ramsey were sent out as part of a work gang,
given picks, and shown where to dig. Reluctantly,
Whitlock had to admit that he didn't mind the
work. He welcomed being outdoors and doing
something after long weeks spent first in the
German stalag and then in the box car on its
endless journey deep into Russia.

However, a few swings of the pick revealed just how soft his hands and muscles had become after those weeks of inactivity. He never had done any real physical labor, and his body soon reminded him of that fact. Within ten minutes he had blisters on top of blisters. He ignored the pain. The sun, weak as it was, warmed his shoulders. Fresh air filled his lungs. It was all he could do to stop himself from whistling.

Ramsey was having a harder time of it. Having been imprisoned longer, and undernourished from the poor diet the Germans fed POWs, he was struggling to swing the pick. Every few minutes, he doubled over with a coughing fit. It was going to be a long day for Ramsey.

Whitlock looked around. There were armed guards, but they were lazing around, smoking cigarettes. A big Russian was in charge, and tucked into his belt was a short whip that Whitlock didn't like the looks of. He had seen some of the other guards use them on prisoners.

There was no way he could know that it was a Cossack whip or *nagyka*, with a long handle that resembled a billy club and a thick length of braided leather, ending with the leather braided around a lead slug like a big fishing weight. Thirty-six inches of pure meanness. The whip was meant for managing the huge horses used to haul freight wagons, but it happened to double as a cruel weapon. Just the sight of it made the prisoners cringe.

The big Russian also carried a rifle with a telescopic sight, which he used now and then to scan the horizon.

Volki, Whitlock heard some of the Russians say.

When he repeated the word to another prisoner swinging a pick beside him, raising his eyebrows in the universal gesture for *what the hell does that mean*, the man had given a low howl in imitation of a wolf.

Given that fact, the guards seemed redundant. Where could anyone escape? The Russian landscape was imposing. An empty plain stretched before them—apparently they were to lay railroad tracks across it. In the distance loomed deep forests. To escape meant death by starvation. Or exposure. Or wolves. Letting a prisoner escape into the wilderness would be the same as shooting him, although a bullet would be faster and more humane.

Whitlock kept swinging the pick, ignoring the pain of his torn hands.

He and Ramsey were the only Americans, but there seemed to be a hodgepodge of prisoners laboring on this railroad to nowhere. Some spoke Polish and looked European; their only offense was being the citizens of a conquered nation. A few had the furtive look of actual criminals.

Toiling nearby were a few intellectual types whom he understood to be political prisoners who had dared to disagree with Stalin. A handful of prisoners had asiatic features and spoke a language that didn't sound Chinese, but that certainly was not Russian. Mongols, perhaps? These groups of prisoners stayed separate, working together, and shunning the others. Whitlock and Ramsey didn't fit in with any of the other groups. They were on their own.

"How long do you think we'll be at this?" Ramsey asked wearily. Already, his swings of the pick had become weaker and weaker.

Whitlock glanced at the distant horizon that the tracks would have to cross, and then at the sun, which still had to reach its zenith for the day. "Hang in there until lunchtime, and you can rest," Whitlock said.

But there was no lunchtime. At mid-day the prisoners were given water, but no food. They were allowed to sit quietly for a few minutes while the Russian guards ate. The only food that the prisoners could expect would be a piece of bread at the end of the day, or a bowl of thin soup.

The big Russian gang boss sat apart from the others, alone except for a small fellow who seemed to follow him around like a loyal dog. The two men were as different in size as Mutt and Jeff —or maybe David and Goliath. *He looks like a*

154

rabbit, Whitlock thought, studying the smaller man. But no—that wasn't quite right. The man moved with a fluid grace that was vaguely menacing. Not a rabbit, then. Maybe a mink or a fisher cat like they had in the New England woods—some predatory furbearer with small, sharp teeth.

The guards ate a peasant meal of chunks of black bread, raw onions, and some cold sausages, but the spicy, smoky smell of the meat made Whitlock's stomach rumble. The guards passed around a bottle of vodka. And then all too soon, it was time to get back to work.

Because of the raw skin from the burst blisters, Whitlock's hands felt like they were on fire when he touched the pick handle again. His hands soon began to leave faint red stains on the worn wood.

Beside him, Ramsey continued to swing the pick, but each of his swings grew weaker. One or two of the guards glanced in Ramsey's direction. If Whitlock had learned anything so far in his short career as a POW, it was that you were better off not attracting any attention to yourself.

"You've got to keep going," Whitlock urged him. "Just a little longer."

"I'm all played out," Ramsey said.

"None of that now," Whitlock said. "We've only got an hour or two yet."

That was a lie, of course, for Ramsey's

benefit. It was just past mid-day and they would be working on the railroad bed for hours to come.

But Ramsey had had enough. He tried to raise the pick. The iron head weighed perhaps ten pounds, but it was too much for Ramsey. He gave up and slumped over the handle, panting with the effort. Two guards started toward them, their heavy faces expressionless as those of a couple of bulldogs.

It was the big Russian, the work gang boss, who got there first. He moved fast for a big man. He grabbed Ramsey by the shoulder and flung him to the ground. The Russian was shouting. Whitlock didn't know the language, but the man's words needed no translation. He was clearly cursing Ramsey, or maybe insulting him.

Up close, the man was big as a bear, heavy through the shoulders, and his angry Russian words sounded like mortar fire. He smelled like onions and alcohol. He kicked Ramsey with a muddy boot, nearly sending him airborne. Ramsey cried out in pain. He drew back his foot to kick Ramsey again.

"Stop that!" Whitlock shouted.

The big Russian turned to regard him. Like Whitlock, he didn't need to know the language to understand the meaning. He tugged the Cossack whip from his belt and started toward Whitlock. The whip was no more than a yard long, so the Russian had to come in close. He struck Whitlock almost casually across the shoulder, but the stinging force of the blow drove Whitlock to his knees. The Russian's arm went up again and Whitlock put up his hands to protect his face.

The whip never fell.

A guard shouted urgently, and the Russian's arm sagged. To Whitlock, the man's bicep looked big around as a tree trunk.

The guards were pointing and shouting, unslinging their rifles. Whitlock was as curious as they were and looked in the direction that they were pointing, though he kept one eye on the whip. Was it a wolf? When he looked, he saw the figure of a man running away across the empty plain.

One of the prisoners had taken advantage of the commotion to make a run for it.

There was nowhere to go. The empty landscape stretched in all directions. The escapee's only hope was to run for the forest, nearly a mile away. If he got into those trees, he might have a chance.

Some of the guards raised rifles to shoot, but the big Russian barked something at them and they lowered their guns. Whitlock felt a faint sliver of hope for the man. Were the Russians allowing him to escape?

Then the big Russian unslung his rifle.

The escapee was getting farther and farther away. He was really covering ground. Running for his life. The guards didn't seem all that concerned. Some were even grinning and laughing, shouting as if urging the runner on.

The big Russian wrapped an arm through the sling of his rifle to steady it, and then put his eye to the telescopic sight. Whitlock thought the man was too far now for the Russian to hit him, even with the telescopic sight.

Even the Russian seemed to have his doubts. He called over the small man, who stood stock still as the Russian rested his rifle across his shoulder. The way that they worked together made it seem as if they had done something like this before.

Whitlock tried to guess the distance. Four hundred feet? Five hundred? The man was increasing that distance every few seconds, running flat out.

The Russian held very still, his bear-like heaviness seeming to shift and settle like a boulder. Then the rifle fired.

Across the distance, the runner seemed to hit an invisible wall. He flung out his arms as he came to a full stop, and then toppled forward.

Whitlock stared in disbelief. How had the Russian shot a running man that far away? He wouldn't have thought it was possible if he hadn't seen it with his own eyes.

Then the Russian slung his rifle again, walked over to Ramsey, and kicked him almost casually. He started toward Whitlock again, Cossack whip in hand. Once more, Whitlock raised his arms to protect his face. But instead of whipping him, the Russian grabbed one of Whitlock's wrists and held his bloodied, blistered hand aloft, yelling something in Russian. The others laughed.

The small man came over. "Hands like woman," he said to Whitlock in broken English that was mostly a snarl. "You both go to the infirmary."

CHAPTER 14

The small man did not mean for them to go to the infirmary immediately. They were allowed to visit the infirmary at the end of the working day, after they were marched back to the Gulag. By then, Whitlock's hands resembled raw meat. Ramsey was reduced to working on his knees, scrabbling at the soil without actually having to lift the pick.

Whitlock thought the Russians were just being cruel by making them work. But then at mid-afternoon another prisoner, this one Polish, had dropped his shovel, too weak from exhaustion to work anymore. The big Russian dragged the man a few dozen yards into the empty taiga and then beat him senseless with the *nagyka*. He and Ramsey had been spared that much. Whitlock could only think that it was because they were American. Not only were they prisoners, but they were pawns.

The walk back to the Gulag was several miles long, a distance that to the weary prisoners seemed to stretch endlessly. Ramsey put an arm across Whitlock's shoulders and just barely managed to make it, forcing himself along by sheer willpower. They had to walk back along the railroad bed that they had dug that day, and Whitlock was surprised by how little distance they had covered, despite all of their efforts. They worked with nothing but hand tools— picks, shovels, and wheelbarrows. With even a few pieces of heavy equipment they could have been far more productive, but the Russians didn't seem interested in anything resembling efficiency. Who needed a tractor when you had slave labor?

They walked past the depressing little village outside the gates of the Gulag, and then into the Gulag itself. From there, the weasel-like man pointed them in the direction of the camp infirmary and let them find it for themselves.

Compared to the other buildings in the Gulag compound, the infirmary was a palace. Whitewashed walls, clean and well-lighted in the dusk, smelling of disinfectant. Beds with actual sheets, so blinding white that Whitlock blinked a few times at the sight of them.

He thought about the crowded and uncomfortable prisoner barracks. How did such a place as this infirmary even exist alongside the rest of the Gulag? There were several empty beds, although these could easily have been filled with the sick and injured. He wondered if those clean beds were mostly for show. Actual sick and injured *zeks* would sully those boiled sheets.

Most radiant of all was the nurse who came to help them. It was not so surprising that she was a woman—there were a few women working in the camp, but most were old and clad in shapeless clothes on par with burlap sacks. These women were more like potatoes with arms and legs. This nurse was entirely different. A rose in the potato patch.

For one thing, she was young—maybe her early twenties—Whitlock's own age. Blond hair framed her pretty face and she did not wear the typical *babushka* head scarf, but a proper nurse's hat. Whitlock had become so used to the company of men that for the first time in months, he keenly felt the fact that he was filthy, wore little more than rags, and smelled like a goat.

The young nurse stood there, waiting, her face an expressionless mask.

Whitlock knew that trying to explain anything in English was hopeless, but he tried anyway. "My friend, he is very weak," Whitlock said slowly.

The nurse nodded, and then replied clearly in only slightly accented English. "He looks feverish. Let us get him into a bed."

Whitlock was astonished. Was this infirmary nothing but one miracle after another?

"You speak English," he said.

The girl looked around furtively. She knew that the *babushkas* in this place watched her jealousy. "I speak English only to do my duty," she said in a loud, deadpan voice.

He helped her get Ramsey undressed and into a hospital gown—again, blindingly white and clean—and then into a hospital bed. By then, Ramsey had drifted off.

"What do you think is wrong with him?"

"I think he has a fever, and he may be malnourished as well," she said.

Whitlock just stared. Other than Ramsey, he had not heard anyone else speak English in months. "It didn't help that he was worked like a dog today."

The girl took hold of Whitlock's wrist and turned it to reveal his raw hands. She made a sound like oh. The mask that she had forced her face into slipped. "Let me do something about those hands," she said.

She sat him down and bathed his hands in a basin of warm, soapy water. The water soon turned pink. Then she smoothed ointment over the sores, and wrapped his hands in bandages. Whitlock couldn't take his eyes off her.

"A Russian who speaks English," he said. "Imagine that."

"Half Russian," she said. "You see, my father was an American."

Whitlock wanted to know more, but the small, weasel-like man appeared to usher him out. The Russian out of place in the white-washed and well-scrubbed surroundings.

He grabbed Whitlock's bandaged hands and stared at them as if in disbelief, muttered what was clearly an oath of disgust, and then gave him a shove toward the prison barracks.

• • •

Whitlock thought that he might never see his Russian angel again—or Ramsey either, for that matter. Although the prisoners were given a fair amount of freedom to wander the compound in the small amount of free time they had, the infirmary itself was off limits, guarded by stern Russians with rifles that had fixed bayonets. Mostly, Whitlock marched out every day to the work site and swung his pick, helping Uncle Joe Stalin build his railroad.

It was lonely, not having anyone else to talk to. The other prisoners mostly ignored him. Two bunks over was a *zek* who was in the habit of talking to his chunk of bread every evening. The poor man would stroke the bread, smile at it and spoke soothing words. Whitlock could not translate the words, but he understood the tone. And then the man would devour his scrap of bread in a few bites, smiling with a look on his face that bordered on ecstasy.

Whitlock wondered how long it would take him to end up like that.

One evening a week later, he returned from digging the railroad bed to find Ramsey back in his bunk. He did not quite look rested or fit, but he was in much better shape than he had been.

"They nursed me back to health," Ramsey said. "So that they can work me to death again. What's the sense in that?"

Whitlock did notice that Ramsey's hacking cough seemed to have subsided. "Well, you sure as hell sound better than you did."

"It wasn't the cough that carried him off, it was the coffin they carried him off in." Ramsey winked. "In other words, I'm not dead yet."

Whitlock grinned. "Glad to hear it."

He was even happier when the nurse from the infirmary appeared in the barracks.

"I came to check on your hands," she explained. "And on your friend."

The air inside the barracks was cold and foul, but at least they were out of sight of the jealous nurses and definitely out of earshot of anyone else who could speak English. She asked Ramsey how he was doing. Her bedside manner was businesslike.

The nurse had brought along a bag with more ointment and fresh bandages. Whitlock's hands were still a mess from the unrelenting labor. Given time, they would harden into leather. For now, he was glad to let her spread more ointment and wrap his hands in more bandages.

"I'm Harrison Whitlock," he said. "My friends call me Harry."

"Inna."

"EE-nah," he repeated. "Just Inna?"

"Inna Mikhaylovna." She hesitated, then added, "My last name is Turner."

Whitlock raised his eyebrows. "So, your father really was American."

"Michael Turner. He emigrated here," she explained. "Some Americans did that, thinking that Communism was the best hope for the future."

"What about you? Were you born here or in the states?"

"I was born here. My mother was Russian."

"So I guess that makes you half American. Your father must have been an idealist to move to Russia."

"No, he was a fool. I loved my father, but he should have stayed in America."

She finished bandaging his hands. The last item that her bag contained was a book, a battered copy of *The Spoon River Anthology* by Edgar Lee Masters. She glanced around before taking it out. "This is what I know of America," she said. "That is, besides what my father told me. I thought you might want something to read. Please don't tell anyone I gave it to you. American books are forbidden."

"My lips are sealed." He examined the book and his face lit up. "Thank God. The only thing I've been able to get my hands on were some pamphlets on Communist Party speeches translated into very wooden English. Some kind of propaganda, I gather. The worker is the backbone of society and all of that. Dreadful stuff."

They talked for a while about the poems, and about life in the camp. Inna had completed her medical training, but now that the war was over, she had been sent here to northern Russia instead of the front lines.

"Lucky you," Whitlock said. "It doesn't seem like the best place to end up."

"Having an American for a father does not always serve one well. It means I am under constant suspicion."

Whitlock nodded. "It's awfully kind of you to

come see how I was doing," he said. "Will I see you again?"

"As soon as I can," she said. "But not everyday. Someone would grow suspicious."

He held up his newly bandaged hands. "Good as new," he said. "Thank you, Inna Mikhaylovna."

Inna wished them good night. She left the bandages—and the book.

Whitlock watched her go, and then said to his friend, "Maybe she's some sort of spy."

"Harry, you really are an idiot," Ramsey said. "The only thing she's spying on is you, my friend."

• • •

Whitlock was right to be suspicious. Here in the Gulag, there really were spies everywhere. Information was traded for a few pieces of bread, or maybe a warmer coat, or an assignment to an easier job that kept you out of the weather. Under Stalin, with money having little value or use, the real currency of Soviet society was treachery.

Thus it was that no sooner had Inna entered the barracks than Barkov knew about it. He'd had his eye on the pretty young nurse for some time. He wasn't interested in using her as a spy, however. He had other uses for her in mind. Barkov was a man used to getting what he wanted. He would try the gentle approach first. If that did not work, then he would take what he wanted.

He was waiting for her outside the barracks when she emerged after her visit with the Americans, her so-called patients.

"Good evening, Comrade," he said, blocking her path. "It is good to see that you are so dedicated that you make house calls."

The big man loomed over her. No one else was around, not even the small man who was like Barkov's shadow. She shivered, and not entirely from the cold. She knew him, just as everyone in the camp knew one another. He had a reputation for being cruel. She eyed the whip stuck carelessly into his wide belt. If something happened out here, it would be her word against his. As a woman, her word was worth next to nothing.

"I was told it is important to make sure that the Americans stay in good health," she replied.

"They are weak," he said. "I am not sure that they will survive the winter. I would not get too attached to them."

"Thank you, Comrade," she said. "That is good advice."

She started to move around him, but Barkov took a step back to block her path again. "If I have any aches or pains, perhaps I could have you tend to them," he said.

"I am not terribly skilled. Perhaps it would be better if Olga Ivanovna or Darya Alexandrovna helped you." Those were two of the weathered crones who worked in the infirmary. They had as much sympathy for the sick and weary of the camp as magpies for a carcass. Mostly, they were angered if a patient dared to sully their white sheets.

"It is very kind of you to worry so much about the Americans." Barkov finally stepped out of her way. "Good evening, Inna Mikhaylovna. I shall be keeping my eye on you."

CHAPTER 15

The team waited at a remote airstrip in Finland for the go ahead. Flying was a new experience for Cole. It turned out to be one that he had enjoyed. The thought of soaring through the sky excited him. Jumping out of an airplane was going to be another first, but he tried not to think too much about that one.

Their Douglas C-47 Skytrain had flown over empty country ribboned with rivers and covered in forests. Cole had gazed out the window of the plane, mesmerized by the vacant landscape. This was his kind of place. Finally, the plane touched down in a godforsaken place in Lapland.

To the south was Europe; Sweden and Norway lay to the west; to the east Russia awaited; to the north was the Barents Sea and Arctic Ocean. Already, the weather was turning wintry this far north. At night, the stars shimmered in clear, cold skies. The sun did little to warm the day, and it was only late October. The locals were saying they were one good storm away from the onset of winter.

The airstrip was gravel. Nearby squatted a couple of low-slung buildings. It was just the four team members, plus Major Dickey and the pilot and co-pilot. There were a couple of Finns who lived on site to maintain the airstrip. One of them spoke broken English, but the words he did know made it clear that he hated both the Russians and the Germans. Finland had managed to declare war on both countries in the recent conflict, and now kept an uneasy peace with its powerful neighbor.

One of the Finns was married to a shriveled peasant woman who didn't speak much at all, and certainly not in English. She served them the same black bread and stew for breakfast, lunch, and dinner. Vaccaro swore it contained reindeer meat. Cole shrugged; he had eaten worse.

Picking at his stew, and thinking about the sausages and beer they were missing back in Germany, Vaccaro asked, "Why are we doing this?"

"A rich old man wants his grandson home, and we're gonna get him," Cole said, then thought it over some more. "I reckon it's more than that. The Russians kept some of our boys. It ain't right."

"I'd like to go home, but nobody listens to me. Why did I ever listen to you, anyhow? I ought to be back in Germany, making love to some sweet *Fräulein*."

"Shut up and eat your reindeer stew, Vaccaro."

When Cole examined it, he realized that being here was better than sitting around the barracks, wrestling with boredom. Back in Germany they were all in a waiting game—waiting to be sent home. The mountain shack near Gashey's Creek wasn't exactly calling to him.

Also, on some deeper level, the idea of Americans being held captive by the Russians, and them lying about it, made him angry. He didn't need to know Whitlock to be mad as hell about it. It just wasn't right. Maybe Lieutenant Whitlock couldn't do a damn thing about getting out of that place, but Cole sure as hell could.

If the food in Finland was lacking, at least the weather was good. It was colder this far north, with skies so blue they seemed scrubbed clean, and crisp nights that made the stars sparkle.

Honaker took the weather as a good sign, and told them so at breakfast the next morning. He was making some attempt at being the leader. "I'm telling you, these blue skies are a sign. It's going to be a milk run."

The Finn who knew some English listened to Honaker's little speech and laughed.

Honaker glared at him. "What the hell is so funny?"

"In our country we have a saying: 'Don't praise the day until evening; a girl until she is married off; a sword until it is tried in battle; ice until it has been crossed; or beer until is has been drunk.' "

"I don't know what the hell that's supposed to mean," Honaker grumped.

"He's tellin' us not to count our chickens before they hatch," Cole said, giving the Finn a rare grin. "That's what we say in our country. All in all, it's good advice. Now, somebody pass that reindeer stew."

• • •

Major Dickey gathered them just before dusk on the second day. Despite the Finn's earlier warning, Cole had almost thought it safe to praise the day, but he changed his mind when Dickey explained that the team was going to make a night drop.

"The Russians don't have radar stations this far north, at least not yet," Dickey said.

"However, they may have spotters keeping watch for enemy planes. Darkness will give us some cover."

"Where's Honaker?" Cole wondered.

"You tell me. He couldn't have gone far." Dickey waved at the nearby forests to make his point. "Grab your gear, everyone. You take off in an hour."

"You're not coming with us, sir?"

"Not me." He tapped his head. "If the Russians captured me, there are too many secrets up here."

"What about what's in my head?" Vaccaro wanted to know. "Aren't you worried about what the Russians will learn from me?"

Dickey looked at him, trying to gauge whether Vaccaro was serious. "Not really."

Cole had already packed and re-packed his gear and cleaned his rifle. He was ready, even eager. He carried his pack down to the C-47 waiting to fly them deep into Russia.

That's where he found Honaker, sliding down from one of the wings.

"What the hell you doin' up there?" Cole wanted to know.

"Just checking the plane."

"You know how to fly one of these things?"

"Nope. Just curious, is all. I thought I saw where some flak damage had been patched, and it looked a little sloppy to me."

"That plane got us here from Germany," Cole said. "I reckon it will be good enough to jump out of."

"I don't know. Let's just hope it makes it that far." Honaker grabbed him by the shoulder in what was meant to be a genial gesture. He grinned. "Look at you, all packed up and ready to go, like a good Boy Scout."

Cole took a step back so that Honaker's hand fell away. He didn't like being touched. And he sure as hell wasn't Honaker's buddy. "Dickey said we're taking off at dusk."

"Show time, then." The grin slid off Honaker's face. "Listen, Cole, you know that Dickey made me the squad leader. The two of us aren't going to have a problem, are we?"

"Why would we have a problem?"

"Because you seem like the type of fella who likes to do things his way. Just so you know, we have got to work together if we're going to get home in one piece."

"You mean, if we're gonna get Lieutenant Whitlock home in one piece. That's our mission, ain't it?"

"Hell, you know what I mean, Cole. Are you going to be a problem for me?"

Cole looked Honaker up and down. He was built much like Cole, so he didn't really have a physical advantage. What Honaker did have, Cole decided, was that look of someone who was always calculating to get an advantage over you, like a buyer at a lumber mill or a fur dealer. Cole decided then and there that he didn't trust Honaker worth a damn. He wished he had seen it sooner.

"Somebody has got to be in charge," Cole said. "I reckon it may as well be you."

"There. You see that, Cole? Me and you will get along fine."

The others appeared, carrying their gear and weapons. It had already been agreed upon that Samson would haul most of the extra ammunition. Honaker carried the winter gear intended for Whitlock, along with the bulk of the rations.

Dickey insisted on gathering them one last time on the tarmac, along with the pilot and co-pilot. The C-47 was flying with a bare bones crew.

"All right, men. I've said everything there is to say at this point," Dickey began. "You know that if you fall into Russian hands, you'll be joining Whitlock in the Gulag—or worse. Nobody is coming to get you."

"That's not exactly reassuring," Vaccaro said.

"Consider it an incentive not to get caught," Dickey replied. He paused, as if building himself up to something. "Of course, I doubt that's going to happen. The four of you would not have been chosen for this mission if you weren't the very best. Gentlemen, I will see you in two weeks at the border."

Nobody had much to say after that. Having spent two days together in the Finnish backwoods, they were talked out. Instead, they went about stowing their gear with the easy competence of men who had been on more than one combat mission.

The plane's two Pratt & Whitney radial engines together generated twenty-four hundred horsepower, giving the C-47 a cruising speed of one hundred and sixty miles per hour. As they gained altitude, the woods and hills disappeared into the dusk below. It took the plane less than a minute to reach cruising altitude before it leveled off and flew east.

Conversation was difficult in the noisy belly of the C-47. There were hardly any creature comforts. They settled themselves into jump seats that folded down from the bulkhead. Looking down from the plane, the countryside below was a dark expanse uninterrupted by a single light. When Cole looked up, he could see the stars illuminating the clear night sky. It was like being on a mountaintop. It all felt more than a little unreal for someone who was used to having his feet planted firmly on the ground. *You ain't in Gashey's Creek no more*, he reminded himself—not for the first time since coming ashore on D-Day.

Cole felt good about the team. He knew he

could trust Vaccaro with his life. Samson seemed dependable, and he was sure as hell solid. Honaker had some sort of bug up his ass about being in charge, but Cole could live with that as long as the man did his part when their boots hit the ground.

He glanced around at Vaccaro and Samson, who both looked to be sound asleep. Honaker was peering at a map by the dim glare of a red map flashlight. Being the leader.

Cole closed his eyes. He figured he could let his guard down on the plane—whatever happened up here wasn't in his hands, but the pilot's. It was damn cold, though, and he tugged his coat more tightly around him. Maybe winter was just a couple of weeks away on the ground, but it was winter sure enough 20,000 feet up. He nodded off.

• • •

Cole was awakened by a change in the rhythm of the plane. They had been flying smoothly enough, but now the plane seemed to shudder and struggle through the air. What was going on?

He looked around. Samson and Vaccaro still slept soundly. In the dim light he saw Honaker unbuckle himself from the jump seat and make his way toward the cockpit. Cole undid his own seatbelt and followed.

To his surprise, the cockpit was actually quite small—not much room for anyone but the pilot and co-pilot, but Honaker had managed to squeeze in. Cole stuck his head in over the man's shoulder, and Honaker looked up in surprise. He hadn't noticed Cole following him.

There was a bewildering number of controls, all dimly lighted. Beyond the windshield, Cole could see the clear unblinking stars. It did not inspire confidence that the co-pilot was busy flicking toggle switches, while the pilot was wrestling with the yoke in his hands. His knuckles glowed white where his fingers wrapped around the controls.

"This don't look good," Cole said.

"Yeah, we've got a problem," the pilot said. His voice sounded strained. "We lost oil pressure in one of the engines. There's over thirty gallons of oil in there, but it must have all leaked out. I can't understand how it happened. We had to shut the damn thing down."

"Must be an oil line that went bad," Honaker said. "We should turn back. We're too far from the drop zone to make it."

Cole looked out, straining to see the engines. Although the plane still struggled, they didn't seem to be losing altitude. The other engine sounded strong enough. "Can this bird fly on one engine?"

"Buddy, we *are* flying on one engine. I think

you would be sure to notice if we couldn't," the pilot said.

"Then we ought to keep flying," Cole said. "We're ready to go. Just get us to that drop zone."

"Cole, are you crazy?" Honaker demanded. "We need to abort this mission."

"What for? If we don't do this tonight, and that bad weather moves in, we might have to sit on our asses in Finland for days. By then, we might need snowshoes to get back out. To hell with that. I say we just keep flying."

"Man's got a point," the pilot said. "There's no telling how long we'd be grounded. We'll be fine as long as the engine doesn't overheat. We're close. Might as well go for it."

"And if the engine overheats?" Honaker asked.

"Then you're going to have some company jumping out of this crate."

Honaker and Cole cleared out of the cockpit. Honaker did not look pleased. "Goddamnit, Cole. I thought you and me had an agreement that I was in charge on this mission."

"In case you ain't noticed, Honaker, there ain't no mission to be in charge of yet. Once we get on the ground, you can be the goddamn leader if that's what makes you happy."

They were both shouting to be heard over the engine noise, but that was just an excuse. They would have been shouting at each other in a library, too.

The loud exchange left Cole's throat feeling raw. Cole made it back to his jump seat, although the bumpy air made the walk a little challenging. It was even noisier back here, which was just fine with him—it meant Honaker would have to shut the hell up. He buckled himself in again and waited. The plane lurched and shook, but then corrected itself. The pilot had seemed confident enough that he could get them to the drop zone. *Don't worry yourself into a corner*, his pa used to say. *Better to leave the door open for good luck to walk through*. The man used to talk sense when he wasn't guzzling his own 'shine.

Cole settled down to wait.

Next stop, Russia.

CHAPTER 16

Honaker signaled the team that they were approaching the drop zone. They got into line near the door and Honaker snapped them onto the static line. He didn't seem anxious in any way and acted as if he had done this a hundred times. Maybe he had. He gave them a thumbs up. Then he slid open the jump door. The wind shrieked like a banshee.

"You got to be kidding me!" Vaccaro shouted.

If anyone heard him, they ignored him.

When the green jump light came on, Cole felt his insides liquify. Cole was not easily rattled, but looking out an open hatch at the darkness beyond would make anyone hesitate. He had reached a point where it was too late to second guess what he was about to do. It was time to go —now or never. He'd be damned if he let Honaker see him look too scared to jump.

It was somewhat reassuring that they were jumping with a static line using a T-5 parachute. In their brief training, he had been reassured that all he had to do was get out the door—the parachute would do the rest.

Samson went first. His shoulders were so big that he had to pivot sideways to get through the hatch. He tumbled out and dropped like a boulder.

Vaccaro was next. He reached the door easily enough, but then froze with arms on either side of the opening. He even took a step back.

Cole gave him a mighty shove and Vaccaro was gone. The wind barely drowned out his scream of pure terror.

Cole knew just how he felt, but he wasn't about to give that son of a bitch Honaker an excuse to give him a shove out the door. They had been told to jump within a second of the man in front. The idea was to land close to one another, and with the C-47 still moving at around ninety miles per hour, any delay meant the jumpers would be spread out over hundreds of yards on the ground below.

Cole closed his eyes and leaped.

He went out the door all wrong, the weight of his pack throwing him off balance. When he looked down at his feet, expecting to see the ground below, he saw the plane beneath his boots instead—which meant he was upside down. Honaker still hadn't jumped.

The static line pulled his parachute, and snapped Cole upright with a jerk better suited to a hangman's rope. It was not a pleasant experience, but he felt a sense of relief as the parachute deployed. Now all he had to do was ride it down.

The darkness was disorienting. Rushing air took Cole's breath away. The cold felt brittle and sharp as an old stone arrowhead. Beneath the circular parachute, he found himself swinging in circles, which did not do much to improve his mood.

It was hard to see the ground, but he knew it was down there, waiting. The question was, how hard was he going to hit? He felt like an egg headed for the hard bottom of a cast iron skillet. Was he going to end up sunny side up—or scrambled?

Then all at once he saw the ground. Images took shape—lighter patches that might be dried grass or brush. The thought that he might be headed toward the trees was more worrisome. The last thing he wanted to do was get hung up like a treed coon. It was all coming toward him way too fast and he braced himself for the impact.

He hit the ground and rolled, but the shock still knocked the breath out of him. It was a thing he'd heard of, but that had never really happened to him before. One second he could breathe, the next he couldn't—he was like a fish tossed up on a river bank, gasping. Fortunately, it was not a sensation that lasted long. His lungs started working again.

Somehow, he had managed to get tangled up in the parachute and the cords. It was damn near impossible to tell what was what in the dark, so Cole unsheathed his big knife and chopped at whatever lines he could reach. The knife was razor sharp, and the chute fell away.

He bundled it up as he had been taught, then shoved it under a bush. Then he crouched down and looked around as he got his bearings.

He seemed to have come down in an expanse of emptiness. Although it was dark and he could see no more than his hand in front of his face, he could feel the barren landscape surrounding him. He had the sensation of being in a vast, open space. He stood still, just listening. He heard the noise of the C-47, fading away. He wished those flyboys luck getting home on one engine. Then all he heard was the sigh of wind.

He definitely didn't hear any warning shouts

in Russian, which was a good sign. They had been told not to worry about the Russians—nobody was expecting them, and their landing zone was just about exactly in the middle of nowhere. For once, the so-called intelligence seemed to have been correct.

He just hoped that the other three men had landed in the general vicinity. How the hell were they supposed to link up? It all sounded so much more sensible back in the warm, well-lighted planning room than it did here.

He decided to take a chance and click on his flashlight. He flicked the switch on and off a couple of times. He was relieved when he saw a light flick on and off in answer about three hundred feet away. An even more distant light appeared, then clicked off again. That accounted for two of the others, but what about the third? He waited tensely, wondering if anyone hostile had seen the light. There were no warning shouts or gunshots. With any luck, nobody had seen them arrive.

Cole flicked his light again and then began moving in the direction of the nearest answering light.

He had not gone more than a dozen steps when he realized he was not alone. It was hard to say how he knew, exactly. You couldn't spend time in the woods without experiencing that feeling at some point—and learning to trust it.

Cole froze. He unslung his rifle, being careful not to make any noise. There was nowhere to run or hide out here in the open, so he got down low, where he would not be silhouetted against the sky. Then he held his breath.

Someone went past him in the dark. He could just see the figure in the starlight. Definitely one person. It was not a body type he recognized as another team member. He had the impression of someone a little older and thicker—not a soldier, then. But stealthy all the same.

He rose up, took three silent steps, and put his rifle muzzle between the other man's shoulder blades.

The man halted. Slowly, he raised his arms from his sides. One held a rifle. "Do not shoot Vaska," the man said in heavily accented English.

Cole pulled the rifle back. "Turn around and keep your hands just like that."

The man did as ordered, swiveling slowly around to face Cole. "I am to be your guide," he said.

"I like blueberry cobbler," Cole said, remembering the first part of the password.

Vaska thought a moment. "With vanilla ice cream."

Cole lowered the rifle. "Do you always go around making as much noise as a herd of elephants?"

The guide shook his head. "You must have

the ears of a lynx. Where are the others?"

"Scattered around."

"Come, let us find them. There are only a few hours until daylight, and everything must be hidden by then."

Cole and the guide moved toward where Cole had last seen the light. That's where they found Vaccaro, still wrestling his way free of the tangled parachute lines. "You pushed me out of the plane, you son of a bitch."

"Shut up, Vaccaro. By the way, it's good to see you, too."

Vaccaro nodded at the guide. "Who's this?"

"This here is Vaska."

Vaccaro flicked on his light. "No offense, Vaska, but you look old enough to be my grandpa."

Vaska shrugged.

"Come on, let's go find the rest of us," Cole said. He flicked the light and got another answer flash, so they moved in that direction.

Soon enough, they found Samson. He was limping, but otherwise no worse for wear.

Honaker was nowhere to be found. Cole flicked his light again, but got no response.

"What do you think if I give him a shout?" Cole wondered. "Vaska, are we near anyone who ain't supposed to hear us?"

"You are in the taiga," Vaska said, and offered another shrug, as if that explained everything.

"Fire a cannon if you want."

"All right then." Cole filled his lungs and shouted, "Honaker!"

They listened; when no one replied, he hollered out again. Cole had a high, ringing shout that could carry across a mountain valley back home, but the vastness of the dark plain around them seemed to swallow up the noise like padded velvet. He decided against firing his rifle.

"Maybe I'm not the only one who got cold feet and there was nobody to push him," Vaccaro said. "He was last."

"Nah, he got blowed off course is all. Vaska, are there any woods 'round here?"

"To the west, about three kilometers away, there is a forest."

Cole nodded. "If he come down in them trees, he might have got hisself hung up. Vaska, how big is that there forest?"

"It would take many days to cross it."

They stood around, thinking about that. Honaker could be hung up in a tree, either tangled up or injured. There were stories about that happening behind enemy lines to paratroopers who managed to reach their jump knives and then cut their own wrists so that they could bleed out quietly rather than become prisoners, tortured for their secrets. Not to mention the fact that there were wild animals. A badly injured man was just another meal to some varmint.

The fingers were most vulnerable. Then the face. It wasn't a pretty picture.

"Goddamnit," Cole said. "We ain't off to what you'd call a real good start."

"Listen, we can't wait around," Vaccaro said. "You heard Vaska. It's gonna be daylight soon. We can't be seen out here, but maybe Vaska can come back and look for him. He won't attract attention like we would."

"*Da, da*, I will come back," Vaska said. "For now, we must hide you."

First, they collected the parachutes. Vaska had already thought ahead and knew of a sink hole that they stuffed the parachutes into. Then they started off across the vast plain. It was still too dark to see much of anything, but Vaska led them confidently, keeping a brisk pace.

"He moves fast for an old man," Vaccaro muttered, panting.

After an hour, they came to the edge of a village. A dog came out and barked at them, but lost interest when Vaska fished around in his pocket and tossed him a scrap of dried meat. Vaccaro opened his mouth to make some comment, but Vaska cut him off by putting a finger to his own lips. They followed him to a small house—more of a shack, really. It reminded Cole of a Russian version of his own family's mountain shack, hammered together out of rough-cut lumber, scrap wood, and discarded metal sheeting.

But inside it was warm enough. There was an old-fashioned ceramic oven rather than a fireplace, over which an older Russian woman tended something good-smelling in a pot. She watched them without emotion, except for her eyes. They drifted over Vaccaro, narrowed at the sight of Cole, but grew large when Samson entered the house. He seemed to fill the tiny space.

"Vaska's house," their guide announced. "Now, you eat, and then you hide."

The woman, whom Vaska did not introduce, served them bowls of fish stew. It was a bland, almost tasteless fish. Lumps of potatoes and onions mingled with the fish. The stew needed salt, but they ate hungrily enough. Samson held out his bowl eagerly for a second helping, which seemed to improve the old woman's mood.

"Burbot," Vaska explained. "I catch them in the river here, from the riverbank in the summer and right through the ice in the winter. When I catch a little extra, I sell the fish to the camp. If not for burbot, we would starve. It is a blessing and a curse, you know. It is a blessing because it feeds us and a curse because it is all we have to eat."

"I thought you were a guide," Vaccaro said. "I thought that meant you were a hunter, too."

"Hunting is hard," Vaska pointed out. "In the winter, you must travel far from the village. Game is scarce. There are wolves. You don't always have something to shoot, but there is always a fish to catch. One burbot feeds us for two days, maybe three."

Cole saw the wisdom in that.

"Wolves?" Vaccaro wondered.

"Wolves," Vaska said with another shrug, although it may have been a shudder. He glanced at their empty bowls. The old lady didn't offer seconds. "You have eaten. Now you must hide."

He took them to a pantry door in the tiny kitchen. They helped him shift bags of potatoes and a few canned goods marked with unidentifiable Cyrillic characters until the back of the pantry was accessible. Vaska pulled aside the boards to reveal an opening. They stepped through it into a tiny, windowless space just big enough for the three of them to lie down in. Vaska had already provided some blankets and a bucket.

Vaccaro looked dubiously at the bucket. "Is that for when the roof leaks? Wait, tell me that's not for—"

Vaska replaced the boards, sealing them in darkness.

CHAPTER 17

Hours later, Vaska returned to let them out. When they emerged from the secret room, they were surprised to find Honaker in the kitchen.

"You made it!" Vaccaro said. "What the hell happened to you?"

"My jump line got hung up, and by the time I jumped you guys were nowhere in sight. I went out of the plane upside down, and the shock of the chute flipping me upright ripped open my haversack. I lost most of my gear."

"Damn."

"Some of it was what we had for Whitlock,"

Honaker said. "It was on top, and when the pack opened—well, out it went. Lost his sleeping bag, his winter coat, some of the rations. I'd still be wandering around the goddamn middle of nowhere if Vaska here hadn't found me."

Vaska was warming himself by the cookstove. His wife hefted a big, steaming kettle and made them all tea. Out the window, they could see that it was getting dark again. The autumn days here must be very short. She was setting out more food—a fish pie this time, featuring chunks of burbot with potatoes and onions, all under a thick blanket of crust baked in a rectangular pan. Cole wasn't a big fan of fish—he preferred red meat—but his belly rumbled all the same at the smell of the food.

They sat down to eat with Vaska around a battered homemade wooden table as the wife served them. This time, she was not so stingy with the food. She did not say much and in any case did not seem to speak a word of English, but she had that universal look of pleasure that came to any cook's face upon seeing hungry men devour the food she had prepared. Cole sopped up the juices with a chunk of thick black bread.

After the meal, there was more tea served in chipped mugs with spiderwebs of fine cracks across the surface. Vaska lit a pipe and a couple of the Americans smoked cigarettes.

They could have been simple supper guests, if

their real purpose had not been to spirit an American prisoner out of the nearby Gulag compound. Listening to Vaska's occasional comments, there was something Cole couldn't figure out. "Vaska, how come you speak English?" he asked.

The old Russian grunted. "You are not the first Americans that I have come across."

That got their attention. "What in the world are you talking about? Have there been others before us?"

Vaska chuckled. "There were others back in 1919. Almost thirty years ago. I helped the Americans fight the Bolsheviks near Archangelsk."

The men look at him blankly.

"Someone must have left that chapter out of the history textbooks," Vaccaro said.

"The Americans lost," Vaska explained. A faraway look came into his eyes as he remembered. "Perhaps that is why you have not heard of this battle, because it was not one that anyone wished to remember, but Vaska was there. We could hardly move in the deep snow and the Bolshevik snipers picked us off. Many Americans were killed and the wounded ones froze to death."

"That was a long time ago. So what's in it for you now?" Cole pressed. "You get paid?"

Vaska nodded. "It is not so easy living here.

There is no way to get extra food unless you have some money. So I get people things they need but that they are not supposed to have."

"So you're a smuggler."

Vaska shrugged. "If I were younger I would move north and trap sables, away from all of this." He waved his hand at the village beyond the window, as if it were a teeming metropolis rather than a collection of humble backwater dwellings. He looked at Cole. "I would be a hunter, like you."

"What do you know about me?" Cole said. It came out snarly—he didn't like the idea of someone prying at who he was, even some old Russian.

"I can see what you are in your eyes," Vaska said quietly. "You have the look of the wolf. You tell me if I am wrong."

As the silence around the table grew uncomfortable, Vaccaro spoke up. "Vaska my friend, I just hope they paid you enough to help us so that you don't go changing your mind."

Vaska shrugged. "What is money? A little goes a long way here. No, Vaska helps you for the same reason I helped to fight the Bolsheviks in 1919. They were no good. Stalin is no good. But I keep such thoughts to myself, or I would end up in the Gulag over there."

Cole went to the window, lifted the shade, and peered out. It was dark enough now that he would only be a silhouette to any passerby. Beyond the village he could see a complex of low buildings, ringed by watch towers and barbed wire fences. Dim lights lit the perimeter. It was his first glimpse of the Gulag where Whitlock was being held. He gave a low whistle—the place looked formidable as a state prison. No way in. No way out.

"We are gonna need some help to get our boy out of yonder prison."

"We need an insider," Honaker agreed. "Maybe there is someone who works inside the Gulag who sees things like you do."

Vaska sucked deeply on his pipe, exhaled a cloud of smoke, and nodded, thinking the problem over. He then spoke to his wife in Russian. She was busy clearing up the dishes and seemed not to have heard, busy as she was scraping the plates and washing them in a bucket of soapy water. She turned to Vaska and smiled. Again, they needed no Russian to understand that an idea had come to her. The old guide and his wife talked together for a while, thick as thieves, oblivious to the men in their kitchen.

"My wife says there is a girl who comes into the village from time to time. She works in the infirmary. She is in love with one of the American prisoners. She will help us."

"In love with him? How does your wife know that?"

Vaska shrugged again. "How does a bird know how to build a nest? Women know what they know. They know when a girl is in love," he said. He looked toward his wife again and smiled. In fact, it was almost a leer. Cole felt a little embarrassed—and surprised. Mrs. Vaska was no looker. But Vaska must have been a randy old bastard as well as a smuggler. He sucked on his pipe again and added: "And a smart man listens to his wife in such matters."

• • •

Inna continued her visits to the Americans, especially Whitlock. She used her concern for their medical care as an excuse, but that was beginning to wear thin with her Soviet colleagues. Two weeks later, Barkov was waiting outside the barracks for her at dusk. Her stomach clenched at the sight of his imposing, dark shadow.

"I have been feeling poorly," he said in a hearty voice that indicated nothing could be further from the truth. "I may come see you soon at the infirmary."

"You do not have to wait for me, Comrade Barkov. There are others who can—"

"No, it is you I want to help me, Inna Mikhaylovna. Be nice to me, and I will make sure your weakling American friends stay alive, at least for now. But if you are not so nice to me, you should know that railroad construction is very dangerous work. Accidents can occur. Men can die. They can be maimed."

Nodding, heart pounding, Inna hurried away. It was very clear what Barkov wanted, but she had no intention of giving it to him. To be a woman in the Soviet Union was to be powerless, and to be a woman assigned to a remote Gulag was to be helpless. She would have to be careful, and somehow string him along without completely rebuffing his advances. The lives of Whitlock and Ramsey, even her own life, might depend on it.

• • •

The next morning, Inna went into the village for supplies. Sometimes the villagers would have a few eggs to trade, or fresh meat. Inna had no money, but the inventory at the infirmary was not closely watched. She always had a few items to barter.

One of the villagers who sought her out this morning was Bruna Ivanovna, the wife of a local hunter and trapper named Vaska. She was an old *babushka* if ever there was one. Inna had chatted with her from time to time, and had previously mentioned the Americans to the *babushka*, only because it was common knowledge in the village that a long time ago, Bruna Ivanovna's husband had fought with the Americans against the Bolsheviks. After Inna had swapped some liniment for two fresh rabbits, Bruna Ivanovna lingered a moment, as if she had something else to say.

"What is it?" Inna finally asked, sensing the woman's reluctance to leave.

"How is your American friend?"

"He is fine, or at least as good any anyone can expect to be in that place."

Bruna Ivanovna nodded sagely. She looked around furtively, as if to make sure that they were not being overheard, although no one was in sight. "How would you like to help get him out of that place?"

Inna tensed. She kept her face carefully neutral. It was a fact of life in Russia that one must be cautious about whom you trusted. She did not want to end up as a zek in the nearby Gulag, at the complete mercy of someone like Barkov. "What do you mean?"

"I am saying that my husband can help him."

Then Bruna Ivanovna explained, and Inna nodded, faster and faster, as the possibilities took shape. "What happens now?"

"Come back tomorrow," the hunter's wife said. "Bring some more liniment. It helps my old bones, which ache so from the cold. And see to it that you are not followed."

CHAPTER 18

The barking of Vaska's dog told them that someone was at the door.

The dog was not allowed in the house no matter how cold it got. This was some sort of rural Russian tradition. It also meant that nobody got near the front door without the dog making a ruckus.

Cole tightened his grip on the Browning 1911 in his hand and Samson shifted his bulk to cover the door with his shotgun. The dog's bark turned to a happy whine as whoever was out there made friends.

Vaska approached the door armed with nothing more than his tobacco pipe. Seconds later, he was beckoning in the woman who stood there. She appeared to be alone, so Cole and the others relaxed enough to take their fingers off their triggers.

Vaska's wife had set up this meeting with the woman who worked in the Gulag infirmary. Cole still didn't know the wife's name, so in his head he just referred to her as Mrs. Vaska. Maybe Vaska had introduced her at some point, but Cole had either missed it or couldn't remember the Russian name.

Inna Mikhaylovna was a lot more memorable.

She entered the small house, keeping her head down and wrapped in a head scarf, like an old *babushka*. She had come under cover of darkness to avoid as many prying eyes as possible. Cole didn't know how much good that would do—if the Russian village was anything like Gashey's Creek, people talked, and not much got by them. He just hoped there weren't too many villagers spying for the Gulag.

The woman took off the scarf and sat at the kitchen table. She had dishwater blond hair and lacked the roundness of face that he had come to expect in the local Russians. Her eyes took in the faces around the table. Her gaze settled on Cole, who sat at the head of the table next to Vaska. So this was the girl who was in love with Whitlock?

Lucky bastard, Cole thought.

Mrs. Vaska served tea solemnly, as if they were all distant relations gathering to discuss something serious, like the sale of property—or maybe the details of an arranged marriage. She did not serve food. Food always seemed to be in short supply. There sure as hell weren't any cakes or cookies to pass around. You couldn't share what you didn't have. Cole felt right at home.

"Are you in charge?" she asked Cole.

Honaker practically leaped out of his chair as he announced, "That would be me." He asked what was now obvious, a tone of surprise in his voice: "You speak English?"

"Yes. Just the four of you?" she asked, looking around the table again doubtfully. Her English didn't have much of an accent—she could almost have passed for an American. Who'd have thought, out here in the north of Russia?

"We're enough, honey. Believe me," Honaker said, sounding boastful.

"Sometimes a small group attracts less attention," Cole explained. "We are glad for your help, miss."

"Inna," she said, pronouncing it EE-nah.

"Cole," he said. He rattled off the names of the other men, but she looked too nervous to remember all the names. He doubted that she was any kind of spy—and if she had been, the Russians would have been right behind her and rounded them all up by now.

Honaker was about two steps behind Cole's thinking process. "Why should we believe you are really trying to help us?" he demanded.

"I am not helping you," she said, some snap in her voice that Cole liked. "I am helping Harry."

By "Harry" she meant Harrison Whitlock IV, grandson of a United States Senator and the golden boy of a New England family that was richer than Jesus.

"Then we're in luck," Cole said. "We need to break him the hell out of that Gulag, so we could use your help."

Her eyes went back to Cole. Honaker had said he was in charge, but her eyes stayed on Cole. "I have a plan," she said.

"Miss Inna, I do love a woman with a plan," Cole said before Honaker could open his mouth, which earned him a scowl. "Let's hear it."

Quickly, she explained the layout of the Gulag compound and its basic security. Cole began to understand that it was really more like an old-fashioned frontier stockade than a proper prison. The Gulag compound had just one watch tower. There were searchlights, but to save electricity they were rarely turned on. There was at least one machine gun up in the watch tower, as far as she could tell, although they never had been fired at anyone trying to escape. Prisoners did escape from time to time, but they never got far. Where would they go, anyhow, in the middle of the taiga, in the dead of night? In effect, the taiga itself served as the prison walls.

"Then there is Barkov," she said. She shuddered. "He is a hunter and he tracks down anyone who escapes. He is a cruel man."

"Is he the commandant, or whatever you call it, of this Gulag?"

"No, but he is like the overseer. He chases down anyone who escapes."

"Sounds like a hunting dog."

"He is more like a bear," she said. "He was a sniper in Stalingrad and then in the offensive into Germany. He should be a hero of Russia, but they sent him here for the things that he did in Germany."

"What kind of things?" Vaccaro asked, sounding nervous.

Inna shrugged, leaving that to their imagination. They could imagine a lot. This Barkov had probably done all that, and worse, to get himself sent to this place.

"He's nothing we can't handle," Honaker said.

Cole wasn't so sure. This girl didn't look as if she scared easily, but it was clear that Barkov concerned her. "I reckon we need to get a head start to give us a chance against Barkov," Cole said. "How do we get Whitlock out?"

Inna explained her plan. The barracks were not locked at night because the prisoners or *zeks* needed to come and go—some worked early shifts in the kitchens, for example. So the problem wasn't getting Whitlock out of the barracks, but out of the Gulag itself. The main gate was out of the question. That gate was mostly for show when important officials came and went, or very large machinery or supplies were brought in. Used more frequently were a couple of smaller gates in the perimeter fence. The gate closest to Whitlock's barracks led to the village, serving as a kind of shortcut for moving between the two.

Vaska nodded when Inna described the gate; he explained that he had used this gate often when bringing in fresh meat to sell.

"One of the regular guards at the gate knows me because I have struck up a conversation with him many times," Inna said. "He knows that I come and go at odd hours—sometimes I come over to the village to check on someone who is ill."

"This guard isn't going let you walk out of there with Whitlock," Honaker said.

"Of course not," Inna said impatiently. "I am going to make sure the guard is missing for a few minutes. I will tie my scarf to the gate as a sign for you and for Harry, and he can escape."

"Where is this guard going to be?"

Inna shrugged. "Busy."

She didn't have to explain how she would be

keeping the guard busy.

"What about you?" Cole asked. "It sounds like this Barkov will figure out right quick who helped Whitlock escape, once he realizes his American prisoner is gone."

"As you say, he will figure it out," she agreed. "But I won't be there. I will be coming with you."

"No, you won't," Honaker said. He shook his head emphatically. "The deal is that we're taking Whitlock with us, and nobody else."

Inna and Honaker started to argue about that.

Cole thought it over. The girl wasn't going to have a chance once Barkov or the camp commandant figured out who had helped Whitlock escape. They didn't have any option but to bring her along.

"She's right," Cole said. "She's got no choice. As long as she can keep up, she can come along."

Honaker was annoyed. "Listen, Cole—"

But it was Vaska who made the decision. "She comes with us. Barkov must not know who in the village helped her. If she is left behind, he will make her tell."

They spent a few more minutes hashing out the details. Then Inna announced that she had to get back to the infirmary before she was missed.

When she had gone, Honaker said: "I don't trust her. Who's to say she won't sell us out?"

Cole wasn't buying what Honaker was selling. He went with his gut. He wasn't sure that he understood love, but he did know loyalty, and he sensed it in this young woman. "We got no choice but to trust her. Besides, if Mrs. Vaska vouches for her, I reckon that's good enough for me."

They glanced at Mrs. Vaska, who stood serenely beside her husband's chair, holding a teapot.

"Inna?" Cole asked, raising his hands in the universal gesture for *what do you think?*

The old Russian woman nodded curtly, like she was pecking at something with her chin. *"Da."*

That settled it.

• • •

Inna thought she had everything planned out, but she was still missing one key piece of the plan —letting Harry know.

So the day after her meeting with the Americans, she packed some medical supplies and made her way toward the barracks where Harry and Ramsey lived. The work crews were back for the day, and it wouldn't be the first time that she had visited the barracks at the end of the day. Most of the guards were never too curious, but she always explained that the Americans were patients. That made sense to the guards— Americans were special.

Walking across the Gulag compound, she thought about how the meeting with the rescuers had gone. They seemed competent enough, although she worried about the tension between the one named Honaker and Cole. Honaker claimed to be in charge, but Cole seemed to be the one who knew what he was doing.

The truth was, though, that Cole made her uneasy. It wasn't that she didn't trust him. But Cole had strange eyes like ice that looked right through you, and a quiet, deliberate manner. Inna had just lived through a devastating war, and she knew Cole's type. There were plenty of soldiers, but maybe one in a thousand was something more. A killer. This Cole was one of them. So was Barkov. Such men frightened her.

The one person who set her mind at ease was Vaska. He had a reputation in the village as a capable hunter and trapper, and quite trustworthy. Did she trust him with her life—and with Harry's?

Lost in thought, Inna didn't see Barkov in front of the barracks until it was nearly too late.

His bulk was unmistakeable, hulking like a bear near the entrance to the barracks.

She had not seen him there these last few days. What did he want? With a sinking feeling, she realized that he wanted *her*.

She recalled an expression that her American father used to say. *Bad news*. Barkov was bad news.

Ducking her head, Inna changed course,

hoping that she hadn't been seen.

Barkov had already run into her before, going to the Americans' barracks. Why hadn't he just gone to the infirmary? Because the Gulag compound was his territory, she thought. The infirmary was run by doctors and nurses who didn't have much patience with him.

Her heart pounding, she ducked into the laundry house. Looking out, it was clear that Barkov hadn't seen her—he was lighting a cigarette and not looking in her direction at all.

Another worrisome thought gripped her. Did Barkov know about the escape plan? It seemed impossible, but there were spies everywhere. People would trade their souls for an extra piece of bread or a bottle of vodka. Maybe someone in the village had seen her go to Vaska's house.

Inna slipped out the back of the laundry and returned to the infirmary. By the time she got there, she already had a plan in mind.

Inna took a piece of paper and composed a poem in English. Well, it would be passable as a poem to someone who didn't know English, but perhaps not to an English teacher. She smiled, in spite of everything, at the thought of writing Harry a poem.

It took her several tries, scratching out words here and there, and when she finished she took a fresh sheet of paper and made a good copy.

She found one of the old *zeks* who worked

around the infirmary because he was too frail for railroad construction. She gave him a heel of bread to deliver the poem to the American. She started to tell him which barracks, and which American, but the old man waved her off.

"The handsome American. Everyone in camp knows him." The weathered old zek winked, as if to say, Ah, love.

· · ·

Whitlock laid down on the bunk and couldn't even think about getting up again. He was that exhausted. He couldn't imagine how Ramsey must feel. Ramsey had a will of iron, even if his body was down to skin and bones. His chest rattled every time he coughed—which was almost constantly.

Not that Whitlock was doing much better. Fortunately, he had stayed healthy, but he had lost weight steadily since last spring, first in the German camp, and especially now in the Gulag, where the labor was constant and the intake of calories did little to replace the ones expended in building the railroad. He didn't have a scale, but he guessed that he had lost twenty pounds in the last few months, and Whitlock hadn't exactly been heavy to start with. At night when in lay in his bunk he could count his ribs, and his shoulder blades grated painfully against the slats of the bunk.

"Maybe your girl is coming by tonight," Ramsey said.

He knew Ramsey enjoyed Inna's company as much as he did, and that was all right—he was willing to share. Ramsey needed every bit of encouragement he could get.

Out of the corner of his eye, he noticed a zek from another barracks angling toward his bunk. The man held a piece of paper in his hand.

Inna, he thought. Who else would send him a note?

He took the few final steps toward Whitlock, a smile on his face as if this were the postman back home rather than a prisoner delivering a message in a prison camp.

A guard materialized to block his path.

The *zek*'s smile vanished. The guard snatched the note from him.

These guards were a rough and brutal lot. It wasn't clear that the guard could read, let alone read English, but every guard excelled at petty cruelty. He studied the note intently.

"Poeziya," the guard said with a sneer.

Then he crumpled the note and tossed it toward one of the stoves that struggled to warm the barracks.

Whitlock felt his heart stop and anger bubbled up in is throat. The son of a bitch was trying to burn Inna's note. His note, goddamnit.

He started to get off the bunk, the exhaustion in his muscles forgotten. What he'd like to do is take his fist and—

Ramsey caught his eye. "Don't even think about it," he muttered.

Fortunately, the guard had turned and wandered off before the note hit the floor. He wasn't all that intent on destruction. Neither was the stove, even though the damn thing glowed cherry red. The note struck the grate that served to keep sparks from burning down the barracks and bounced off, singed but legible.

Whitlock waited until the guard was gone. Then he was off the bunk, snatching the note out of the cinders and dirt on the rough wood floor boards.

The note contained a poem that was one stanza in length.

First Words of Icarus
Escape the great northern sky
Gate beyond the stars
Three wisdoms keep their watch
Midnight in the garden of evil
Tomorrow can't come soon enough
Scarf of the muse if the path is clear

"She sent me a poem," Whitlock said, a little in awe. A woman had never sent him a poem before. In this place, seeing a few words of

English on a scrap of paper was the equivalent of getting the *New York Times* delivered. "It's lovely, even if it doesn't make any sense."

He handed it off to Ramsey.

The other man read it and announced, "Harry, your girl may be a looker, but I hate to say that she's a lousy poet."

"It's the thought that counts."

Ramsey handed back the piece of paper and said in barely a whisper: "It's not a poem, you blessed idiot. It's a message in code."

Whitlock studied it again. "How do you figure?"

"Icarus was a pilot of sorts who escaped the island of Crete," Ramsey explained in hushed tones. In a Gulag barracks, you never knew who was pretending not to know English, but being paid to listen to the American prisoners. "I didn't go to Harvard like some people here, but I know that much. Well, he escaped for a little while. He did crash into the sea."

"How is it in code?"

"The first word of each line."

Once he saw that, it seemed so obvious that he wondered how he had overlooked it in the first place. Whitlock strung the first words together: **Escape gate three midnight tomorrow.**

Gate three was the one closest to the barracks. He didn't need Ramsey's help to figure out the line about the scarf. The muse in the poem was Inna. Inna's scarf. It was to be the signal.

"Pack your bags, Ramsey. This is our last night in the Gulag Hotel."

Then he crumpled up the paper and fed it into the fire, making certain that this time, only ashes remained.

CHAPTER 19

Inna's heart pounded as she approached Gate 3. She wore a cheap wristwatch made by Pobeda —a Soviet attempt at a fashion label of sorts— that showed that it was getting close to midnight. Harry would be expecting her signal. The team of Americans would be in place beyond the Gulag walls.

Everything now depended upon her.

In her ears, her pounding heart now sounded loud as a kettle drum; she was sure that someone else must hear it. She forced herself to walk calmly.

Since her last encounter with Barkov, Inna had taken to carrying a tiny pistol tucked into her boot. Her father had brought the .22 caliber pistol from America all those years ago, and the five shots left in the magazine were the only ammunition she had for it. She felt the weight of it there now, reassuring her.

Although she was afraid, it surprised her how easily she had learned to live this deceptive life. In Stalinist Russia, one had to be good at hiding one's true thoughts and actions. Then again, secretly planning the escape of an American prisoner from the Gulag was an entirely different level of deception.

In her pockets were the tools of her new-found trade, starting with a flask of vodka to help distract Dmitri, the young guard at the gate. The poor boy was drunk most of the time. Who could blame him in this place? He had gotten used to her coming and going at all hours of the night to help the sick people of the village. They had even flirted in the meaningless way that young people did. He was a young man—of course he was interested in her. Many of the guards coerced female inmates into being their "prison wives," but Dmitri was still too young and naive for that.

Her other pocket hid a bright red scarf, which she would tie to the gate once she had dealt with Dmitri.

But as she approached the gate, she sensed

that something was wrong. The man there did not have Dmitri's tall, slim build. As usual, a single bare bulb struggled to light the darkness around the gate. The gate itself was somewhat larger than a normal-sized door so that two men could easily pass through it, shoulder to shoulder. The guard stood just outside the circle of light. As she approached, however, the guard stepped closer, and she saw at once that it was not Dmitri.

Her heart, thrumming now like a hummingbird, skipped several beats in panic. She managed to keep her face carefully blank.

"Where is Dmitri?" she demanded, a bit too quickly.

The guard shrugged. He was an older man that Inna recognized, but had never talked to before. She didn't know a thing about him—she wasn't about to risk her plan by attempting to flirt with him, only to be turned down, or worse yet, raise his suspicions.

Her thoughts went to the pistol in her boot. Maybe she could wrap it in her scarf to muffle and gunshot, and then shoot the guard.

"They put Dmitri in the guard tower," the guard said. "The poor fool who was normally there was sick—vodka flu, most likely. Barkov will skin him with that whip of his if he finds out that he was drunk." Then a thought came to the older guard and he raised his eyebrows. "So, you were hoping for Dmitri? You're the girl from the infirmary. Lucky boy, though he wouldn't know what to do with you, ha, ha. The poor dumb *devstvennitsa*. If you want a man with some experience, come see me."

Despite what the guard said, she doubted that Dmitri was still a virgin. Inna looked away demurely and lowered her eyes, not wanting to encourage his flirting, but not wanting to make him angry. There was still time to shoot him, but she could not bring herself to reach for the pistol. "Mmm, I will keep that in mind. Listen, I am going into the village to help Anna Korkovna. Her child is due any day now and she has been having—"

"Go ahead then," the guard said, waving toward the village. He was not really interested in discussing the particulars of childbirth. "Watch out for wolves, though. They have been seen prowling around the village at night. If you see any, give me a shout."

"Yes, I will."

The guard closed the gate behind her.

She glanced up at the watchtower, but it was too dark to see Dmitri up there. She hoped Harry didn't make a run for it tonight without seeing her signal. If he did, it might very well be Dmitri who would shoot him with the machine gun.

Inna made her way along the path toward the village. Halfway there, a shadow appeared from the darkness. She gasped, remembering the guard's warning about wolves.

"It's me." She recognized the voice as Cole's. She was still startled—he had moved with utter silence. "Where's Whitlock?"

"There has been a problem," she said.

• • •

Midnight came and went in the barracks. The barracks did not have proper glass-covered windows, but only wooden slats over the opening to let in fresh air. Whitlock didn't want to be too obvious about it, but from time to time he peered out the ventilation slats toward the dimly lit gate just beyond the barracks.

No sign of a scarf.

"What do you think?" he whispered to Ramsey. "Should we make a run for it?"

"Not unless you want to provide these Ivans with some target practice. Inna is going to tie her scarf to the gate, as she put it so poetically. Until we see that scarf, I think we should sit tight."

After a while, Whitlock's eyes grew heavier. No one in the barracks owned a watch, but it must have been approaching two or three in the morning. Still, Inna had given them no sign. Exhausted from the day's labors on the railroad, Whitlock could no longer stop sleep anymore than a canoe can keep itself from being swept over Niagara Falls.

"Inna," he mumbled as he drifted off. "Inna ..."

• • •

The American team was forced to wait another day in the secret room within Vaska's house. The four men could barely move without bumping into one another in the dark space. The room was intended to hide smuggled goods, not four men. In particular, whenever Samson fidgeted he jostled the others, making Cole feel like he was trapped in a milking stall with a clumsy cow. They did have flashlights, but there was no point in wasting their limited supply of batteries. Instead, they made themselves as comfortable as they could and waited out the day by dozing shoulder to shoulder in the confined space.

"This is getting old," Vaccaro muttered.

"Sshh."

In building the secret room, Vaska had carefully sealed all the gaps between the planks, but they were thin all the same, most of the wood having been salvaged from packing crates. Beyond the walls, they could hear the business of the village taking place: old men and women conversing in Russian, children at play, laughter, the squeak of a passing cart.

Occasionally, they heard gruff male voices. Soldiers. They held their breath each time, wondering if Vaska had betrayed them, after all, or if a curious villager had somehow ratted them out. Maybe the soldiers had only come to the village to trade. A few kept wives or girlfriends there.

The flimsy walls did nothing to filter out smells. The still air in the hidden room soon became a miasma of woodsmoke, boiled cabbage, vaguely spoiled fish, and horse manure. The atmosphere was not helped by having four men who were overdue for a shower in close quarters.

As they listened, unseen, it felt a lot like being a ghost. Waiting in the house itself was out of the question because Mrs. Vaska had visitors throughout the day who came to gossip. She was quite the agent—no one would have guessed that she was hiding four American soldiers planning an escape from the nearby Gulag.

Finally, the noises outside diminished as the day wound down. The temperature dropped steadily in the unheated room. Cooking smells drifted in from the kitchen, making their bellies rumble.

Night was coming on.

At long last, they heard the sound of the boards covering the narrow doorway to the secret room being removed. They stumbled out into the kitchen, blinking even at the dim glow from the oil lamps.

Mrs. Vaska had prepared the evening meal. Russian black tea and more of her fish pie. She gestured at them to sit.

Vaska nodded at them, and drew up a chair to the table. The men all settled down to eat.

Once they had finished, they gathered their gear. Vaska picked up his hunting rifle and kissed his wife. She would explain his absence by saying that he was on a long hunt, which he was known to do. She would say that he had left two days before the escape.

None of them felt the excitement that they had the night before. Nobody wanted to say it, but the plan was flimsy to begin with. The delay made it feel like tissue paper. They had come a long way to rely on the Russian girl distracting a guard.

Honaker said, "If she doesn't come through tonight, I'm going to knife the guard and tie a goddamn scarf to the gate. I can't take much more of this sitting around in that packing crate behind the chimney."

For once, Cole agreed with Honaker. If Inna didn't deliver tonight, it might be time to try a different approach. The more time that they remained in the village increased the chance that someone would spot them, and then the gig would be up. They would find themselves imprisoned in the Gulag alongside Whitlock—if the Russians didn't shoot them outright.

"We go tonight, one way or another," Cole agreed.

Outside, Cole sniffed the air. It smelled clean and fresh—and felt vaguely damp on his cheeks. Out of the south. Cold as it was, that meant snow. He looked up and couldn't see any stars.

He looked at Vaska. "Smells like snow."

The old man nodded. "Yes, the first snow is coming. Maybe tonight. Maybe tomorrow."

"Got to get out ahead of it," Cole said. "If we leave tracks for these Ruskie sons of bitches to follow, we ain't got a prayer."

CHAPTER 20

Inna shivered as much from fear as from the cold. It was almost midnight as she approached the gate, hoping against hope that she would find Dmitri on duty tonight. She had a rapport with him. He was young and naive—which was important for the success of her plan. The guard last night had called him a virgin. Even better.

She felt a spark of relief when she saw his familiar figure.

He greeted her with a smile. In the dim light, she could see that he was heavily bundled against the late autumn chill. He really wasn't a bad-looking boy, and not unkind. She felt bad about what she was going to do to him, but then pushed the thought from her mind. If this plan was going to succeed, she needed to be single-minded of purpose.

"Inna," he said, obviously glad to see her.

As she stepped closer, she could smell the vodka on his breath, but he didn't seem to be drunk. It was likely that he'd been taking a few nips to stay warm. Out here, who could blame him?

"You were not here last night," she said.

He shrugged. "I was in the guard tower. You were on another mission of mercy?"

"Anna Korkovna is expecting and she is having a difficult time."

"You are good to the people of the village," Dmitri said. "I hope that they appreciate you."

"They do," she said. She produced a flask of vodka from her coat pocket. She knew, from observing him, that his own coat pocket held the key to the gate. "One of them gave me this in thanks, but I do not care for vodka. Let me give it to you for the many times you have opened the gate for me."

He took the vodka gladly. "This will keep me warm tonight," he said.

"I know something else that will keep you warm," she said, stepping closer. "Dmitri, I do not know how to say this ..."

"What is it?"

"Leave your post for a few minutes," she said, touching his arm. "You look so cold. Let me warm you up a bit."

Dmitri grinned. He could not seem to believe his good luck. "You want me to go with you? Right now?"

"I was hoping you could." Inna stood quite close to him as she said it, smiling up at him.

"I suppose one will notice if I am gone for just a few minutes," he said, as if reassuring himself.

"Come on," she said. She slipped her arm around his waist. "I know just the place where we can go."

Dmitri needed no more encouragement. Inna had planned this next step carefully. She led him to the infirmary, then inside to one of the supply rooms. She kissed him deeply, which sent the boy reeling.

"Inna!" he said in surprise.

"Hurry," she said. She tugged at his coat. "We don't have much time."

Getting undressed was no small matter. There were coats, scarves, belt buckles, trousers, boots —

Mostly, Inna helped him get out of all that while only tugging perfunctorily at her own clothes. In between, when they could, they kissed. Virgin or not, he seemed to have a good grasp of kissing. Soon enough, there was a pile of clothes on the floor, and Dmitri stood in just his undershorts, with his anticipation of a passionate interlude made all too clear.

Inna, trying not to stare, put a finger to her lips. "Shh! I think I hear someone in the hall. Wait here. I will send them away."

She picked up his coat and slipped it on as if to keep off the chill, then bundled up his other clothes and moved into the hallway. It was empty; she had only pretended to hear someone outside the door. Inna took a moment to pat down the coat pocket to make sure that Dmitri's ring of keys was there. She had brought the other clothes in case the key was in his pants. Then she locked the door behind her, trapping Dmitri inside.

Inna walked quickly out of the infirmary and toward Gate 3. It was almost midnight.

At the gate, she took out the key ring and selected the bright silver one that unlocked the padlock. The gate was secured by a length of chain, which she undid.

Then Inna tied her scarf to the gate and slipped outside the Gulag's walls.

She had done her part. The rest was up to Harry and Ramsey.

• • •

No more than a couple hundred feet away,

Whitlock lay in his cot listening to the fitful sleeping of the other prisoners around him. Inna had not come to visit and had not risked another note, but as far as he knew, the escape attempt was still on. He and Ramsey had no choice but to hope for Inna's signal.

He had struggled to stay awake until midnight. The barracks was no place for night owls. The Soviets rousted everyone before dawn to set them to work on the railroad to nowhere, or on a hundred other tasks around the camp itself. At the end of the day, exhausted and hungry, sleep was a welcome escape.

He felt a lot like he had as a kid on Christmas Eve, hoping to stay awake for some sign of Santa Claus.

The hammering of his heart kept him from drifting off. His belly rumbled. He and Ramsey had saved half of their bread ration these last three days. It wasn't much, but it might help them survive beyond the Gulag walls.

Whitlock had worried that someone might steal the bread, which they had to leave in their bunks, but no one had touched it. Petty theft was a problem in the barracks—almost any item would be snatched up the second you took your eye off it—except when it came to food. Food was the only thing of real value in the Gulag compound, and it could be a matter of life and death, of survival or starvation. Stealing another man's food was severely punished by a group beating. Even the worst bullies and thugs in the Gulag knew better than to suffer mob justice. This was a rule that crossed all boundaries of nationality and faction within the Gulag's population. Whitlock had witnessed one such beating, so maybe it wasn't all that surprising that their bread supply had gone untouched.

His thoughts drifted to food: Thanksgiving dinners with mountains of mashed potatoes and gravy, hamburgers on the grill, a clambake on the beach at Cape Cod with corn on the cob and lobster ... playing as a boy on the beach ... that time he got so sunburned that everyone called him lobster boy ...

His mind drifted lazily as summer sunshine —

He jerked awake. *Just a little longer,* he promised his exhausted mind and body. *Got to stay awake.*

If he fell asleep, they might miss their opportunity to escape this place.

He glanced over at Ramsey, who *was* sound asleep. Maybe he had tried to stay awake, but poor Ramsey was really suffering from the work, and the growing cold of the autumn days had not helped his cough. Whitlock wasn't sure how much longer Ramsey would last in this place. There might not be another chance.

Whitlock shifted on the bunk so that he could look out the ventilation slats in the barracks. When he moved, the thin blanket fell away, and he was surprised by how cold he immediately felt. Winter was just around the corner.

He looked toward the gate. Was it midnight yet? If not, then it was goddamn close. Gate 3 nearest the barracks was lighted by a single dim bulb. Usually, he could see a guard standing there. He squinted, searching for the familiar bulk of the Russian's uniform.

No one there.

Whitlock stared. As a pilot, he had excellent vision. His eyes could just make out something fluttering on the fence beside the gate.

The scarf.

Inna had said in her message that she would tie her scarf to the gate as a signal. How in the world had she gotten rid of the guard?

There would be time later to ask her about that, he thought. Right now, it was time to go.

He reached toward Ramsey, then paused. Maybe he should just let the poor bastard sleep. Even after his sojourn in the infirmary, Ramsey was getting weaker by the day. How long would he last on the run?

The mere thought of abandoning Ramsey was too much. To have left him behind would be the ultimate cruelty. Whitlock shook him gently by the shoulder and Ramsey startled awake.

"Damnit, I was just getting to the good part,"

he muttered. "I think her name was Betty."

"You can dream about Betty later," Whitlock said. "It's now or never if we want to get out of this place."

• • •

Not long after the stars had come out, Honaker and his team, Cole included, moved into position beyond the Gulag walls. It was Vaska who placed them, hidden beside the dirt road that connected the Gulag to the village. Crouched in the darkness with their guns and knives, they could have been setting up an ambush rather than a rescue.

For the umpteenth time, Cole considered how indebted they were to Vaska. Without the Russian's help, they would literally have been stumbling around in the dark. It was against Cole's nature to trust anyone easily, and it still worried him that Vaska could betray them with a simple word to this Barkov character, or to the Gulag commandant. Maybe Vaska was all right, but if Mrs. Vaska ever got tired of fish pie and wanted something a little better, there might be in trouble.

There was something slow and steady about Vaska that Cole trusted. Vaska was a hunter and a trapper, after all, so Cole had formed an immediate connection with the Russian.

It was hard to tell how long they crouched there in the darkness. At one point, someone came along the road, but it was only one of the villagers who worked at the prison. They could hear him singing. He sounded a little drunk. Oblivious, the villager passed within a few feet of the hidden Americans.

Another hour went by. No one else passed on the road. At night, the road between the Gulag and the village was hardly a thoroughfare. For such a large facility, the Gulag in the distance was oddly quiet. The only sounds came from the village that lay maybe a quarter of a mile away. They heard barking dogs, some shouting between a husband and wife, the sound of someone chopping wood.

"You must have patience," Vaska said. "She is coming."

Cole had to hand it to Vaska, because he himself hadn't seen a thing. He reckoned it helped that Vaska was on his home turf. Also, Vaska had brought along his dog, whose ears were about a hundred times better than their own. From where he was standing, Cole could hear the dog growl. He tightened his grip on the rifle.

Moments later, Inna emerged as a shadow on the road from the Gulag.

She gasped when Cole emerged from the shadows.

"I have done it," she said excitedly. "The gate

is unlocked, and I left Harry the signal. He should be here any minute."

"If he ain't here in thirty minutes, we've got to call it off," Cole said. "We need a head start on whoever is gonna chase us, and the closer we get to morning roll call, the less time we have."

"He will be here," Inna said.

"I sure as hell hope so," Cole said. "For his sake—and ours."

By previous arrangement, it had been decided that Cole would be the one to step out of the shadows while the others still waited, hidden, with weapons drawn, just in case Inna or Whitlock, when he showed up, had accidentally brought along any Russians.

Inna crouched beside Cole, struggling to remain calm. She seemed to be holding her breath. Once or twice she fidgeted or cleared her throat as if to speak, but Cole quieted her with a touch. It was better not to call any attention to themselves. Anyone else might be concealed in the darkness nearby.

She had mentioned this thug named Barkov. What if he had followed along behind Inna, unseen?

Fortunately, Vaska's laika had much keener senses than any of the men. He had told them the dog's name was Buka, which translated roughly to surly. The name fit.

Buka began to growl.

• • •

Whitlock and Ramsey had both had slept in their boots. Other than their tattered coats and their supply of bread, which barely filled a single pocket, they had nothing else to pack or carry.

No one seemed to pay any attention to Whitlock and Ramsey. It wasn't unusual for men to get up during the night to relieve themselves. The door of the barracks was not watched, although the compound itself was guarded. They slipped out into the night.

"I have to tell you, Harry, I don't think I can make a run for it if it comes to that," Ramsey whispered. "You'll need to leave me behind."

"We'll walk," Whitlock whispered back. "If we run, we'll only attract attention to ourselves."

Side by side, they took their time crossing the distance to the gate. They expected at any moment for someone to shout at them to halt. Nobody seemed to be around. Inna definitely was nowhere to be seen. There were a couple of figures moving through the gloom in another part of the compound, but those guards were too far away to identify them as escaping prisoners. They reached the gate, found it unlocked, and walked beyond the Gulag walls.

They had escaped.

Ahead of them, about half a mile away, they

could see a few twinkling lights from the village. Those lights seemed swallowed up by the vast darkness of the taiga beyond. The wind was blowing, and Whitlock found himself shivering. It was late October, but it felt cold as a December night back home in New England. The ground felt frozen under his feet.

Ramsey looked at him and said, "Now what?"

Whitlock didn't have a quick answer for that, but as it turned out, he didn't need one. A figure stepped out of the darkness and said in a twangy Southern drawl, "I reckon you must be Whitlock. It's about goddamn time you done showed up. Who the hell have you got with you?"

• • •

Whitlock was so overcome with emotion at the sound of another American voice that he couldn't even speak.

Beside him, Ramsey spoke up. "Lieutenant William Ramsey, Army Air Corps."

Ramsey seemed to be struggling for breath, even while just standing there. Moments later, he was overcome with a coughing fit, doubling over from the spasms that racked his lungs.

"Where's Whitlock?" the man in the road asked.

"That's me."

Another man emerged from the shadows.

"We can't take him," he said angrily, pointing at Ramsey. "Just you, Whitlock. That's the deal."

"Who are you?"

"Lieutenant Honaker."

"Listen, Honaker, I'm not leaving without him."

The Southerner spoke up. "We ain't leavin' nobody behind for these Ruskie bastards. Now let's get a move on, or we'll all end up in that there Gulag, or worse."

"I like this guy," Ramsey said. "We ought to listen to him."

Inna approached and threw her arms around Whitlock. "Thank God, Harry. I wasn't sure that you were going to make it."

Their reunion was cut short by Honaker. "Listen up, people. I'm in charge here," he said. "We can't take another prisoner with us. This is a rescue operation, not a two for one sale."

"And this ain't Montgomery Ward," Cole said. "If we leave this poor bastard, the Ruskies will kill him—after he tells them about us. We either have to kill him, or take him with us, and I sure as hell ain't gonna kill him."

It was impossible to make out any details of the surrounding faces in the darkness, but it didn't take much imagination to guess the expressions on them as they glared at Honaker.

"Goddamnit," Honaker said.

CHAPTER 21

Honaker wasn't a happy camper, but he could see that nobody was going anywhere without Ramsey. Giving in, he grudgingly introduced the team to the two escapees.

"Let's move out," he said, once the introductions were over. "Vaska, you lead the way."

They expected Vaska to strike out into the surrounding taiga. To their surprise, Vaska brought them back toward the sleeping village. They kept to the road at first, heading toward the houses, then made a wide circle around the village before setting off to the east, directly across the taiga.

"What the hell?" Again, Honaker wasn't happy. He fell into step beside Cole and said in a low voice, "We just walked in a circle. What a goddamn waste of time. What the hell kind of guide have we got?"

Cole had seen right away that Vaska was covering their tracks by taking a roundabout route. "If they put dogs on our trail, all the smells from the village will keep them confused," Cole said. "It will take them a while to figure out which direction we took. That's good. We need to put some distance between us and them. Once they figure out that their prize American prisoners done run off, the Russians will come after us with everything they got. We can use a head start. We need all the help we can get."

Honaker looked doubtfully at the group. He snorted. "All the help we can get sounds about right. That's because this other guy is gonna slow us down, not to mention that woman."

"Ain't nothin' we can do about that."

"It's not too late to leave them behind."

"Wouldn't be right," Cole said with finality.

"Then they are officially your problem," Honaker said. "I wash my hands of those two. If we have to carry Ramsey, then I expect you to do it. Look how weak he is."

Cole quickened his pace to break stride with

Honaker. He had long, rangy legs that were used to eating up the miles. Even loaded down with gear and a rifle, Cole managed to walk with the easy lope of a coyote. It wouldn't be any problem for him to walk clear to Finland.

Honaker was right, even if Cole hated to admit it. Ramsey would definitely slow them down. The jury was still out on Whitlock, but if Cole had to issue a verdict, he would guess that Whitlock was more than likely a soft, rich boy whose feet would blister up after a couple of miles.

Cole was less worried about Inna because he had the impression that the half-Russian, half-American woman could hold her own. Those two halves had made a pretty good whole.

Whitlock fell in beside Cole. "I can't thank you enough," he said. "Inna has told me everything that all of you did to get here. It's amazing."

"Don't thank us yet," Cole said. "We ain't even out of sight of the Gulag."

Goo-lahg. It was another one of those foreign words that Cole had come to know since landing in Normandy more than a year ago. The way it sounded made it catch in your throat like a bad piece of meat, matching the bleak atmosphere of the Soviet prison camp perfectly.

"Listen, I wanted to thank you for sticking up for Ramsey back there," Whitlock said. "He's tough, but he hasn't been well. It doesn't help that these goddamn Russians have been working him nearly to death and feeding him scraps. I know Honaker isn't thrilled about it, but I couldn't leave Ramsey behind."

A few paces back, they could hear Ramsey coughing. He moved quickly enough, keeping up, but he walked with a stiff gait.

"You done the right thing," Cole said.

"So what's the plan?"

"We walk east for the next six days. When the sun comes up, that's the direction we move in. We stay ahead of the Russians, then get across the border into Finland. Simple. Sound all right to you?"

Whitlock nodded. "Simple is good," he said.

They continued to walk mostly in silence, until faint streaks of pink showed on the horizon. The wind had a bitter edge, chilling them all to the bone, despite the exercise. On the Russian plain, the weather felt more like December than mid-October.

Finally, Honaker called for a halt. "Let's get some sleep, maybe get some food," he said. "It looks to me like Whitlock and Ramsey could use it. Hell, we could all use it. Then we'll head out again when we have some daylight."

The group flopped down as if the ground was covered with a rich carpet, rather than the brown and withered grass. Samson broke out some food, just black bread and cheese courtesy of Mrs. Vaska, but the two former prisoners devoured it. Their faces had that too-thin look brought on by constant hunger. Cole had seen plenty of that among the mountain people before the war. The Depression had hemmed them in, starving them out. He reckoned there were all kinds of Gulags in this world.

Cole sat apart from the others and put his rifle to his shoulder, scanning the horizon through his scope. Although it was dark, he figured that whoever was coming after them would have lights. Vaska lit a pipe and stationed himself a few feet away, his ancient hunting rifle across his knees.

"You need to relax, Hillbilly," Honaker complained. "There's no way they caught up to us that fast."

"I just want to see them before they see me," Cole said.

As the light grew, the surrounding taiga was revealed for the first time. Since leaving the village, the landscape had grown more hilly and rugged. Rocks and boulders pushed up from the frozen ground like the knuckles of an old man's hand. In between the high ground lay swaths of swampland. Nearby, a pool of standing water had formed between the rocks. A skim of ice reached most of the way across. Trees marched down the slopes toward their camp: spruce, pine, and a kind of tree that Vaska had told him earlier was a larch. In the United States, it would not have been unusual to find a few hardscrabble homesteads in the most remote area, but most Russians lived in villages. Away from the village, the land was an uninhabited wilderness.

Vaska sucked at his pipe. He had noticed Cole surveying the landscape. "It is what we call pustynya," he said. "Nothingness."

Cole nodded. He didn't mind pustynya. He thought that he and the Russian taiga would get along just fine.

• • •

Honaker got them all up an hour after sunrise. Cole had never gone to sleep, but had kept watch. They were still too close to the Gulag camp for comfort.

He hadn't been alone. Vaska sat nearby, nursing his pipe, his old rifle across his knees. Watching the horizon for any sign of light or movement.

"Barkov will be the one coming after us," Vaska explained. "It would be just like him to come sneaking through the dark. He moves quietly, for such a big man."

Cole kept his eyes trained on the darkness. "Just who is this Barkov?"

"He is a deadly shot. In Stalingrad, the

Germans called him the Red Sniper." Vaska spat. "He is also a throat cutter."

Cole thought that Barkov cast a long shadow. Inna clearly feared him, and he even seemed to worry Vaska. It would be just fine with him if he never got to experience Barkov for himself.

Now that it was full daylight, they felt more secure. The horizon was nearly unbroken under low clouds. They would see anyone coming from a long way off.

The laika dog raised his head and sniffed the air. Vaska nodded. "He smells the change in the wind."

"Coming out of the southeast now. Smells like snow."

"We will get some snow, maybe a dusting. That will help to cover any tracks that we left."

"Early for snow," Cole said.

Vaska laughed. "You are in Russia, my friend. First it will snow a little, then it will get cold. If the wind shifts around to the northeast we will have a bigger snow. That is how the winter begins."

"Good thing I wore my long johns."

The others were getting up. As soldiers, Vaccaro and Samson had long since learned to sleep wherever they could, whenever they could. They awakened instantly when Honaker kicked at their boots. Inna and Whitlock were more sluggish. Cole noticed they had slept side by side, but not touching. Ramsey took a while to wake up, like he was dazed. Finally, Whitlock had to reach down and shake him roughly.

Cole thought that what Ramsey needed was to sleep for a week straight in a decent bed, with someone to give him soup every time he woke up. His mama's rabbit stew would have fixed Ramsey right up. His mama hadn't been much of a cook, but she could make a damn good rabbit stew with onions, carrots, potatoes. Cole provided the rabbit. His stomach rumbled at the memory. Most of the time, there had been more broth than meat or vegetables. Even so, a few bowls of that would have Ramsey back on his feet.

They didn't have stew. Or a bed. Ramsey coughed so much that the air frosted around him like it was smoke.

"All right, we have got to get a move on," Honaker said. "We don't know how much of a lead we have on the Russians, but we want to stay ahead of them. We'll keep moving as long as there is daylight."

• • •

A few miles away, Barkov looked out over the empty taiga. "Which way?" he asked the Mink.

He and Barkov had been in pursuit since not long after dawn, when the guards had discovered the escape after assembling the prisoners for the walk to the work site. The Mink sent the guard to check the barracks, fully expecting to find the Americans' dead bodies in their bunks. The Americans wouldn't have been the first to die of exhaustion, and wouldn't be the last to be worked to death.

The guard came back shaking his head.

The Mink couldn't believe it. How did the Americans even have the strength to get more than a few kilometers?

Barkov questioned the other men in the barracks, using his whip as encouragement, but no one seemed to know anything.

Then someone had found one of the guards locked in a storeroom at the infirmary. The young man was nearly naked. He had a wild story about being tricked by Inna Mikhaylovna.

She was nowhere to be found.

Barkov had the growing realization that the bitch had helped the Americans to escape. He'd had his suspicions that she had grown too fond of the American, Whitlock. Foolishly, she must have acted on that.

Then, a woman's scarf was found tied to Gate 3. Inna's scarf. He recognized it by the color—it had been red once, but washed so many times that it had faded to pink. It was clearly a signal of some kind. Together with her absence and the young soldier's story of seduction, it was damning evidence.

When informed of the escape, the commandant had simply ordered Barkov to handle it. He was a soulless bureaucrat who saw each prisoner as a unit to be accounted for, like a can of beans in a storeroom. He busied himself with ledger books that tallied camp expenses and work output. He kept careful records on how many miles of track were laid each month. In the eyes of Moscow, it made him the perfect commandant.

Quickly, Barkov assembled a team to pursue the escaped Americans and Inna. In between barking out orders, he hummed happily to himself. Someone else could lead the work party today; he and The Mink were going hunting.

• • •

Prompted by Barkov's question, the Mink considered the empty landscape. There was no indication of the direction taken by the girl and the escaped prisoners. The Mink thought about that as he smoked an unfiltered cigarette that seemed to be one part cheap tobacco and three parts sawdust. What lay to the north but arctic wastes? Hundreds of miles to the south lay Moscow, which seemed an unlikely destination. China and Mongolia were hundreds of miles distant. But to the east, Finland was barely two hundred miles away.

If you were an American, your only hope lay in that direction.

The Mink jerked his chin that way, then exhaled a cloud of the foul cigarette smoke toward the sun, still hovering above the eastern horizon.

"Ah, that makes sense," Barkov said. He waved his arm toward a squad of soldiers in a *follow me* gesture. "They won't have gone far."

Barkov led the way. They did not get far because there was no clear trail to follow.

Along with Barkov and the Mink there was Bunin, a local tracker who had brought his dogs, and six soldiers detailed from the Gulag garrison. Barkov hardly thought that they would need half a dozen soldiers to help catch the escapees—he and the Mink could do that handily—but the soldiers would be good workhorses to carry back any bodies. Normally, he wouldn't have bothered with that. However, the Americans were special prisoners, so the Gulag commandant might need bodies to show some commissar if there was interest from Moscow. Barkov sighed. If he had been given his way, those annoying Americans would have been dead some time ago. That was politics for you.

One of the soldiers detailed to Barkov's squad was Dmitri, the luckless boy whom the witch Inna Mikhaylovna had tricked into abandoning his post.

"You are growing soft," the Mink said, nodding at the young man, who by all rights should have been taken out and shot.

"This is a much better punishment," Barkov said. "Besides, do you think he is the first young man to be misled by his *khuy*?"

Barkov was thinking about the incident in Berlin that had got them sent to this Gulag camp months before. Most commissars would have shot them to avoid the paperwork. They had gotten a second chance—Barkov was willing to give Dmitri a similar opportunity. He was young.

"Soft," the Mink repeated.

"The war is over. We can afford to be generous."

The Mink was not so sure. "If he gives us any trouble, I will cut off his *khuy* for him."

Barkov laughed. "Cheer up, my friend. We are on a hunt! What could be better?"

Barkov was in an ebullient mood. There was nothing that was so much sport as chasing a prisoner. His only concern was that this hunt would be over all too soon. He doubted that the Americans or Inna had gotten very far. In fact, he was surprised that they were not visible somewhere on the horizon. He put his German-made binoculars—a prize from the sack of Berlin—to his eyes. Nothing but trees, rough open ground, and more trees.

He turned to Bunin, whose trio of dogs

sniffed halfheartedly at the ground. No trail yet. They had expected to pick up the trail near the gate, but that had not been the case. The frozen ground was inscrutable. Not so much as a footprint to give them a clue.

"Those dogs of yours are worthless," Barkov said. "Don't expect me to pay to feed them."

Bunin grunted. He was a big man—as tall as Barkov, but not as heavy through the shoulders. From a distance, it would be easy to mistake one for the other. But size was where the similarity ended. Though Bunin had a fierce face, weathered by sun and wind, he was soft and gentle at heart, known to prefer the company of his beloved dogs to that of people.

"There is no scent," he said simply.

Barkov had given him the scarf that Inna had tied to the gate, and Bunin had made sure that his dogs got a snout full of her smell. The dogs had followed the scent toward the village, then lost it.

"The village?" the Mink wondered. "Do you think they are hiding there?"

Barkov shook his head. "Who would be foolish enough to hide them? Besides, the Americans wish to escape. It would be like a fish hiding in a net. No, there is nothing for them in the village."

What Barkov did not admit, even to the Mink, was that he was reluctant to search the village. The Gulag compound relied on the village much more than the village relied on the compound. Some of the prison guards, right up to the commandant, had taken "outpost wives" there. No one would take kindly to a disruptive search. Barkov knew better than to kick a hornet's nest.

"No, they are on the run. Let us give chase! Ha, ha!"

He called Bunin over and had him work his dogs between the prison gate and the village on the eastern side. First, they moved a couple hundred feet off the road that connected the Gulag camp and village so that they could pick up a fresh trail away from the well-traveled road. Then the dogs worked back and forth, back and forth, moving in expanding circles as Bunin nudged them along with low, gentle words. Barkov was no expert on dogs, but he had to admit that it was fascinating to watch them work. Grudgingly, he thought that perhaps Bunin did know what he was doing, after all.

Barkov looked up at the leaden sky. "We haven't got all day, Bunin!" he called.

"You cannot make bread bake faster," Bunin said.

The Mink laughed. He was simple that way, Barkov thought.

Instead of laughing, Barkov cursed. They were losing precious daylight hours to Bunin's lazy dogs while the prisoners increased their lead.

The nights were getting colder. He sent Dmitri back for rations and blankets in case they had to spend the night on the taiga, telling him to run all the way.

Finally, one of the useless dogs had a hit. The dog yelped with a new, excited tone. Bunin raised an arm aloft with the scarf, as if to mark the spot.

The other dogs joined in. At first, they followed the road toward the village, which confounded Barkov and the Mink. Had the prisoners escaped into the village, after all?

But the trail did not go as far as the houses. Bunin called the dogs back to where they had first caught the scent.

"Clever," Barkov admitted, seeing what the prisoners had done. They had muddled their trail by backtracking to the village, partially circling it, and then striking out at a random point. It created a confusing trail to follow. They had anticipated the dogs and bought themselves more time with that simple maneuver. Barkov had the niggling thought that perhaps he had underestimated his quarry. Where did an American pilot learn to outsmart hunting dogs?

No matter—Bunin had found the trail. Now they had to wait until Dmitri returned with supplies.

"What took you so long?" Barkov demanded in frustration, once the young soldier returned.

Barkov took out his whip and beat him a few times for good measure.

Then he shouted to Bunin, his voice like a starting gun at a race: "After them!"

CHAPTER 22

By mid-morning of the following day, the wind had picked up, with a wet edge that promised snow. None of them had slept well. Above the incessant wind in their ears they could now hear barking in the distance.

"Dogs," Honaker said. "The Ruskies have dogs. Goddamnit. How the hell did they catch up to us?"

"They must have stayed on the move last night," Cole said. "They ain't lazy, that's for damn sure."

"Barkov," Vaska said. "That is just what he

would do."

Cole had new respect for Barkov. If he'd been in Barkov's shoes, it's just what he would have done.

Inna looked up at the mention of Barkov's name. To Cole's surprise, she shuddered—and not from the cold. "Maybe this was a mistake," she said. "Maybe we should not have escaped. What have I gotten us into?"

"Are you kidding?" Harry touched her shoulder. "Don't let yourself think that for a minute. Nobody should be at that Gulag. Not me, not Ramsey. And definitely not you."

"But Barkov—"

Cole spoke up. "You let me worry about Barkov."

"He is the devil," Inna said. "No one can stand up to him."

"I reckon we'll see about that," Cole said. He shouldered his rifle. "Them dogs are gonna be on top of us before long, but I ain't too worried about dogs. This Barkov is gonna be right behind them. From everything I've heard, he sounds like the problem. Let me see if I can slow him up. Miss Inna, maybe you can help."

"Me?"

"Give me that scarf you're wearing."

Inna had left a scarf at the Gulag gate, but had worn an extra one against the cold. Cole took it, pulled his knife, and cut the woven scarf in half. He returned what was left of the scarf to Inna. "I just need half, darlin'. You can use the other half to stay warm."

Next, Cole asked Whitlock and Ramsey for their scarves. They looked puzzled, but handed them over. He cut pieces off and handed them back.

Vaccaro spoke up, "You're not doing this alone, Hillbilly. I'm coming with you."

"To hell you are."

"To hell I ain't," Vaccaro said, in a fair imitation of Cole.

Cole grinned. "All right, then."

Honaker was having none of it. "Cole, you can't just march back there and pick a fight with the Ruskies."

"Why the hell not? If nothin' else, it will buy you some time. Now go on, you need to make tracks. Vaccaro and I can handle this."

Without another word, Cole walked off in the direction they had come from, with Vaccaro trailing behind.

The sound of barking dogs was growing stronger.

"He is such a son of a bitch," Honaker said, fuming.

"Maybe, but he's *our* son of a bitch," Whitlock said. "Let's get a move on before those dogs get here. Cole is doing us a favor, so let's not waste it."

• • •

Just two miles away, Barkov and the Mink walked at the front of the squad, with Bunin and his dogs leading the way. Now that the dogs had a scent to follow, their random barking had taken on a more musical note.

Barkov paused to light a cigarette, then offered the pack to the Mink.

"Do you remember the schoolteacher?" the Mink asked, after lighting one of the harsh Russian smokes.

Barkov grinned. "Who could forget?"

That incident had barely been a few months ago, but already it seemed like an eternity. Time ran more slowly in this place.

The schoolteacher had escaped not once, but twice. He was a true political prisoner, given to writing pamphlets about Stalin's failure to adhere to the ideals of a true socialist state (which was true, but only a fool went around putting such thoughts into words). Because he was a fool, he had simply been caught and put back to work building the railroad—after being given a sound beating by Barkov, of course.

The man had worn round eyeglasses and had narrow shoulders and a little potbelly like cushion stuff under his shirt. Not a robust specimen of manhood. He had a long neck like a girl, or perhaps a chicken. But he didn't so much as flinch when Barkov hit him. Then hit him again. And again. His fortitude had forced Barkov to reconsider his view of intellectuals as soft-fleshed cowards.

"Do you think the Americans and that bitch Inna even got as far as he did?" the Mink wondered.

"Let us hope so, or where's the fun in that? I will bet you a bottle of vodka that they did not even make it as far as that schoolteacher."

They reminisced about how the schoolteacher had escaped again. That second time, he had gotten out of sight of the Gulag camp, except for the watch tower that was still visible on the horizon. A late cold spell made it bitter out. He had seen them coming and stopped, waiting for them. He did not even have a coat or a blanket.

The schoolteacher berated them. "You are a tool of the state and you do not even know it! You can take me back, but I will only escape again. Maybe you should just shoot me."

"No, we are not taking you back. You are not welcome. We are not going to shoot you, either, Comrade Schoolteacher."

Puzzled, the schoolteacher watched as Barkov and the Mink built a fire and made tea, then handed steaming mugs around to the handful of soldiers that made up Barkov's squad. When he approached the fire, intending to give himself up, the soldiers prodded him away with bayonets and curses.

The schoolteacher was no fool. He understood. Escape across the taiga was impossible. Return to the Gulag compound was not possible. He sat down in the snow fifty feet away, took out a tattered book that he had somehow smuggled into the Gulag, and began to read. He did not beg, as Barkov had expected. Men tougher in appearance would have. The schoolteacher acted as if the life-saving food and warmth did not even exist.

As daylight faded, the temperature dropped cruelly. Soon, night shrouded the scene and the schoolteacher was lost from sight.

They found him the next morning still sitting there, the book clutched in his stiff hands, dead from exposure.

Barkov and the Mink stood quietly smoking, lost in reverie.

The memory of that curious schoolteacher did not stop Barkov from wishing for a horse. A horse would be just the thing in this terrain. But there were no horses at the Gulag. What would they be fed? The taiga was too rough for a truck, and there were no roads. So they walked.

When the watch tower of the Gulag compound had disappeared from view, the Mink said, "Comrade Barkov, you now owe me a bottle of vodka. They have made it farther than the schoolteacher."

"I am impressed," Barkov said. "But, Comrade Mink, *two* bottles says we shall catch sight of them within an hour."

"Agree." Barkov laughed. "I am working up a thirst."

When that hour passed away, the Mink said, "Why don't you bet me three bottles that we will see them before nightfall? When we get back, I can throw quite a party."

Barkov didn't answer. He shouted at Bunin, "Those mutts of yours are useless."

"They are perfectly good dogs," Bunin said.

"Maybe they are good for hunting squirrels or woodcock," Barkov said.

"The Americans had a head start of several hours."

"We tracked them through the night. Your mutts should run faster. And don't give me any of that baking bread nonsense!"

The Mink was laughing in his soundless manner. His shoulders shook in mirth. "What about those three bottles if we don't catch them by nightfall?"

"I won't take that bet," Barkov grumbled. "But I will bet you a case of vodka that we catch them by noon tomorrow."

"Where would either one of us get a case of vodka?"

Barkov finally laughed. "When I win, that will be for you to worry about."

• • •

Cole and Vaccaro worked their way across the taiga. Cole was satisfied to see that despite the size of their group, they had left little trace of themselves moving across the frozen ground. Here and there, he could detect where a broken branch or the shadow of a footstep marred the brown grass, but he had sharp eyes for such signs. The question was, would the Russians?

Listening to the dogs, he realized that it might not matter what the Russians saw. Those dogs would follow their noses right to them.

It was up to Cole and Vaccaro to slow down the pursuers.

"What's your plan, Hillbilly?" Vaccaro asked.

"I seen a hill back there that would give us a good view. I say we get up there and pin them down for a while. After that, they might not be so hot and bothered to come running straight for us. They will take their time if they think we might be keeping them in our rifle sights."

"Sounds like a plan, just as long as we don't have to shoot any dogs."

Cole nodded. "Them dogs is just makin' a livin'. I say we shoot the people first. We'll only shoot the dogs if we ain't got a choice."

Vaccaro gave him a sideways look. Cole could be awfully matter of fact when he talked about killing. Not for the first time, he was glad that Cole was on their side.

"I never took you for an animal lover."

"Oh, I got a plan for them dogs."

"You know, just a few months ago, the Russians were supposed to be allies and the Germans were the enemy."

"Vaccaro, don't you know by now that you can't trust nobody?" Cole nodded toward the higher ground. "This way."

Though the terrain was rough, Cole navigated a path through the boulders and brush.

The gray clouds seemed to nearly touch the horizon, and even the air itself felt thick. The wind had dropped to nothing. Snow coming.

Soon, they reached a ridge that was fifty feet higher than the plain before them. Had they really walked all that way in the dark last night? They half expected to see the Gulag itself, but the horizon was empty of any man-made features.

Cole circled around to the front of the hill, walking almost casually. He took the scarf he had taken from Inna out of his pocket and dragged it along the branches he passed. He gave Vaccaro the items from Whitlock and Ramsey.

"What are we supposed to be doing?" Vaccaro wondered.

"I want to leave the dogs a trail and stop them

here," he said. "When you run a dog, first you give him a noseful of what you want him to run after. I reckon the Russians gave them dogs something that belonged to one of these three, so they'll pick up the scent right here."

Spoken in Cole's mountain accent, the last two words ran together out as "rye-cheer."

They walked along, rubbing down the branches they passed with the scarf. When they came to a small clearing, Cole collected the scarf and speared it overhead on the tip of a broken branch. Then they walked back the way they had come, following the same trail.

When they reached the point where they had started near the base of the hill, they turned and began to climb.

It took them less than a minute to reach the open, rocky top. The hilltop was mostly devoid of trees and brush. It was as if a giant had dumped a wheelbarrow full of rubble up there. The place would be sunbaked in the summer and windblown in winter, but there was good cover for a shooter.

There was also a commanding view of the surrounding landscape. Maybe half a mile off, they could see a handful of pursuers. Racing ahead of them were three dogs. They appeared to be the same breed as Vaska's dog—somewhere between a husky and a mutt, with maybe a little wolf mixed in. What the locals called a *laika*.

These dogs were all pointy ears and snout, curved tail, and eagerness. They also looked mean.

"Cole, I have to say, I don't like the looks of those dogs."

"That makes two of us. But I reckon I like the looks of them Russians a whole lot less."

Cole put the rifle scope to his eye. He counted nine men. Six of the pursuers appeared to be soldiers, but three of them wore civilian clothes. One of the men in civilian clothes was small and slight, but the other two were big men. Both carried rifles slung over their shoulders. Which one was Barkov?

Cole moved the crosshairs from one man to the other. They were just within range. Normally, this would be farther out than he would prefer to shoot. But he needed to buy the others time. If he missed, he told himself that it was no big deal. The Russians would still be slowed down.

Then he thought, *I ain't gonna miss*.

"Cole, they're too far away," Vaccaro muttered. "Let them get a little closer."

"Which one do you think is Barkov?"

"The big one."

"I see two big ones."

"If you're not sure, then save Barkov for later."

"My pa always said to drink the good whiskey first," Cole replied. "That's what I aim to do."

"You and your sayings. I ought to write them

down and put them in a book."

"Who the hell would buy that?"

"City people," Vaccaro said. "They think you country people are full of wisdom."

"They'd be right about that much."

War movies made it look as if every soldier was a marksman who never missed a shot. In fact, nothing could be further from the truth.

Using a rifle to hit a target more than a short distance away was a complex process that required skill and practice.

It was why machine guns and hand grenades were a whole lot more effective. Close wasn't good enough with a rifle, but it worked out fine with a fragmentation grenade.

Cole got comfortable for the shot. He had set up behind a boulder and rested the rifle on top of the stone. He took off his mittens—gloves not being worth a damn once it got really cold—and slid them under the forearm of the rifle to cushion the wood. He nestled the butt of the rifle firmly into his shoulder and pressed his check against the comb of the stock. In a strange way, it was almost like a lover's embrace. He had done this so many times that the rifle felt like part of his body.

Bone and stone.

Just what he needed to make this shot.

CHAPTER 23

Barkov called a halt. Immediately, the half dozen soldiers flopped to the ground. The time for any semblance of military order was gone. They were tired of walking and running—mostly running—in the wake of dogs that never seemed able to catch the escaped Americans. Flasks of vodka appeared and the soldiers passed them around. In spite of the hardships, the soldiers still seemed eager for the chase. Barkov thought that it might be a different story once the vodka ran out.

"Do you hear them singing?" Bunin asked, a

contented smile on his face.

Confused, Barkov looked at the men, who did not appear very musical. It took him a moment to understand that by *singing*, Bunin meant the baying of the dogs.

"It is about time," Barkov said. "I was beginning to think that those dogs were worthless. I was going to shoot them rather than have to feed them again."

Barkov, Bunin, and the Mink stood apart from the men. Rifles slung over their shoulders, they were turned in the direction of the dogs. Bunin was right about them singing—their barking had taken on a more musical note that made it clear they were on the trail of the escape prisoners and Inna.

"What will those dogs do once they catch them?" the Mink wanted to know.

Bunin answered with a question. "What does a dog do when it catches a sable?"

"I am thinking that they do not sit down and have tea, Comrade Bunin, but you tell me."

"The dog, he shakes that sable until he breaks its neck."

"A man is much bigger than a sable," Barkov pointed out.

"Then maybe the dog grabs a leg and does not let go until we arrive. What I want to know is—"

Bunin never finished his sentence.

• • •

Cole settled his crosshairs on the man to the right. At this distance, it was impossible to see their faces. Both men looked tall and heavy in their winter coats. The group of soldiers paused; some lit cigarettes or drank from flasks of vodka. Maybe the booze kept them going. It was possible that they were listening to the dogs; the two tall men and the shorter one seemed to be conferring about something.

He adjusted the crosshairs about a foot above the distant target to account for the drop that the bullet would make. Some officer had called it the bullet's trajectory, but Cole knew it was simple gravity. When you threw a rock, it fell to earth, and a bullet was no different. A bullet traveled a whole lot farther, but it was falling just like that rock the moment it left the barrel. The air, though heavy with the promise of snow, was barely stirred by the wind, so that much, at least, was in Cole's favor as he took aim.

He held the crosshairs steady, unwavering, and slowly squeezed the trigger, gently applying pressure with the pad of his right index finger.

Through the scope he could see all three men talking, oblivious.

Cole felt a familiar rush. This was the part of being a sniper that no one ever spoke about. Most people saw how a sniper would be satisfied in the ability to hit a distant target. Cole almost took that part for granted anymore—hitting targets was like pulling on his boots in the morning. He just did it. Without thinking much about it. However, that sense of holding a life in your hands—well, it was an almost god-like power. That part of being a sniper never faded or got old. It was what thrilled him about putting his finger on the trigger.

Focus, he warned himself.

By now, his body was operating on autopilot. He had done this so many times that it was like sleepwalking. Thinking too hard at this point only spoiled the shot Better to let training and instinct take over.

His finger applied the last fraction of the nine-point-eight pounds of pressure needed to release the trigger.

What happened next was a complex chain reaction that had changed little from the days when a twelfth century Chinese warrior fired a stone projectile from what was essentially a pipe. Thanks to modern technology, however, it was now a chain reaction that took place instantaneously.

Within the mechanism of the rifle, the firing pin shot forward and struck the center of the round in the chamber. That firing pin caused the primer in the base of the brass cartridge to explode, which in turn caused the gunpowder in the cartridge itself to ignite. The cyclone of hot gases drove the bullet down the barrel, in which the rifling gripped and spun the bullet until it emerged at a speed of more than two thousand feet per second. The spinning bullet honed in on its target like a supersonic hornet.

It all happened faster than Cole could think it.

Bullseye.

• • •

Bunin was still asking Barkov and the Mink his question when a neat round hole appeared in his chest. Barkov watched Bunin open his mouth in surprise once, then twice, before he sank to his knees.

Traveling at just a little under muzzle velocity now, the impact of the bullet released more than eighteen-hundred foot pounds of energy into Bunin's chest. His lungs exploded and his heart shattered, killing him instantly.

"Sniper!" Barkov bellowed, mostly for the benefit of the soldiers who lolled nearby. He was diving for cover behind a clump of bushes before Bunin's dead body hit the ground. Right about then, the noise of the rifle shot finally reached their ears.

The Mink had found a boulder to shelter behind and had gone to one knee, his rifle to his shoulder, scoping the vast open taiga for a target.

The soldiers were still busy putting away their vodka. Two or three, including young Dmitri, gawked at Bunin's body. They were too shocked and surprised to move.

"Get your heads down, you fools," Barkov shouted at them.

They finally stirred themselves to action and scrambled behind what shelter they could find. If the sniper had fired again, he could have killed at least one more.

But he did not fire.

Sniper. The word ran through Barkov's mind again. Only a sniper would fire once, and then keep his finger off the trigger.

"That shot was from a long way off," the Mink announced from his hiding place, several feet away. "Whoever it was knew his business."

"See anything?"

"Bushes, rocks, grass. That is not what you meant, is it?"

"The prisoners had no weapons."

"Maybe Inna took Dmitri's rifle," the Mink suggested.

"No, she did not. Besides, what could anyone hit with that piece of shit? You saw what happened. One shot, and Bunin is dead."

"Maybe not such a good shot," the Mink said. "Whoever it was, was trying to shoot you."

"What are you talking about?"

"Think about it. Who looked like you from a distance?"

Barkov nodded. As usual, the Mink made sense. But that still did not answer the question of who had shot at them. "Let's go see if we can find this sniper," Barkov said.

He didn't care about Bunin, beyond the fact that someone else would now have to care for the dogs. What he did care about was that somehow, his quarry had turned the tables on him.

• • •

Cole and Vaccaro watched the Russians in the distance. "How long do we wait?"

"Long as we need to."

"Do you think you got Barkov?" Vaccaro asked.

"I would say that's a fifty-fifty chance," Cole said. "I shot a big man. Was it Barkov? Flip a coin."

"If he's half the sniper he's supposed to be, he's already on his belly down there, trying to worm his way toward us."

"Let him come on," Cole said. "If someone shoots at us, then we know it ain't Barkov that I shot down there."

"The dogs are getting closer. You hear them?"

Cole nodded. "Them dogs are gonna be a problem."

Down below, some of the soldiers had not hidden themselves well. Cole picked out a fellow who was lighting a cigarette.

Shot him.

• • •

Barkov gave orders for the men to stay put. There were no arguments after a second bullet killed one of them. Nobody did anything as stupid as light a cigarette after that. Barkov kept forgetting that these men had not experienced war, until today.

He and the Mink began to work their way forward, using the terrain for cover. It was likely that the sniper had fired from the high ground just ahead. By working around to the left, they could follow a depression—not quite a gully—that brought them closer to the hill without exposing themselves to the sniper.

Barkov was beginning to have the nagging thought that perhaps, just perhaps, there was more to this escape than he had perceived. He thought about the fact that their quarry had somehow managed to cross miles and miles of taiga at a punishing pace. How was that possible? One of the trio had just picked off Bunin. With what weapon? None of it made sense.

He pushed aside his doubts and followed the Mink through the brush. True to his name, the

Mink moved almost soundlessly. When people thought of a mink, they thought of fur coats. However, a mink was not cuddly. By nature, a mink was in fact a predator, and ruthless.

Being bigger, Barkov kept getting hung up on briars and had to bull his way through the brush. Barkov paused to listen for the dogs. They were somewhere on the hill ahead, baying in excitement. Poor Bunin. He would have liked to hear that. He really had been proud of those worthless mutts. The dogs sounded excited, as if they were very close now to the quarry.

"The dogs must have found them," the Mink said.

They moved in that direction, careful to stay low in the gully.

A rifle fired from the vicinity of the hilltop.

They heard a yelp.

"Now he is shooting the dogs," Barkov announced. "Good. He will be worried about those dogs, and not about us."

Still, he was a little surprised that the Americans would be so heartless—even Barkov wasn't sure that he could bring himself to shoot a dog. He had killed men without a second thought, but never a dog.

They picked up the pace, moving toward the sound of the excited dogs. Close now. The dogs were near the base of the hill, which surprised Barkov, because he was sure the last rifle shot had come closer to the top of the hill. Then again, it could be that the trio they were pursuing had split up. Even now, Bunin's dogs might be snapping at that bitch Inna Mikhaylovna. She might even be glad to see him if he called off the dogs. The thought made him smile.

The Mink stopped, then jerked his chin at the noise ahead. They could just see the dogs through the brush, barking as if they had someone cornered. Barkov nodded and pushed his way through the undergrowth. Though the twigs and branches clutched at him, he managed to move almost silently.

Then the dogs were *right there*. Barkov stepped out into a clearing in the brush, the Mink right behind him. No one there. He did, however, see a bright red scarf tied high up in a bush. The dogs milled about under it, barking furiously, jumping to get at it, but the scarf was just out of reach of their jaws. One of the dogs was dead, shot by the Americans.

Barkov kicked the dogs out of the way and reached for the scarf.

From behind, the Mink gave him a shove.

An instant later, a bullet carved the air where Barkov's head had been.

From the corner of his eye, Barkov caught sight of a muzzle flash.

Instantly, Barkov put his rifle to his shoulder. Through the telescopic sight, he caught just a glimpse of a figure on the hilltop. As soon as his post sight touched the target, he pulled the trigger. It was a sloppy shot, more by instinct than aim. Then he rolled away into the brush, out of sight.

• • •

Vaccaro had been in the middle of saying, "I don't think you got—"

He had not finished his sentence when the bullet struck a rock inches from both their heads, and a moment later came the crack of the Russian's rifle. Vaccaro took his time looking through the binoculars again.

"Goddamn, but that was close," Cole had to admit.

"That Russian can shoot."

"I guess that does answer the question."

"What question is that?"

"The one about which Russian I shot. If that was Barkov down there, then I reckon the one I shot was the wrong one."

"Now you know for next time."

When he had fired at Barkov just now, the man had managed to shoot back in a split second. The Russian had been shooting as a reflexive action. And yet, the bullet had *pinged* off a rock just inches from Cole's head. That was some shooting.

Pinged really wasn't the right word. A high velocity bullet ricocheting off a rock a foot from your head was a noise that turned your guts to water and made the back of your skull tingle. He puckered his asshole tighter. Wasn't really a single word to describe all *that*.

"Let's get the hell out of here," Cole said.

They could have stayed in position and tried to pick off Barkov and the other Russian. However, if Barkov was half the sniper he seemed to be, it wasn't likely that he was going to let himself get picked off that easily. Cole had set out to buy the others some time, and that was just what he and Vaccaro had done. The dogs were confused now, milling about the clearing where Cole had tied the scarves. Barkov himself wouldn't be in any hurry to continue the pursuit if he thought Cole was still occupying the hilltop. What they needed to do now was let Barkov worry about that while they slipped out the back door.

They made their way back down the hilltop on the opposite side from where the Russians were hunkered down. The others would have a huge lead on them. If they were going to catch up, they would need to hurry.

"You ready?" Cole asked.

"Let's hoof it. I've got to admit, that Barkov makes me nervous."

They set off at a trot across the taiga, hoping

to catch the others before nightfall.

• • •

The Mink lay prone nearby, scoping the hill, hoping for any sign of movement.

After several minutes he said, "He is gone."

"Did I hit him?" Barkov asked.

"Maybe, maybe not, but you at least gave him something to think about."

He and the Mink settled deeper into the brush. A dead dog lay nearby. Barkov looked again at the scarf overhead. He realized that the Americans had made a false trail to lead the dogs here, tied the scarf in the brush, and waited. He and the Mink had walked right into the trap.

"Those three aren't that clever," the Mink said. "They should not have a rifle. They would not have set a trap. Someone is helping them."

Barkov agreed. Everything was not what it seemed. When they rejoined the others, he planned on seeing what else the boy Dmitri knew. Perhaps he had not told them everything.

He stood up, sure that the sniper was gone from the hilltop. Taking his whip from his belt, he snapped it at the remaining dogs, driving them away. Then he reached up and untied the scarf. Pressed his nose into it and inhaled deeply. Smelled wool and a hint of perfume like apple blossoms, and a little of the warm bread smell that women had. Inna.

While he admired the cleverness of the trap, he felt anger at allowing himself to be fooled by it. He coiled his whip and hung it on his belt. When he caught the Americans and Inna, he would use the whip to strip the skin from their bodies. Until then he looked forward to taking out some of his frustrations while questioning that young fool, Dmitri.

CHAPTER 24

In northern Russia, on the cusp of winter, the daylight hours lasted slightly longer than the flavor in a stick of chewing gum.

Cole and Vaccaro reunited with the others in the final waning hour of daylight. Cole was pleased to see that they had put some distance between themselves and the Russian soldiers. He and Vaccaro had only managed to catch up by maintaining a steady trot. His legs sure as hell could feel that.

As if the day hadn't had drama enough, the weather took a turn.

Just before dark, ice pellets began peppering their faces. Stinging and cold. The ice turned to snow. Along with the snow came the wind. They wrapped up their faces and covered their ears so that just their eyes looked out from between layers of damp wool flecked with ice. Still, the cold and the snow managed to sift in.

Vaska's dog stopped, perked up his pointy ears, and growled. They thought at first that Buka sensed the Russian dogs were back on their trail. Then they heard the distant howl carried on the wind.

There came another howl. And another. The sound cut through the snow and wind. It was hard to say where the howls were coming from, but it was clear that the wolves were on the move.

Honaker looked around at the growing darkness. "What the hell is that?"

"Wolves," Cole said. He paused to listen. Something deep in him thrilled at the sound, even though it represented danger. Cole had never seen a wolf. The had long since been hunted to extinction in the Appalachians.

"First it's Russians, then it's dogs, now it's wolves," Vaccaro complained. "Jesus God, I hate this place. It sounds as if the whole pack is out there. I would sure as hell feel better if we had a fire."

"If we light a fire, we'll have worse than

wolves to worry about. The Russians might see us from miles off."

Vaska nodded. They both knew Cole was right, even if Vaccaro didn't look convinced.

Honaker looked at Vaska. "How much snow can we expect?"

Their Russian guide shrugged. "This will not amount to much. We call it sugar snow. There is sometimes a heavier snow that follows in a day or two. Certainly, if the wind shifts to be out of the southwest, we can expect a heavy snow."

Honaker shook a finger at the guide as if the storm was his fault. "It's late October!"

Vaska nodded. "Yes, it is late October ... in Russia."

• • •

The snow was just as hard on the pursuing Russians. Twilight arrived like a shade pulled down across a window, and the temperature dropped. The soldiers looked expectantly at Barkov, but he did not call a halt. They had been on the move now for more than twelve hours.

"They must have wings on their feet," he said, referring to the Americans. "We will keep going. Just be careful not to trip over them in the dark."

The men were not happy, but nobody was going to argue with Barkov.

The Mink called the dogs back as night came

on. "Wolves," he explained, putting on the dogs' leashes. Over the wind, they could hear distant howling. The men kept looking anxiously into the gloom, their rifles at the ready. In the remote regions of the Soviet Union, wolves were not something out of fairy tales. They had all seen them hanging around the work gangs and even the Gulag itself, keeping just out of rifle range.

The dogs were still on the Americans' scent, practically dragging the small man along.

They kept at it for another hour until it was fully dark.

Barkov wanted to keep going, but even he had to admit that it wasn't possible. The men were tired. The terrain had grown more rugged, making it difficult to move at night.

"We must stop here for the night," the Mink said quietly, away from the others.

"You are right," Barkov said grudgingly. He called a halt and told the men to set up camp. Wind-driven snow now raked them cruelly, even though most of it blew away and barely coated the ground. They had not even brought a tent. The men wrapped themselves in blankets and huddled together for warmth.

During the encounter earlier that day, the sniper's second shot had killed one of the soldiers, leaving the five survivors jumpy, half expecting death to come looking for them out of thin air. Barkov knew all about that—for much of the war, it had been his job to create just that feeling in German soldiers.

Without Bunin, the dogs lacked guidance. He watched the Mink feed them chunks of burbot that Bunin had brought along in a sack for just that purpose. The fish smelled spoiled, but the dogs didn't seem to mind.

Now that it was snowing, they would need light to see where they were going. Lights, however, would make them targets for the American sniper who must still be out there. So, they would have to wait for daylight.

One good thought. The snow meant that in the morning, there would be tracks.

Barkov allowed his men a small fire. They gathered around it and drank the last of the vodka. He and the Mink stayed well away from the fire, just in case the sniper had prowled back. Better to be cold and breathing than to be a warm corpse.

He glanced over at Dmitri, who sat on the ground, chewing on a piece of cold bread. It was time to question the boy and see if he had left out anything important about his encounter with Inna. For example, had he forgotten to mention that Inna had stolen a rifle along with his clothes? He knew that Dmitri's rifle had not been stolen, but had she taken someone else's?

Barkov stood and walked over to the boy, tugging the whip from his belt as he went.

Dmitri saw him coming. His eyes grew wide.

Smiling, Barkov made the whip sing. The exercise warmed him better than any fire.

• • •

That night, the snow squall hit the Americans as sharp and fast as a right hook. They slept fitfully, shivering in the cold—there was no possibility of lighting a fire, because that would give them away. They awoke to find a landscape transformed by the light snow. As Vaska had predicted, it was no more than a dusting, light as the coating on a jelly doughnut back home. But now the landscape looked exponentially more cold and forbidding.

They were divided into three distinct groups. The rescue team huddled together, with the exception of Cole, who was talking something over with Vaska. Whitlock sat with Inna and Ramsey, who was doubled over, coughing.

"Man, what I wouldn't give for a hot cup of coffee right now," Vaccaro grumped, shivering in the cold.

"Have a cigarette and a drink of water," Honaker said. "That's a real soldier's breakfast."

"You go ahead and order the soldier's breakfast, Honaker," Vaccaro said. "I'd rather have the bacon and eggs."

Honaker tossed him a package. "We're

already running low on C-Rations," he said. "Split that with somebody, why don't you."

"Running low?"

"I lost some gear in the jump, remember?" Honaker reminded him. He jerked his chin at Ramsey. "We have two extra mouths to feed between this guy and the Russian doll."

"Maybe Vaska or Cole can catch us a rabbit," Samson suggested. He was so quiet most of the time, that despite his size, it was easy to forget that he was there.

"Samson, you ever see how much meat there is on a rabbit? We would need a bushel of rabbits just to feed you," Vaccaro said, then considered Samson's size and added diplomatically, "No offense."

A flicker of movement on the horizon caught Vaccaro's eye and he reached for rifle.

"Relax," said Cole, breaking away from Vaska. "It ain't the Russians. It's a wolf. They've been hanging around since first light."

"I liked 'em better when they were howling."

"Cole, why the hell would wolves be hanging around us?"

"Well, unlike us, they ain't got K-rations to eat."

"You know what, Hillbilly? That part how you said to relax? Forget about that."

Cole leaned away and spat. "Wolves are the least of our worries. You see this snow? It's gonna make it easy for them Russians to follow us once their dogs pick up our trail again. Vaska says there's more snowing coming. This was just a taste."

"Then we had better get a move on," Honaker said.

Everyone was on their feet in minutes, with the exception of Ramsey. He started to get up, but sank back down to his knees as his body was wracked by another coughing fit.

Cole stepped over to help Whitlock get Ramsey to his feet. Vaccaro gave Ramsey his half of the rations.

Looking on, Honaker just shook his head. "Wasting food," he muttered.

Cole shot him a look. "Shut up, Honaker," he said.

Honaker's mouth opened in an angry twist, but he bit back whatever response was on his lips when he saw Cole's steady gaze on him. He looked away and said: "I can't wait to get out of this place. Nothin' but rocks and shrubs. Hell, even the Russians won't live here if they can help it."

CHAPTER 25

Before the day was out, the group's luck took three more turns for the worse.

It started with the threatening skies.

They had suffered through yesterday's snow squall, which hadn't amounted to much, barely dusting the ground. Now the air felt warmer—and wetter. The wind had shifted around to blow out of the southwest.

"It does feel like more snow, Hillbilly," Vaccaro said.

"You would be right about that, City Boy," Cole agreed. "Maybe a lot of snow."

The heavy gray skies seemed to press upon them, but the snow held off. They covered as much ground as they could, knowing that once the snow started to fall, it would slow their progress.

"Hasn't started yet," Vaccaro pointed out. "Maybe it will blow over."

Cole didn't answer. Morning blended into afternoon. The miles passed in a blur, with the only stops for water. Nobody even bothered to light a cigarette—they were too winded.

Just before nightfall, fat flakes the size of silver dollars began to float down lazily out of the sky. Within minutes, however, the snowflakes diminished in size and began to come almost straight down. It was as if a million down pillows had been ripped open in the heavens above.

They kept going in the dusky light, hoping to add another mile or two to their progress.

"We ought to stop," Cole announced. "We'll need some light to build shelters from this snow."

Honaker ignored him. "No, we keep going," he said. "We have flashlights if we need them."

Gloom surrounded them. A dark shape flashed past, and then another. Vaska's laika growled, the raised ruff around his neck feathered with snow.

"Did you see that?" Vaccaro asked nervously. "Some kind of animal. A *big* animal."

"We ought to stop soon and make shelter,"

Cole said. "The Ruskies ain't the only thing on our trail."

"We need to keep going as long as there's any daylight," Honaker insisted. "For all we know, those Russians could be right behind us."

Despite the need for shelter, Honaker made no sign of stopping. He acted as if he could somehow leave the snow behind, if only they kept moving.

The landscape was changing. They left the rocky, shrubby terrain and entered a marshy area, with hummocks of grass frosted by snow, interspersed with frozen ponds and pools, their frozen surfaces covered by a neat layer of snow, like a white tablecloth at a fancy restaurant. They were lucky that the temperature was below freezing. The bog would have been impassable in warm weather.

"Stick to the grass," Cole warned. "There's no telling if the ice is thick enough to cross."

The trouble was that in the growing darkness, it was hard to find sure footing. In the murky twilight, each step was becoming an act of faith. The grassy hummocks were too narrow in some places for the entire group to pass easily.

Whitlock was crossing one of the frozen pools with Ramsey hanging off his shoulders. The new snow squeaked under his boots. One man might have made it, but the weight of both men was too much. The ice cracked with a noise like a gunshot.

Whitlock felt the ice going, and half-shoved, half-threw Ramsey toward the grassy bridge being crossed by Inna. An instant later, he plunged through the ice. They had a glimpse of Whitlock as he bobbed up and gasped for air.

His hands scrabbled at the edges of the hole, and for a few seconds it looked as if he might get a grip on the ice.

But his hands slipped.

And then he was gone.

It all happened so fast. By the time Inna shouted in alarm, the dark water had already claimed him.

The glacial kettle pool was deceptively deep, because not so much as Whitlock's head was visible. All that remained was a patch of black water, surrounded by cracked ice.

Cole was the first to react. Water was Cole's worst nightmare—he had nearly drowned as a boy when he was caught in one of his own beaver traps in a wintry creek. The fact that he had survived the creek and the cold trek home had taught him a valuable lesson about keeping calm. He had often felt since then that if he could survive that near-drowning, he could handle just about anything.

He rushed past Inna and threw himself down on the ice, which crackled ominously. Seconds later, Whitlock's head bobbed to the surface like a cork. His hands scrabbled for a hold at the slick edges of the ice. Cole grabbed the collar of Whitlock's coat and heaved for all he was worth.

He had been hoping to drag Whitlock onto the ice, but it was pointless. The ice was cracking apart under him so that he couldn't get any leverage. The muscles and tendons all along Cole's arms and shoulders popped with the strain, but Whitlock outweighed him, and now the other man was soaking wet. It was all Cole could do to keep Whitlock's head above water, never mind haul him to safety.

The ice crackled ominously. Another few seconds, and Cole was going to join Whitlock in the water.

Just then, someone got a firm grip on Cole's ankles. He heard Samson's deep voice boom, "Hang on!"

Cole felt a mighty tug on his legs. He glanced back. The others had formed a kind of human daisy chain across the ice and onto the firmer ground of the grassy hummock. Samson was stretched out across the ice behind Cole, hanging onto his ankles. Vaccaro was bent over, holding onto Samson, and it looked like Vaska was, in turn, gripping Vaccaro's feet. Even Ramsey was doing the best he could, tugging weakly at one of Vaccaro's legs. Inna stood nearby, hands held to her face in an expression of horror. Honaker simply watched, his rifle cradled in his hands.

Cole had the uneasy thought that all Honaker needed to do to take them all out was level the weapon and start shooting. Why on earth would that thought even come to mind—and at that moment, of all times?

Already, the cold sapped the strength from Cole's wet hands, but he wasn't about to let go of Whitlock. He forced his grip tighter, imagining that those weren't hands at the ends of his wrists, but steel traps.

Slowly, laboriously, Cole felt himself being pulled across the ice. He couldn't even use his elbows, so all he could do was hang onto Whitlock. It was soon clear that steady pressure wasn't enough. They needed one good yank to get free of the hole, just like you would use to land a fish.

"On the count of three, everybody pull!" Vaccaro shouted. "Cole, hang on! One, two—"

It felt as if his legs were being tugged right out of the hip sockets. His shoulders screamed in protest.

Whitlock came out of the hole and flopped on the ice, water streaming from his clothes. Still, Cole didn't release his grip. There was another giant tug, and then they were safely off the ice.

They all stood around, panting, hearts hammering, exhausted from the effort.

Cole took stock. Sharp as glass, the edges of the ice had made some cuts on his wrists that stung even worse in the cold, but the bleeding was nothing serious. More troubling was the fact that his hands were just about frozen and he was wet to the elbows, but the rest of him was mostly dry. He'd be all right as long as he kept moving. Whitlock was soaked to the bone. Saved from drowning, he now shivered uncontrollably in the cold.

The narrow hummock in the middle of the bog was no place to make camp for the night. However, a quarter mile off he could see a dark line of trees in the gathering dusk. Solid ground.

"Come on," he said. "Let's find some shelter in those trees yonder and then get Whitlock out of these wet clothes before he freezes to death."

"We can camp right here," Honaker said. "Whitlock might not make it to the woods. It's goddamn cold out."

"Then I reckon we had best get a move on," Cole said. "The trees will block the wind."

Ignoring Honaker's protests, Cole grabbed Whitlock's left arm. Vaccaro got the idea and grabbed Whitlock's other arm. It was as if they were giving him a bum's rush. With Whitlock's own legs working as best they could, they crossed the bog and headed toward the woods. The others followed, with Samson hauling Ramsey in a fireman's carry.

For the first time since the escape from the Gulag, Cole began to wonder just how the hell they were ever going to make it to Finland.

It wasn't a good sign that Whitlock's legs were mostly dragging now.

Vaccaro stumbled, almost dropping Whitlock. He must have been having the same thought about the mission, because he managed to pant, "Goddamn, Whitlock, you better not turn into a popsicle on us."

"Faster," Cole grunted.

They reached the forest and the trees closed in around them. Immediately, Cole felt safer here, more protected than they had been in the open. The thick evergreen boughs filtered out some of the snow, causing it to fall more slowly. Although it was dusk, the snow reflected what light remained.

They dumped Whitlock in a wet, shivering heap in the snow. The others gathered around.

"We need to build shelters," Cole said. The time had come to give them all a crash course in building shelter. He nodded at a fallen log about three feet off the forest floor. "That deadfall there is a good start. For another shelter, we can set a pole in the fork of a tree. Then cut these here pine branches to make the roof. If you have time, cut a few boughs for the floor, to get yourself out of the snow and off the cold ground."

Cole drew his big Bowie knife and began hacking at the evergreen boughs in the understory. The heavy, razor-sharp blade easily chopped through branches as big around as a broom handle. He began to pile them so that they slanted from the deadfall to the ground, creating a sloped roof. Despite the cover of the forest, snow began to pile up on the branches he cut.

The others set to work making two-man shelters. Honaker and Samson teamed up, first wedging a long branch into the fork of a tree so that it sloped down to the ground, then piling branches against it. Vaska had done this before and worked with efficient strokes of a hatchet to build an evergreen cave for himself and Buka. Cole and Vaccaro completed the shelter using the windfall in minutes.

Cole's arms and chest had gotten wet trying to pull Whitlock out of the water. The activity of building the shelters had kept him warm at first, but now the cold setting in with nightfall was quickly sapping his body heat. He stripped off the wet shirt and thermal top and put on dry clothes, although he had to make do with putting his damp coat back on. He wished they could build a fire to dry out, but it wasn't worth the risk.

As if reading his mind, Honaker said, "We ought to build a fire."

"If we start a fire, them Russians will be on us fast as ants on sugar," Cole said. He pronounced the word as *far*. "Do you reckon this is a good time to tangle with them?"

"If we don't start a fire, Whitlock is gonna freeze to death," Vaccaro said quietly. "Look at him."

Hypothermia set in when a person's body temperature fell by ten degrees. The plunge into the bog had easily done that to Whitlock's core. He shook uncontrollably. When he tried to speak, the words emerged in a thickened stammer. His movements appeared sluggish.

"There is another way," Cole said. "Body heat. Skin to skin, wrapped up in a blanket."

"Don't go looking at me to when you say that," Vaccaro said. "What do I look like to you, some kind of Nancy boy?"

"It ain't like that," Cole snapped. "It's about keeping Whitlock from freezing to death."

Inna stepped forward. "I will do it."

"All right. Let's get his clothes off."

Getting Whitlock out of his wet clothes wasn't easy—the wet cloth stuck to his sluggish limbs, and it didn't help that their own hands were freezing. Their numb fingers fumbled at the buttons. Finally, they were able to get him out of his wet clothes and wrap him in a blanket.

Inna was already stripping down. Cole held up a blanket to give her some privacy.

"Thank you," she mumbled, draping the blanket around herself. Cole bundled up her clothes to keep them out of the snow, and handed them to Inna. He happened to notice the tiny pistol in her boot and pulled it out. The gun barely filled the palm of his hand.

"Why, Miss Inna, what's this for?" he asked, amused. "You could maybe shoot a rat with this little thing."

"What would you Americans say? It is insurance."

Then she and Whitlock crawled into the deadfall shelter. "You need to get right against him and then wrap the blankets around yourselves."

"I know," she said, sounding slightly annoyed. "Hillbilly, do not forget that I am the one who worked in the infirmary."

"Roger that."

Although Ramsey had not gotten wet, he was also shivering—when he wasn't wracked by bouts of coughing. "Too bad we don't have an extra nurse to wrap herself around me," he said with a smirk. "Some guys have all the luck."

"Go on in there and huddle up against them as best you can," Cole advised. "It's the best we can do without a fire."

Ramsey did just that, and Cole cut more boughs to close off the front face of the deadfall shelter. The falling snow would add another layer of insulation.

"Now what?" Vaccaro asked, tilting his head into the falling snow. In the growing darkness under the trees, Cole could barely see him.

"Smoke 'em if you got 'em," Cole said. "We ain't goin' nowhere until daylight. The snow ought to cover our tracks soon enough, so I'm not worried about Barkov. Let's get some sleep."

"All right, but don't go spooning up against me now," Vaccaro said.

Cole cackled. "When it gets right cold in the middle of the night, City Boy, ain't gonna be no strangers."

•••

Huddled inside the shelter, Inna felt like some forest creature. The rough-cut fir boughs smelled pleasant, and in the silence she could hear the soft patter of snow accumulating around them. It reminded her of how she had built forts out of blankets and chairs as a child. She had felt safe then. Cozy.

There was something reassuring, too, about sharing simple body heat with Harry. Although it was wrong, she had to admit that she had dreamed of such a moment, when she could be flesh on flesh, skin to skin, with this man. He still shivered, and she wrapped her legs and arms around him as if she could soak right into him, her belly pressed into his back.

"Inna, I—"

"Shhh," she whispered. What was there to

say? She was simply glad that he was alive.

A few spasms still worked their way through his body. Inna maneuvered so that she lay on top of him, like a blanket. She could feel every contour of his body, every rib and muscle. She could feel that he was a man, stirred by her warm body. She took his cold hands and guided them to the warmth between her thighs. He flinched. To his icy fingers, the heat felt like a furnace.

Their lips brushed, and then Harry was kissing her, deeply and longingly. His lips still trembled with the cold. It was a kiss that had been delayed for weeks and months by the ever-watchful eyes surrounding them in the Gulag. Indeed, it had proven easier to escape than to steal a few moments of such intimacy.

They held their breath, not wanting to be overheard. Ramsey lay nearby, wrapped in a blanket, already passed out from exhaustion, judging by his measured breathing. Perhaps he was just pretending, hoping to give them some measure of privacy.

She spread her legs and took him into her, which only seemed natural and beautiful. They lay that way for several minutes, simply coupled together, sharing warmth. She clenched him tight inside her. His hips shifted and lifted her, up, up, again and again, both of them moving together, struggling to be as quiet as possible. Inna smothered her cries in his shoulder. Finally, they both seemed to melt into the other. She lay there listening to his heart thudding in his chest, thinking that, just perhaps, it was not such a bad thing to be here in this snow-covered shelter forever.

Together, they drifted off to sleep.

• • •

Cole crawled into his own shelter, glad of the slight warmth it offered. Vaccaro was already sound asleep. Cole had thought he might stay awake for a while, standing guard, but exhaustion seeped through his limbs and he found himself falling asleep. Before he did so, he looked up at the sky through the gaps in the branches that made up the roof of the shelter. Snow had a way of reflecting the light, so that the sky was more gray than black when framed against the treetops.

Many times as a boy he had slept rough in the woods rather than return home to face his drunken pa. He would wedge himself under some rocky outcropping and look up at the shimmering stars, picking out the shape of the constellations that his pa had taught him when sober. When you knew the names of the stars in the sky, you were never alone. Orion the Hunter, with his bright belt of three stars in the southern sky, and Cassiopeia the vain queen, kept him company.

The snow must have been letting up, because he thought he glimpsed a single star through the thinning clouds. It was a comforting sight. The clouds drifted across again, and Cole slept.

• • •

Cole always had been a light sleeper. He couldn't say what woke him. Maybe the sleeping part of his brain detected the almost inaudible crunch of snow crystals under a paw, or possibly some part of his subconscious heard the sound of the wolf's warm breath turning to fog just beyond the opening of his shelter.

That was all the noise that the predator made, but Cole's eyes flicked open. He held himself perfectly still. The snow created a soft, suffused glow like starlight, and against the backdrop of the forest he saw the wolf looking in.

Slowly, he raised himself to a sitting position facing the opening in his shelter. The eyes that stared back could have been cousins to his own. They glittered in the light reflected by the falling snow. Cole tried to see something in the wolf's eyes, some glimmer of intelligence. They were a hunter's eyes, but far from human.

Cole observed the long snout, felt the warm breath inches from his face. The wolf watched him back. They seemed to glare at each other like two old gunfighters, each daring the other to make a move.

The moment was broken when, quick as a copperhead's strike, Cole balled his fist and struck the snout. The beast yelped and fell back, momentarily stunned, before baring its teeth and approaching the shelter in a crouch, growling. Now, there was no mistaking the wolf's intent. Cole went at him again, making a snarling sound that wasn't quite human, this time with his long, gleaming knife in his fist.

He slashed at the wolf and the beast fell away. In the clearing, another ghost-like shape went past, and another. The silence of the lithe shapes was more unnerving than the sight of them.

The camp was under attack, not by Russians, but by wolves.

• • •

Not more than twenty feet away, Inna woke because feather-soft snowflakes dusted her face. She blinked awake, surprised that it was not entirely dark; the fresh snow all around them in the forest reflected the light and suffused the air with a kind of soft glow. Harry was sound asleep. Ramsey too.

More snow hit her face, not so gently now, and she thought it must be Cole or one of the others shifting the outer boughs of the shelter.

"What is it?" she whispered, but there was no answer.

She propped herself up on an elbow and peered at the boughs as they separated, expecting to see a familiar face. Instead, two yellow eyes appeared, and then a long, dark snout. It was the face of a wolf, wide as a shovel, fetid canine breath steaming in the narrow space of the shelter.

Inna screamed.

CHAPTER 26

A full-grown Eurasian wolf was more than one hundred and fifty pounds of gristle and sinew, fur and fang. In mid-winter, it would not have been unusual for the hungry wolves to haunt the fringes of the remote villages, hoping for easy prey, whether it was a stray goat or a wandering child. But it was only autumn, and this was the first real snow.

These wolves had grown bold. Aggressive even. The only explanation was that the long war had left a deficit of hunters, allowing the wolves to grow bolder than normal. They had forgotten their natural fear of humans.

No wonder. What did they have to fear from the humans they encountered? Some of the packs ran to thirty or forty wolves. Fortunately for Inna and the others, this was a smaller pack of a dozen animals, led by an alpha male whose rough coat was the color of dusty coal.

It was this big male that had thrust his head into the shelter. Inna's scream did not deter him. With a growl, he fastened his teeth on the blanket twisted around her feet and tried to drag her through the opening in the shelter. Only the fact that Harry shared the blanket with her kept the wolf from being successful.

Inna screamed again, and this time Harry finally woke from his slumber.

"What?" he shouted, still groggy from the aftermath of hypothermia and Inna's efforts to warm him to the core. "What is it?"

"Wolf!"

Harry sat up, instantly awake. He found himself in a living nightmare, confronted by a snarling wolf. The space was too confined to use any sort of weapon; in any case, his pistol was somewhere outside with his wet clothes. He punched the wolf, but the blow was not well aimed and bounced harmlessly off the shovel-sized head. The wolf did not let go. Harry hit him again.

By now, Inna's screams had awakened the

others. Cole slipped from his shelter, shirtless in the cold, his lean muscles corded like rawhide across his arms and shoulders. His only weapon was a hunting knife. A gray shape rushed him and Cole's knife flashed; the wolf yelped and fell away. Cole's lips pulled away from his teeth, contorted in a snarl that made him seem just as vicious as one of the attacking wolves.

Vaccaro tumbled out after him, but saw Cole's savage face and took a step back, half afraid that Cole might stab him. He gulped and leveled a pistol at one of the gray forms whirling around them, but Cole grabbed his arm.

"No guns!" he shouted, loud enough to be heard by everyone. "If we start shooting, the Russians will know where we are."

"Goddammit, Cole! How are we supposed to fight off these wolves?"

"Like this," Cole said. He ran forward at a crouch, right at the big coal-colored wolf that had its head buried in the shelter from which Inna's screams emanated. He rammed a knee into the wolf's shoulder, pinning it down, and drove his knife into the wolf's belly. The beast snarled and twisted its head, trying to get at Cole, but he put more weight on the wolf and plunged his knife in again, hilt deep. The wolf yelped and with a new surge of power shook Cole off, snapping at him, then disappeared into the trees, trailing blood.

Nearby, Samson had emerged from his own

shelter and stood head down, like a big, raging bull. Two wolves launched themselves at Samson. The first fell away when he struck it in the head with a full canteen swung at the end of a webbed belt, but the second wolf latched itself onto the big man's leg.

This second wolf was the alpha female, so opposite in coloring to her mate that she was nearly the color of the snow, except for a ridge of gray that ran the length of her back. She had jaws like a vise and she bit down until Samson felt her teeth grate his shin bone. He hit her with the canteen, again and again, until the wolf gave a final shake of her head, tearing out a chunk of flesh the size of a fist, and raced off into the trees.

In moments, the awful attack was over, the wolves having discovered that these visitors to their woods were not such easy prey. The wolves disappeared into the trees, leaving only blood-stained snow and frightened humans behind.

They took stock, nursing their wounds. Inna and Harry emerged from the shelter, tugging on clothes. Ramsey followed soon after. Even after hours of sleep, he could barely stand.

"Are you hurt?" Cole asked them.

Harry shook his head. "Scared the hell out of us, but the worst that happened is that the wolf chewed a hole in our blanket. Look at you—Jesus, Cole, you're bleeding."

Cole touched the place where the alpha

male's teeth had raked him. "It ain't deep. I just hope that damn wolf don't have rabies."

Samson came hobbling over. He had gotten the worst of the attack. He leg bled freely where the wolves had ravaged it. Seeing the blood and torn flesh, Inna attempted to choke back the sound of dismay in her throat, then set to work binding up the wounds.

Cole looked around. "Where's Vaska at?"

In the aftermath of the fray, they had forgotten about the Russian hunter. They found him kneeling in the snow beside his laika. Buka lay motionless, his throat and side torn. Nearby was the body of a wolf.

Cole felt a chill in spite of himself—even in death, the wolf looked menacing. The beast's mouth gaped open, revealing strong, sharp teeth. Even Vaska's tough laika had been no match for it. A wolf that big could easily have dragged Inna from the shelter. It must have weighed almost as much as Cole.

Beside him, Vaccaro gave an appreciative whistle. "Look at the size of that motherfucker."

"Vaska, are you hurt?" Cole asked.

"No," he said without looking up. With a bloody hand, he stroked the ruff of the dog. "When the wolf went for me, Buka fought him. He was a good dog."

A tear streaked the leathery face of the Russian hunter.

Honaker appeared, standing apart from the group, his weapon half raised toward the others. Something about the way he was looking at them made the hair on the back of Cole's neck stand at attention. He suddenly felt naked—not because he was only wearing a blanket across his shoulders, but because his rifle was still in the shelter. Again, Cole wondered why he felt that Honaker was trying to get the drop on them. It didn't make sense—they were all on the same team here.

Then Honaker looked off into the shadows. "Maybe we should risk building a fire," he said. "We don't want those damn wolves coming back."

"Maybe a small fire," Cole agreed. It was a risk, but they had all seen the size of the dead wolf. "We can warm up, dry out, and keep the goddamn wolves away until first light."

"What about the Russians?" Vaccaro asked. "What if they see the fire?"

"You want a two-legged problem or a four-legged problem? Take your pick."

Vaccaro's eyes went to the dark trees surrounding them. Dawn was still hours far away. "Let's build that fire."

• • •

Cole had a fire burning within a few minutes,

having scrounged dry wood from deep within a windfall. The shelters were abandoned in favor of crowding around the fire, not so much for the meager warmth it offered, but for the circle of light it cast. None of them liked the idea of going beyond the firelight, where a wolf might be lurking in the shadows.

It was also the perfect time to eat an early breakfast, but Honaker had some bad news for them.

"There's a problem with the rations," Honaker announced, once they were all gathered about the fire.

"What problem?"

"The food is gone. I had everything in my rucksack, and now it's gone. A wolf must have dragged it off."

"Maybe you dropped it back at the bog," Inna said.

"To hell if I know," Honaker said. "All I'm sure of is that our food is gone."

"We could go look for it," she suggested.

"What's this we business?" Honaker snapped. "I'm not going anywhere until it gets light. Those wolves would like nothing better than to turn *us* into food."

They had to admit that Honaker had a point. Nobody blamed him for the loss of the rations— Whitlock's near drowning, followed by the wolf attack, had created utter chaos. It would have been easy enough to lose the rations.

They took stock of what they carried in their pockets. Vaccaro had a chocolate bar, Inna had a handful of foil-wrapped beef bouillon cubes, and Vaska had a pouch filled with jerky. Everybody had a few cigarettes or sticks of gum. It was all enough to stave off hunger for a few hours. Nobody had any real food.

"Damn, but I'm hungry," Vaccaro said. "Do you think roasted wolf is any good?"

Cole shrugged. "I could skin it out and—"

Vaccaro raised a hand. "I'm joking, Hillbilly. I'm not going to eat a wolf."

"It would be damn stringy, anyhow. Maybe we can do better than wolf meat." Cole looked over at Vaska, who nodded. The Russian understood just what Cole had in mind.

For the next couple of hours, they dozed, keeping one eye on the shadows beyond the fire. Near daybreak, when there began to be enough light to navigate the woods, Cole and Vaska moved into the trees to set snares.

A snare was the simplest of traps. A loop of thin wire was draped across a rabbit trail, with one end tied to a sapling. Even during the snow, rabbits had left a few tracks. When the unsuspecting rabbit ran its head through the loop, its struggle to get away tightened the noose. Within minutes, they had four snares set around the woods near the camp.

Cole wasn't satisfied with the possibility of a few rabbits. Looking around, he spotted a windfall log that had caught against another tree so that it hung a few feet above the ground.

"Vaska, what do you say we try to catch something bigger?"

"What, like a deer?"

"Like a Russian."

Cole explained what he had in mind. A deadfall trap.

If a snare was simple, a deadfall was only slightly more complex. Vaska built them all the time to trap sables in the north country. The deadfall they built now was intended for larger prey. Vaska took a stick four feet long and cut it to a flat point, like the tip of a screwdriver. He then cut a notch in another stick that ended in a fork.

They recruited Vaccaro to help pull the windfall log free and lift the one end high over their heads while Vaska carried out the delicate act of supporting the log using the two sticks— one end of the stick with the screwdriver point was on the ground, the point itself jammed into the notched stick, which at the forked end supported the log. The tip of the notched stick extended downward a few inches, and Cole baited it with an empty cigarette pack. Then he disguised their handiwork with a few well-placed branches. It was good enough to fool someone careless.

The trio stepped back to admire their handiwork. Vaska was grinning for the first time since the wolves had killed his dog.

"Whoever grabs that cigarette pack is going to end up with one hell of a headache," Vaccaro said, looking at the log overhead. At the slightest touch, it would come crashing down.

"With any luck, it might take out one of these Russians and even the odds for us," Cole said.

They moved back to the campfire, hoping that the rabbits would soon be stirring to forage in the new snow. After an hour, they checked the snares, but came up empty.

"I reckon it's chewing gum and cigarettes for breakfast," Cole said.

When they returned, the campfire was only smoldering now that the others were preparing to leave. Cole looked around the group. Samson was limping. Ramsey was being propped up by Whitlock, who looked rejuvenated for a man who had only recently escaped being both drowned and frozen. Inna must have been a mighty fine nurse.

The morning light usually meant that they were greeted by the sound of pursuing dogs. This morning, there was only silence.

"Maybe the Russians gave up," Vaccaro said.

"Barkov does not give up," Inna said.

"Then what happened to their dogs?"

"The same thing that happened to our dog. Wolves."

Although it was some relief not to hear the dogs on their trail, it was also disconcerting. In a way, the dogs had helped them keep tabs on their pursuers. The Russians could be miles away—or else creeping up on them.

"Better get a move on," Cole said. His belly clenched in hunger, but there was no choice but to ignore it. He had a sudden recollection of the many hungry nights he had spent as a boy in Gashey's Creek, where he had learned to ignore the rumblings of an empty belly.

Food was more than mere comfort; out here, it was fuel. They still had many miles to go. If there was time later, he might try to circle back and check Vaska's snares.

"Maybe there's a diner up ahead," Vaccaro said.

"Short of that, the best we can hope for now is to get across that border as fast as possible," Cole said.

CHAPTER 27

Not more than a mile away, Barkov was up at first light, kicking his men awake. They were down to one bottle of vodka, so he let them all have a swig along with their hunk of cold black bread that served as breakfast. It was just below zero degrees celsius. Typical autumn weather. In a few weeks, it would be so cold that a cup of water froze instantly when poured onto the ground.

"No sign of the dogs?" he asked the Mink.

The Mink shrugged.

Last night, a she wolf had come to the edge of camp and lured the dogs away. Barkov suspected that she had been in heat. How could a wolf be so clever? It almost went beyond animal cunning.

Since they had seen no sign of the dogs since then, Barkov assumed that the wolves had gotten them. There had been two dogs, but a dozen or more wolves in the pack that they been roaming around them. Not good odds.

He liked to think that the dogs had escaped the wolves and run back home. Maybe they had run all the way to Moscow. Barkov wished them luck.

Without the dogs to do their tracking, he was worried about losing the prisoners' trail. The snow was deep enough that it had buried any trace of their footsteps. All that Barkov could do was head west from the last point where the trail had left off. The good news was that if they found the trail this morning, it would be a simple matter of following the prisoners' tracks through the snow.

As usual, the Mink seemed to sense what Barkov was thinking. He nodded, as if in agreement to Barkov's thoughts.

"If we find their tracks, we won't need the dogs," the Mink said. "A child could follow their trail."

"Even Dmitri could follow their trail in the snow!" Barkov said, and laughed. The clear, bright weather, and the promise of another day of hunting, had put him in a good mood.

First, they had to find the trail.

Barkov ordered them to fan out, each man about twenty meters apart, so that they could cover the most ground in hopes of picking up the prisoners' tracks. All around them, the taiga was covered in a blanket of unbroken white.

Barkov did not mind the cold or the snow. He did not mind having to find the escapees' trail. It was much better to be the hunter than the hunted. And the day was young.

• • •

It was clear by now that Ramsey wouldn't last long. There was something wrong with his lungs. His breath dragged in and out, rattling like chain being dragged down a gravel road. Ramsey had seemed to rally after the wolf attack, but that had sapped all his energy. Now he was wrapped in a blanket. Inna had put his head in her lap, in the way that one might comfort a child. Every now and then his eyes fluttered open.

You didn't need to be a doctor to know he had pneumonia, or something just as bad. Whatever was wrong with Ramsey, it wasn't something they could cure a hundred miles from nowhere.

None of them was in great shape. They were a cold and miserable bunch. Samson nursed the leg where the wolf had ripped a chunk from his calf.

Vaccaro nervously scanned the horizon, clutching his rifle. The wolf attack had left him more shaken than an artillery barrage. Honaker was even more jumpy and irritable than usual. Whitlock huddled beside Inna and Ramsey, shivering.

Only Vaska and Cole seemed calm, both men sitting apart from the others. Vaska scraped out his pipe and tamped it full of tobacco again, making a ritual out of lighting it. Cole had an unlit cigarette clenched in his teeth. He was convinced that cigarettes were leaving him too winded, so he was giving them up. Both men kept rifles across their knees.

Honaker walked over and joined them.

"He's not gonna make it," Honaker said in a low voice, nodding at Ramsey. He acted as if he didn't want the others to hear, but that was futile —they were only a few feet away. "We are just carrying a dead man."

"What would you suggest?" Cole asked, making no effort to rein in his contempt for the man. He knew damn well what Honaker was going to suggest, and he didn't like it. Honaker was someone who always took the easy way, but not necessarily the right way. The mountain folk back home would have said that he lacked sand.

Thinking about it now, Cole realized he hadn't seen Honaker during the wolf attack. He puzzled it out until he realized that Honaker had likely stayed in his shelter, out of harm's way until the wolves scattered.

"He's not going to make it."

Cole didn't even bother to keep the contempt out of his voice. "What do you want to do, Honaker? Leave him for the wolves? Shoot him?"

"I'm just saying, is all."

"Say it to somebody else," Cole said. "Nobody gets left behind. Now, you had best tell everyone to get on their feet. We need to keep a move on."

Honaker glared at Cole, but after a minute he gave the order. Everyone was too cold and tired and hungry to protest. They knew that the only way out was to keep moving.

Ramsey's eyelids fluttered open again. He struggled to get himself propped up on an elbow. "I'm staying right here," he announced.

"The hell you are," said Cole. "Come on. I'll help you up. I'll carry you if I have to."

Ramsey shook his head. "Look at me. We are still days away from Finland. No, give me a gun and I can buy you some time. I can take out a few of those Russian bastards before they get me."

Cole shook his head. "You ain't in no shape to fight."

Samson spoke up. He had not said much since last night. "I'll stay with him. You've seen my leg. How far do you think I'd get? It looks like hamburger."

"You two can't stay here." Cole pronounced it

cain't, as if it rhymed with *ain't*.

"Sure we can stay. It's the easiest thing in the world," Samson said. He grinned. Injured leg or not, he remained a force to be reckoned with. "Besides, you and whose army are gonna stop me?"

"Hate to say it," Honaker said. He didn't look at Ramsey or Samson, but spoke as it they weren't there. "That gives the rest of us a fighting chance."

"Shut up, Honaker," Cole said sharply. "Nobody asked you."

Honaker wouldn't be put off that easily. He snapped, "Listen up, Cole—"

"No, you two listen to me," Samson said. "I've already told you how it's gonna be."

Cole didn't like it. Deep in his bones, he downright hated the idea. However, he wondered how much of his opposition had to do with the fact that he didn't like any idea that Honaker supported. He looked over at Vaska's grave, stoic face. The old Russian sucked on his pipe and nodded. Vaccaro wouldn't meet his eyes, which meant he also favored the idea.

"Goddamn," Cole said, feeling that he had been outvoted. He needed someone to take his side against this damn fool idea. He looked at Whitlock and Inna. "You two all right with this?"

Ramsey interrupted. "It's not up to them. I've already decided. Harry, give me all the extra bullets you have for that Browning of yours."

Whitlock fished in his pockets, came out with a handful of shells. "Along with what's in the magazine, that gives you maybe twenty rounds." He knelt down beside Ramsey and pressed the bullets into his hand, then held it for several moments. "I hate for it to end like this."

Ramsey pushed himself up higher and grinned. "Are you kidding me? Harry, this is like the Alamo. I get to go out in a blaze of glory. Just like Davy Crockett."

Inna spoke up. "But—"

Ramsey cut her off with a wave of his hand and his best effort at a happy-go-lucky smile. "Take care of yourself, Inna. Watch out for this one here."

Whitlock was getting choked up. "I don't know what to say."

A shadow passed across Ramsey's face. "The only thing that bothers me is never getting home again. When you get back, will you at least put up a headstone for me? I doubt the Russians will give me a proper burial."

Whitlock nodded, and the two men shook hands.

"Hold on a minute," Cole said. He walked over to Inna and handed her his penknife and one of the brass shell casings for the Springfield. "I want you to scratch Barkov's name on that shell. In Russian letters. Let's send Barkov a message."

Inna was done in a couple of minutes. Cole took the shell and pressed it into Ramsey's hand, then gave Ramsey and Samson a nod. His pale eyes were hard to read.

Then they walked off into the taiga, leaving Samson and Ramsey to their fates.

• • •

Barkov was so intent on looking for tracks in the snow that he wasn't paying attention to his surroundings. It was a mistake that nearly cost him his life. He was just passing a boulder, with one of the soldiers from the garrison a few feet behind him, when a shape that was alien to the natural landscape caught his eye. It took him a split second to recognize the fat black muzzle of a shotgun, thrust out from behind the rock.

Barkov reacted without thinking, throwing himself into the snow. An instant later came the shotgun blast. He heard screaming. The soldier at Barkov's elbow had picked up some buckshot. A second blast clawed the air overhead, followed by several shots from a pistol.

"Ambush!" Barkov managed to shout. "Take cover!"

His men did not need to be told twice. But it was too late for the soldier nearest Barkov. The second shotgun blast nearly cut him in two. More shots followed in rapid succession. Just two guns, he thought, but it sounded more like twenty.

Barkov and his men were on the receiving end of a military issue trench warfare shotgun. The Winchester Model 12 pump action shotgun could be slam fired—that is, as long as the trigger was depressed, the gun fired each time the action was pumped.

The fire slackened. Then a pause. Time to reload? Barkov sprang to his feet, remarkably agile for a big man, and bulled ahead, rifle at the ready.

He found a big man behind a rock, hurrying to feed shotgun shells into the gun. He got it loaded and leveled it at Barkov, who threw himself flat as the man fired twice. Just two shots —either the man hadn't had time to fully reload, or he must be out of shells.

Barkov got to his feet, taking his time.

The man shouted something at Barkov in English—*American*, Barkov thought—then threw the shotgun at him in frustration, and pulled a knife.

Barkov almost sneered as he leveled his rifle at the big American's chest. A knife? He was about to pull the trigger when he caught movement just beyond the big man. Another man crouched there with a pistol at his side. Why didn't he shoot? *Because the gun was empty*, Barkov thought.

His eyes locked on the man, whom he

recognized immediately as one of the escaped prisoners. The one called Ramsey. Barkov took his finger off the trigger and shouted at the others not to shoot. It would be so much more satisfying to take them both alive.

Alive for now, anyhow.

Barkov knew about six words of English, one of which he spoke now: "American?"

The big man said something that started with *Yeah*, which was another one of the words Barkov knew. The others were *no, booze, gun,* and *sonofabitch*. He couldn't understand the rest. He was trying to get his head around the fact that there was an American out here who was not an escapee from the Gulag compound. What was going on?

Then the prisoner named Ramsey shouted something at the big man. What Barkov heard was Samson. That sounded like a name to him.

He handed his rifle to the Mink and took out his whip. His eyes met those of the big American. Barkov didn't see any fear there, just a challenge. Smiling, he advanced toward the American in a wary crouch.

The two men were almost equally matched, both of them well over six feet tall and heavy through the shoulders. Hands out, heads down, they resembled two bears about to rumble. Samson was maybe a little bigger, but he was limping, favoring a leg that was wrapped in bloody rags. Barkov took note of that.

They circled each other, looking for an advantage, knife against whip. It wasn't just any knife. The American had one of those wickedly sharp combat knives that resembled a medieval dagger. When the Americans and Russians had met outside Berlin, those knives had been freely traded for vodka and even Russian pistols. If the American managed to stick that thing into him, the fight would be over.

Barkov did not plan on letting him get in that close. The whip was an ideal defense against a knife attack. When Samson lunged, Barkov stung his hand with the whip and pulled back. The whip was made of braided leather, thick as a broomstick near the base and taping slightly down its two-foot length. It had some weight behind it.

Samson feinted left, then lunged from the right. Barkov slapped him away again.

Cautious now of the whip, the American circled just out of reach. Barkov held the whip cocked back by his ear, and gestured with his left hand for the American to come on. The American really had no choice but to attack. His shotgun blast had killed one of the Russians, but there were still four of them with their guns trained on him. It was attack, or die.

He steamed forward like a bull.

Barkov was ready with the whip, but as it

hissed down, the American instantly tossed the knife from his right hand to his left and caught the whip in his open right hand. It must have been painful, but he did not let go. Instead, he dragged the whip down and pulled Barkov off balance, then stabbed down with his left hand.

Barkov felt the blade slice his shoulder. Fortunately for him, the American was not accurate with his left hand. Most of the damage was done to his winter coat.

The American wasn't finished. He drew back his left hand for another go at Barkov.

The Russian saw it coming. He turned sideways and kicked the American's injured leg out from under him.

Samson went down to his hands and knees like a bull felled by a matador, but one hand still grasped the whip. He was using it to pull himself back up.

Barkov let go, and the American went toppling backwards. Barkov did not give him a chance to recover. As the American got to his knees, Barkov punched him in the back of the head so hard that his knuckles screamed in pain. The American went down again. Then Barkov kicked him. The American rolled onto his back.

Barkov got down and straddled him, pulled back a fist to punch the man, but was surprised when the American's hands shot out and locked around Barkov's throat. Instantly, he felt his airflow cut off as the American's hands clenched around his windpipe. His opponent's grip felt like a vise.

He grabbed the American's wrists and pulled. The grip around his throat did not loosen. Starbursts and spots swam in front of his eyes. Letting go with his right hand, he groped on the snowy ground for any kind of weapons. A rock. A stick. Instead, his fingers closed around the knife that the American had dropped.

Barkov had it in his grip in an instant, and plunged it down at the American.

For a big man, the American was quick as a viper. He let go of Barkov's throat and grabbed his wrist instead before the knife could strike home.

They went back and forth, both of them straining as if the knife weighed a thousand pounds, when in reality it was the sheer muscular resistance of them struggling against one another. Barkov had the advantage of gravity and pressed the tip down, down, toward the American's throat. Then the American rallied and pushed the knife up, up, turning it with bone-cracking strength until it was pointed at Barkov's eye.

In spite of himself, Barkov was impressed. The American was incredibly strong. Strong as a bear. Strong as Barkov.

Dimly, he was aware of a pair of legs beside him. Then a rifle barrel reached down and touched the American's temple. The American's eyes widened, but he shoved the tip of the knife toward Barkov's eye with one final wave of strength.

That's when the rifle went off. Loud as a thunderclap in Barkov's ear. The American's grip went slack instantly.

Barkov rolled to his feet, so angry that he was shaking. The Mink stood nearby, nonchalantly working the bolt of the rifle.

"What have you done?" Barkov demanded. "He was mine to kill!"

"You were taking too long. We need to get moving," the Mink said. He lowered his voice. "Besides, he almost had you."

Barkov looked down at the dead man. Unlike most bodies, it did not look any smaller in death. Then he look around for the American prisoner, Ramsey, who was still slumped against the rock. His eyes went from his comrade's dead body to Barkov's eyes. Barkov tried to read something there—fear or defeat—but saw only defiance.

Well, he would fix that. "Dmitri," he called. "Bring me my whip."

"Let's just shoot him and be done with it," the Mink said.

"Look at him. He's already half dead. This won't take long."

The boy scurried to do as he was told, pressing the cruelly braided leather grip into

Barkov's hand. The boy eyed the whip nervously, having been on the receiving end of it.

Barkov made the whip sing. He struck the American prisoner across the face hard enough to draw blood.

He pulled back his hand for another swing and froze.

Ramsey now had a pistol in his hand. Nobody had seen it before. He leveled it at Barkov, but then seemed to reconsider. Instead, he put the gun to his own head and closed his eyes. An instant later, it was done. Barkov felt cheated for a second time.

The Mink bent over and pried the gun out of the dead man's hand.

"He must have had just one bullet left," the Mink said. He seemed to find the situation amusing because he gave one of his rare smiles. "I think I would have saved that last bullet for you."

Barkov grunted, unhappy that both Americans were dead. There were many questions he would have liked them to answer.

They searched the pockets of the dead men. One soldier took the big man's wristwatch. He had a wallet with a few American dollars in it. What did he plan to buy out here on the taiga? There was some identification that one of them could read. The Mink kept the wallet and let the paper money flutter away on the wind.

Ramsey's limp hand had opened in death. It

turned out that he did have one more bullet, but this one was for a rifle. Something was etched into the brass casing. The Mink picked it up and squinted at it, then shook his head and held it up for Barkov to see.

The etching read: "Barkov."

"The dead one here was not the sniper," the Mink said.

"How do you know?"

"What would a sniper be doing with a shotgun? No, this isn't him. If I did not know better, I would say that the American sniper is sending you a message."

"It's just nonsense," Barkov said. He tossed the bullet away. Then he looked across the expanse of taiga ahead and all the open places they would have to cross. He felt a chill, imagining the American sniper's crosshairs on him.

"What are other Americans doing out here?" the Mink wondered.

Barkov coiled the whip and tucked it into his belt. "We need to get moving," he said. "Let's catch up to them and find out. Then we will kill them just like we killed these two."

CHAPTER 28

It wasn't long after they had been ambushed by the two Americans that Barkov found the signs in the snow of where the others had started out that morning. He counted six sets of tracks. He knew that two of those sets of tracks belonged to Inna Mikhaylovna and the escaped American pilot. But who else? He felt a twinge of apprehension, not knowing exactly whom he was chasing.

"Not so far ahead of us now," he said.

Even so, they might have missed the campsite if Dmitri had not stopped to relieve himself, and being shy, had moved into the woods away from the others.

"Over here!" the boy called, frantically buttoning himself up. "There is blood all over the snow!"

Barkov could see that Dmitri had found where the Americans had set up a rough camp and built shelters. Barkov was more astonished to discover that the camp had been the scene of a battle—or so it seemed. It was just as bloody as any skirmish site he had seen during the war, but he quickly saw that this had been a battle between man and beast. The snow was trampled. Blood flecked the drifts. He saw a dead wolf, and a dead dog. He was sure that not all the blood belonged to the animals.

The Mink walked up next to dead wolf. It looked nearly as big as him. The beast's eyes stared sightlessly, and its jaws gaped open, revealing sharp white teeth.

"When we return, we need to organize a wolf hunt," the Mink said. "These wolves need to be taught fear."

Barkov grunted in agreement. He did not like wolves.

It was disturbing that the wolves had attacked, and yet it was not terribly unusual. The war had all but eliminated hunting because there simply had not been any hunters in Russia—they had all been off fighting in Finland or on the

Eastern Front. Sure, there were a few old men around like that village hunter, Vaska, armed with ancient rifles, but someone like Vaska did not actively hunt wolves. You could not eat a wolf, and the pelts had little value.

Stalin had seen to it that few people had weapons of any kind. An unarmed people were more easily controlled by a dictator. He had left his own people defenseless. As a consequence, the wolf packs had grown larger and bolder. It wasn't unusual to hear of a child being snatched from the edges of a village. Some of the bigger, and hungrier, wolves even attacked adults.

Which was just what had happened here.

"May the devil take them," he said, and spat.

The men spread out to explore the campsite. There was not much to see. He did have to allow some grudging admiration for the work the Americans had done. Their shelters looked snug.

Except for one. He could see the damage where a wolf had dug into a shelter, then forced its way between the branches of the roof. Someone had been sleeping in there, and the wolf had gone after him. Or her.

In spite of himself, Barkov shivered.

One of the men gave a shout, and Barkov saw that he was waving. He had found something. A cigarette pack was speared on a stick.

The soldier reached out to pull the pack free, perhaps hoping that a cigarette had somehow been overlooked inside.

Barkov's warning came too late.

There was a snap, a swish, the sound of something heavy shifting overhead. Instantly, a log above the solder's head gave way. The man's scream was cut short as the log struck him.

Dmitri hurried over and struggled to get the log off the other man, who was quite still beneath it. Barkov shoved Dmitri away, then reached down with two big hands and tossed the log aside as though it were a matchstick.

But it was too late for the soldier. The falling log had struck with enough force to break his neck.

It wasn't even noon, and he had already lost two men today—one in the trap just now, and the other in an ambush.

"Come on," he said gruffly. "Let's see if we can finish this business before the day is out."

• • •

They needed food. Meat. It had been two days since they had eaten any real food. They wouldn't make it another two days. Cole decided to take a chance and double back to check the snares that he and Vaska had set that morning. He left Vaccaro as the rear guard.

He didn't backtrack, but moved in a circle to give the Russians a wide berth. Vaska had offered his snowshoes, but the snow was only about six inches deep—not really enough snow to slow him down, and definitely not deep enough to make strapping on the cumbersome snowshoes worthwhile. He would be able to catch up with the others, if he double timed it on the way back. With luck, he would be gone for an hour at most, maybe two.

Earlier, he and the others had heard the gunshots that would have been Samson's and Ramsey's last stand. An ominous quiet followed.

Part of him burned with a desire for revenge. It was just how he was wired: eye for an eye, tooth for a tooth. Anyone who grew up in the mountains lived by that code. Vengeance ran through the mountain people like a vein of ore. The fact that he had known Samson and Ramsey for just a few days didn't matter.

The bullet he had sent back with Barkov's name on it was more than an idle gesture. He would face Barkov when the time was right. Right now, he and the others needed fresh meat more than they needed a fight with Russians. Samson and Ramsey had bought them time with their lives. Time to get that much closer to the border. Cole and the others would take it.

From the tracks in the snow, he could see that the Russians had found the makeshift camp and searched it, kicking the shelters apart. They either hadn't bothered with the snares, or hadn't seen them. Their tracks went on, following the trail that Cole and the others had left that morning.

One of the snares had caught a rabbit. Cole collected it and took down the wire for the snares, in case it might prove useful again.

With a smile of satisfaction, he noted that the deadfall also had done its work. A Russian soldier lay crushed by the fallen log, the cigarette pack still gripped in his hand. One less Russian to fight later. The Russians had left the body where it lay.

• • •

Carrying the one paltry rabbit, he followed the tracks out of the old camp, wondering how long it would take to get to the spot where Samson and Ramsey had made their last stand.

They were damn fools to have done what they did, but he could understand why they had volunteered to go out fighting. If it looked like they weren't going to make it to Finland, this was just what Cole planned to do.

Ramsey had been done for—hardly more than a dead man walking, and barely walking at that. Samson seemed to like the idea of a showdown, like he was Doc Holliday at the OK Corral or some such place.

The killing ground that Cole found was not the OK Corral, but only a rocky clearing in the snowy taiga. He found Samson's body surrounded by bloody snow. Judging by the trampled ground, it looked as if he had put up one hell of a fight.

Then Cole found Ramsey.

Dead, he was just a bag of skin and bones. He had been shot in the head, but his face was slashed with tiny cuts. Not from a knife. Inna had told him that Barkov liked to carry some sort of sawed-off horse whip. It looked as if Barkov had used it on Ramsey.

Cole felt hollow and sad. He had hardly known Ramsey, but he did know that he deserved better.

He reached down and closed Ramsey's eyes. The last thing he had seen was that goddamn Russian and the snowy taiga. He sure as hell wouldn't ever be seeing home again.

Then the anger came flooding in like a rip tide, along with a current of guilt for allowing the poor bastard to make some kind of half-assed last stand. The anger swept Cole up and carried him away. He started to shake and tremble, not from the cold, but from pure rage. His vision flickered and for a moment he was blinded. He went down to one knee and stayed there until the fit passed.

When he stood back up, the cold taiga wind cleared his mind. He felt like a bar of red-hot iron that had just been dipped in cold water, newly forged.

"Barkov," he vowed to the Russian wind that

moaned across the empty land. "I will put a bullet in you if it's the last thing I do."

• • •

Staring down at Ramsey's body, Cole couldn't bring himself to leave just yet. He thought about what Ramsey had said. That he hated the idea of never getting home again. Cole thought that after everything Ramsey had been through, that it just didn't seem right that his body would be left here on the taiga—maybe to serve as supper for whatever critters happened by. The thought made his belly churn, but there was no way to dig down through the cold ground to give Ramsey a decent burial. He didn't have a shovel, and his knife wasn't up to the task.

"Goddamn," he said, thinking it over.

Cole had brought a blanket with him, just in case he became separated from the others and had to spend the night. Ramsey looked so small laying there, just an empty shell like a corn husk. The hard work and poor food of the Gulag camp had worn him down to hardly more than a scarecrow.

Cole decided that it had been Ramsey's spirit and personality that had been outsized. He spread the blanket on the snowy ground and dragged Ramsey's body onto it, then rolled him up in the blanket.

Maybe he could carry Ramsey, but there was no way he could carry Samson. The man outweighed him by a hundred pounds. He refused to leave Samson to be scavenged by varmints. The Russians abandoned their dead, but not him.

The ground nearby was scattered with stones and boulders, some of them the size of a softball, others the size of a watermelon. Slowly, laboriously, Cole dug through the snow for these stones and piled them around and over Samson's body. The effort took him the better part of an hour. He bashed his fingers between a couple of the larger stones, and ended up leaving bloody fingerprints across the rocks.

When he was finished, Cole hoisted Ramsey's body over one shoulder and set off along the path he had made getting there. He would be a liar if he didn't admit that every step was a struggle. Following his old steps made it a little easier.

In the back of his mind, a plan began to develop. It was so goddamn crazy that it might just work. But he would have to push himself hard to get ahead of the Russians.

He plowed ahead. After a few minutes of laboring through the snow with Ramsey on his back, he realized there was no way that he could circle around Barkov and get ahead of the Russians. That was just wishful thinking. He decided that he didn't need to get ahead of them;

he just needed to make sure that they found him when the time came.

He located a copse of trees on hilly ground. The trees would give him some cover, so that the Russians would have to come in close. It was perfect ground for what Cole had in mind.

He tried to put Ramsey down gently, but the weight of the body was more than he could manage and the body ended up slamming to the ground in a way that reminded Cole of the judo throws they had practiced back in basic training. He shook his head. Judo. A lot of goddamn good that did anybody.

Then he set about building a fire. Cole could build a fire just about anywhere, short of it being in the middle of a blizzard or a hurricane. There was almost always some dry wood to be found, if you knew where to look.

He got a nice blaze going—a real fire to keep the cold at bay. He had to admit that the heat was welcome. The smoke trailed up into the sky like a banner, which was exactly what he had in mind. He tossed on some green spruce boughs to thicken the smoke.

Once the fire was going, he skinned the rabbit. He supposed that this was technically a hare, but if it hopped and had long ears, it was enough to call it a rabbit. He skewered the rabbit on a sharp stick, which he propped beside the fire so that the indirect heat would roast the meat. With a fire that size, the cooking wouldn't take long. *Goddamn, that smells good*, he thought as the meat began to sizzle.

Satisfied with the fire and the rabbit, he knelt beside Ramsey and got to work.

One way or another, Ramsey was going to have his revenge.

CHAPTER 29

Barkov was the first to spot the smoke. He was surprised. So far, the Americans had shown a great deal of discipline in avoiding any sort of fire. Maybe they had finally gotten too cold, or maybe they had something to cook. Any number of possibilities ran through Barkov's mind.

What the Mink said in Russian was the equivalent of, "Can you believe they would be so stupid?"

Barkov told the other three men to stay put, and he and the Mink went out to check on the source of the smoke.

They could see flames flickering through the tree trunks—the fire was no stingy affair. A delicious smell reached them. That explained the fire. The Americans were cooking meat.

They crept forward, using the trees and brush for cover. Barkov made a motion that signaled *far enough* and *quiet* all in one. The two Russians studied the scene before them.

Much to their surprise, there was just a lone figure hunched over the fire. An American sniper rifle with a telescopic sight was propped up within the sniper's reach. It was hard to see the sniper's face, because his neck and the lower part of his face were wrapped in a scarf against the cold. A cigarette hung from his lips. They had expected an entire group, but not one man. Looking around through the scope at the sniper's feet, they could see what was clearly a body wrapped in a blanket. There was no mistaking it. They had seen enough of those over the last few years.

"So that is the American sniper," the Mink whispered. "He's not much bigger than I am. What is he up to, do you think?"

"It looks to me like he is cooking his dinner."

The Mink gave him an annoyed look. "Over a big fire like that?"

"Maybe he does not think we are nearby. Maybe he thinks we gave up. Maybe he just does not give a shit anymore."

The third possibility was plausible. They had seen so many strange things. Soldiers who lost their minds and threw away their weapons and stripped off their clothes in the middle of a battle. A schoolteacher who sat down to read a book as he froze to death. One could only believe what one saw, which was what they were seeing now. One of the Americans sat by this fire, cooking a rabbit, with a dead man rolled in a blanket nearby. Who was the dead man? Nobody —he was dead. It was not an elaborate scenario.

"What are you waiting for?" the Mink asked.

Barkov lined up the sights and shot the sniper through the head. The body sagged.

The Mink stood up. He uncorked his flask of vodka, took a drink, and handed it to Barkov.

"Good shooting."

"I expected more from this one," Barkov said. "In the end he was *nichevo*. Nothing."

Barkov took a drink, handed back the flask.

"I want his rifle," the Mink said. He grinned. "And there is no point in letting that rabbit go to waste. Are you coming?"

Barkov clapped him on the shoulder. "You go ahead. I will start back toward the others, so that the cowards don't run away. I would not care, but we may still need them yet. Catch up to us when you can, and bring me some of that rabbit."

• • •

Cole waited for what seemed like an eternity, holding himself very still and barely breathing. But he was a patient man. He just hoped that the rabbit didn't burn. He would have had time to turn it, too, because it took an hour for the Russians to find the fire. By then he felt cramped and cold, despite the fact that he was wrapped tightly in a blanket, but he ignored the discomfort.

He was positioned with his arms in front of him. His hands held the Browning 1911 pistol.

He neither heard nor saw the Russians approach. He only knew that they had arrived when a single shot ripped out and hit Ramsey square in the head. The sound made Cole wince. It didn't seem possible to kill a dead man any deader, and yet Barkov had done just that. Ramsey's body slumped to the snowy ground just at the edge of Cole's limited field of view.

Now came the tricky part.

He tightened his grip on the pistol.

What happened next depended on what sort of cards he had been dealt. If one or two of the enemy approached, he had a chance. More than that, and this blanket was going to be his shroud.

He waited, his heart barely making a murmur, which was a good thing—it was so quiet in the forest that the flutter of a bird's wings sounded like a hurricane wind.

He had left a gap in the end of the rolled blanket so that he could look out. The problem was that it reduced his world to a narrow field of vision. It was essentially like looking through a tube. Like a rifle scope, as a matter of fact. He felt cramped as the tobacco inside a hand-rolled cigarette.

Cole had positioned himself carefully. A ring of bushes surrounded the camp—nothing too obvious, but there was a gap through which anyone approaching the fire would naturally walk. It was this gap that the open end of the blanket faced, like a rifle barrel.

As for the waiting, it was simply part of the game. He was very good at being still for hours. He just hoped that these bastards came along before he froze to death—or his supper burned to a crisp. His belly rumbled. It would be a damn shame to waste that rabbit.

It was a sign of the Russian's own skill that Cole never heard him approach. He felt him instead; some inexplicable pressure in the air. He was impressed that the big Russian could move so quietly, until he saw that it wasn't the big Russian at all. In a single glimpse as the man passed through his field of view, he saw that it was the smaller Russian. The one that Ramsey had called the Mink.

Everything depended on the Russian stopping cautiously a dozen feet away, coming through the gap in the bushes directly in front of Cole, so that he could get a clear shot.

But without pausing, as if he didn't have a care in the world, the Russian walked right up to the fire.

Too fast to get off a shot.

Then the Mink was gone. Out of Cole's narrow field of view.

Cole couldn't move the gun or even see him at all. He heard him pick up the Springfield rifle and grunt with satisfaction. At any second, the Russian might get suspicious and put a big, fat slug into Cole. He held his breath.

The Mink stepped closer. Too close. But at least some part of him came back into view. Cole could see the man's boots, his legs to his knees, and that was it. Cole began to understand the fault in his plan. His heart beat faster.

Then, he saw the Russian toe the body with his boot.

In another second the Mink was going to realize that he had not shot a sniper, but that he had shot Ramsey all over again. Cole couldn't take that chance. He aimed at the Mink's shin. His hands shook from the strain of holding the pistol so long. He was aiming at the leg just eight feet away, but still far enough to miss.

He pulled the trigger.

At point blank range, the slug splintered the shin bone. The small man went down as if his leg had been chopped by an ax. Belly down in the snow, he looked right into the blanket roll and locked eyes with Cole. Even through the pain and shock, the eyes registered surprise. He didn't make a sound. Then the face tilted away, as the Mink rolled toward the rifle that he had dropped in the snow.

Cole shot him in the top of the head.

Was Barkov out there with his rifle, watching? Cole held his breath, but no bullet tore into him. Cole sat up, feeling like a sausage. He wriggled out of the blanket and scrambled into a tangle of undergrowth nearby.

From the safety of cover, he strained to hear some sound of movement in the surrounding forest, but his ears rang from the pistol shots.

It stood to reason that if Barkov was out there, he would have shot Cole by now.

Slowly, cautiously, he emerged from the underbrush. Crouched. Stood.

Nothing.

That meant the Mink had been alone. But where the hell was Barkov?

Cole built up the fire. He searched the dead Russian and found a flask of vodka. He uncapped the flask and sniffed. The stuff had an oily smell. He jammed the cork back in—he wasn't that hard up for a drink.

He could, however, think of one good use for the vodka. Maybe he couldn't bury Ramsey, but he could give him another kind of funeral.

He splashed the vodka over Ramsey's clothes. Then he dragged the body into the fire, letting the hungry flames spread across the clothing. He piled more wood on top.

He liked to think that Ramsey would appreciate the fact that he didn't have to worry about being cold.

It didn't seem right just to leave; something was missing, so he muttered the Lord's Prayer, the only bit of religion that had survived his childhood. He gave one final nod at the flames, then slipped away into the trees.

Cole didn't bother to do anything with the dead Russian. The varmints could have at him.

• • •

Barkov had already rejoined the others when he heard two gunshots from the direction of the American sniper's campfire.

He was perplexed. Barkov knew with certainly that he had shot the American square in the head.

Dead men did not need killing again.

So who was shooting?

He waited for the Mink's return with growing apprehension.

Half an hour went by, and still the other sniper did not appear.

The two shots could mean only one thing, which was that his old friend had walked right into a trap. Barkov did not know how it was possible, but snipers were full of tricks. He should know. There was no point in going to investigate, not unless Barkov wanted to walk into a trap himself.

It dawned on Barkov that the campfire they had come upon might actually have been an elaborate trap. Set not for the Mink, but for Barkov. Who had set the trap? The same man who had scratched his name into the rifle casing. It had to be the sniper that they had already encountered.

He still did not understand what the sniper was doing here, or why anyone had bothered to rescue the American prisoners. It wasn't the first time that he had found himself caught up in the middle of something bigger than he was, something that he could never understand.

Stalingrad came to mind.

"What were those shots?" Dmitri asked nervously. "Where is the Mink?"

"He is dead," Barkov said. He cuffed the young soldier in the ear, putting some of his pain and anger into the blow, so that he knocked Dmitri to the ground. The youth glared up at him spitefully. That was good. He was showing some spirit. Barkov kicked him in the ribs, so that he did not become *too* spirited. "Now, let us go."

Barkov headed out, following the tracks left by the other Americans. Doubled over in pain, Dmitri did his best to keep up.

The Americans did not wish to stand and fight. Barkov understood now that their only goal was to get across the border into Finland. How many did the Americans have? Five, if you counted the girl. He now had four men—including himself, and the useless youth. It was too bad about the Mink. He had been as good as ten men.

Barkov would have liked more men, but he wasn't about to give up and turn back.

Thinking about it now, he did not care if the Americans had twenty men, or even thirty. There was only one man who mattered to him now. He did not even care about the escaped American prisoner named Whitlock or the Russian traitor, Inna Mikhaylovna. All that Barkov cared about was the American sniper. The one who had apparently killed his old friend with his imperialist tricks. Barkov felt that he might cross to the ends of the earth to put a bullet in that one.

CHAPTER 30

Cole caught up to the rest of the group just before nightfall. No one relished the idea of another night exposed on the taiga, not after the wolf attack. Not with the Russians still hot on their trail. The Mink was dead, but Barkov was still out there.

There could be no fire tonight. Since the loss of the rations, there was nothing to eat. Cole had brought along the rabbit that he had roasted over the fire, but it provided just a few mouthfuls of meat each. Better than nothing, but not nearly enough.

Snow. Cold. Empty horizons. Empty bellies. The landscape caused a pang in Cole's soul—though not a bad one. True, it was a harsh and barren place, but that did not bother Cole. If anything, he felt a kinship with wild places.

But they were not here to admire the scenery. They were here to get across the border to Finland.

Maybe it had something to do with the vastness of the surrounding taiga, but their group looked even smaller and more dejected than before. Honaker wore a scowl as if he wasn't happy that Cole had come back instead of getting himself killed by the Russians, and he didn't do a very good job of hiding it. Inna and Whitlock sat slumped together on a rock. Vaska sat quietly apart from the others, smoking his pipe and gazing out at the taiga. Even Vaccaro had quit wisecracking.

Cole reckoned that they could cross the border in one more day, if they pushed it. Looking at this group, he wasn't sure that they had much push left. Two more days, then. Short of a miracle, they wouldn't make it to three.

Inna looked at Cole expectantly. "What about Samson and Ramsey?"

Cole shook his head.

"Poor bastards," Whitlock said quietly.

"They put up a fight, that's for damn sure," Cole said.

"I hope they got a few Russians," Whitlock said.

"They got one," Cole said. "And I know that I got that wiry one you told me about. Barkov's buddy."

"I heard the shot. You got the Mink?"

"I reckon I did."

Whitlock grinned. "If there was ever anyone who deserved to get shot, aside from Barkov, it had to be that rat-faced son of a bitch."

"But you did not get Barkov?" Inna asked, sounding worried.

"Not yet."

Vaska came over, holding a small bag, which he dug into to produce a handful of jerky. He explained that this was the last of the food he had brought. He cut the dried meat into equal shares. There was enough for one piece each, not much bigger than a stick of chewing gum.

"Chew it slowly," he said. "Then eat some snow so that you feel full."

"Vaska, just what the hell kind of meat is this?" Honaker wanted to know. He looked doubtfully at the jerky. "Are you sure this isn't an old pair of boots that you cut up?"

"If you ain't gonna eat it, give it here," Cole said harshly.

Honaker glared at him. He had long since given up trying to pretend that he was in charge. The hardships they had been suffering had eroded their chain of command. Hunger and exhaustion put them on an equal footing. Cole had shown himself to be the natural leader, out here in his element. That didn't mean Honaker was happy about it. "Cole, I am goddamned tired of you."

Cole bit off a bit of jerky. He had perfectly formed teeth, although he had never been to a dentist before the Army. It was one benefit of growing up in a place where sweets and soda pop were unobtainable luxuries. "You want to make something of it?"

Honaker seemed to think it over, then looked away. "You aren't worth it, you goddamn hillbilly."

"Maybe I am, and maybe I ain't," Cole said. "What I do know is that if we hurry and get across that border, you won't have to worry about me no more. How does that sound to you?"

Honaker didn't respond, but struggled to snap off a piece of jerky, yanking at it with his teeth without success. "You think you've got all the answers. We'll see about that."

"What's that supposed to mean?"

Honaker gnawed his jerky, his jaw muscles working and popping under the skin. "You'll see."

• • •

Morning dawned cold and bright. The sun and sky hinted at warmer weather. And yet it was a cheerless dawn, without anything to eat. Breakfast consisted of a few handfuls of snow. For Cole, it was like old times growing up in the mountains during the Depression with a father who spent most of his days and nights deep in the hills, making whiskey and drinking as much as he sold, not much caring if his children went hungry.

"What I wouldn't give for some hotcakes and sausage right about now," Vaccaro said. "Hell, I'd settle for a cup of coffee."

Cole threw a snowball at him. "Shut up, Vaccaro."

Cole's joints ached and creaked in the morning chill, like he was an old man. He would have welcomed some coffee and maybe some bacon to grease himself up good. Vaccaro had the right idea. His belly rumbled at the thought.

Even their cigarettes were gone. Vaska still had his pipe. He cleaned out the bowl with a short-bladed knife, carefully tamped it full of tobacco, and then puffed away.

Cole glanced toward the horizon. Most of the trees had disappeared, leaving a snow-covered plain before them. It was a barren, unwelcoming landscape.

The only good news this morning was that Finland was a day's walk, if they pushed it.

"May as well get to it," Cole said. "No sense in burnin' daylight."

Vaccaro groaned. "You are like a regular goddamn rooster, Hillbilly."

"You are a ray of sunshine yourself, City Boy."

Cole's attention had been on the horizon to the west. Now he looked back toward the east. What he saw made the frigid air catch in his throat.

Russians. Moving down the face of a long, low slope that Cole and the others had crossed just before dark. He didn't need binoculars or his rifle scope to count five of them. The bigger one out front would be Barkov.

The Russians had not seen them yet because they had made camp for the night in the lee of a spill of boulders. But all that Barkov had to do was follow the tracks right to this spot. Easy as pie.

He considered the rifle in his hands, but this was no time for a last stand. If Barkov was worth anywhere near his salt as a sniper, out here in the open, he could pick them off just as easily as Cole could. No, now wasn't the time to fight.

It was time to run.

Cole sprang to his feet. "Ya'll got to move. Now!"

Honaker seemed annoyed. "What?"

Cole pointed. "The Russians must have kept moving during the night. They come right up on us."

A shock of urgency jolted the team to action.

They hastily rolled their blankets and lashed them to the tops of their packs. Whitlock and Inna rolled up their own blankets, and then tackled Cole's blanket while he kept watch on their pursuers through his rifle scope. Within two minutes, everyone was on their feet and ready to go. Honaker was the only one who didn't seem satisfied.

"We ought to stay and fight," Honaker said, gripping his own weapon.

"If we can keep our distance from them, ain't no need to fight," Cole said. "Our mission is to get Whitlock across the border, not do a version of Custer's last stand."

"I agree with Cole," Whitlock said. "Stopping to fight is just what they want. They must have been on the go most of the night. They'll be tired. We have a head start."

"Enough yammerin'," Cole said. "Let's make tracks."

• • •

Barkov spotted the Americans right away. One moment there was nothing but empty landscape, and the next, there were figures moving in the distance. They stood out against the whiteness of the snowy taiga, but too far to really tell the figures apart.

They must have made camp there for the

night. If Barkov and his men had arrived earlier, the Russians would have walked right up on them in the dark.

Too far to get a clear shot. The American sniper had already proven that he could return fire with deadly accuracy. So now, it was a race. The Americans were close to the border. If they pushed it, they might very well might make it across.

Barkov was not about to let them do that. He had chased them too far to let them escape now. The Mink had died because of them.

"Faster!" he shouted at what was left of his band. "Are you going to go faster, or do I need to use the whip?"

Barkov moved quickly for his size. He was longer through the torso than the legs, yet each step covered nearly a meter of snowy ground. The others had to take an extra half step for each one of his strides.

Since the Mink had not returned, Barkov had been in a bad mood. The others picked up the pace, knowing that he would be more than happy to use the Cossack whip at his belt.

Now it was Barkov who stopped. He unslung his rifle.

Through the magnification of his telescope, he could see the Americans. They looked like ants, or less than ants. Fleas, perhaps. Insignificant. Too far for serious shooting. But the sound of a gunshot would give them something to think about.

He placed the reticule high above their heads to compensate for the distance, and pulled the trigger.

The message was clear. *Barkov is coming.*

CHAPTER 31

The echo of the distant gunshot rolled across the taiga.

"He is shooting at us!" Inna said, panic in her voice. She started to trot through the snow. Not that it would do her any good if Barkov had them in his sights. There was nowhere to hide.

Cole caught her arm.

"Ain't nothin' to worry about," he said. "He's too far off to hit anything."

Whitlock muttered, "That's just what General Reynolds said at Gettysburg."

Cole snorted. "I reckon my great uncle might

have been the one that shot him. I hear tell that he was a Reb sharpshooter. I think he was a lot closer than Barkov, and a better shot to boot. You would have to be a damn sight unlucky for that Red Sniper to hit you at this distance."

"You ought to take a shot at him," Whitlock said, through chattering teeth. "Give him something to think about."

"Too far," Cole said. "Ain't no point in wastin' a bullet. I only got a few left."

Cole pondered how things had come full circle. He had just spent several months taking part in some of the most brutal fighting that could be imagined across France, Belgium, and Germany. The Germans might have been low on planes, but they always had plenty of ammunition, and so had the Americans. If bullets were seeds, there would have been fields of lead sprouting all across Europe.

Things felt different now, closer to his roots. Cole had grown up in the mountains, during the Great Depression. Rifle and shotgun shells cost hard cash that nobody had, although sometimes his pa traded moonshine for a handful of shells.

There had been times when Cole had just one bullet, and if he missed, it meant that he and his brothers and sisters would go hungry that night. When missing a shot meant nothing to eat, you learned not to miss. You learned not to waste a bullet that you might need later.

Cole wasn't about to waste any bullets on Barkov. When the time came, he only planned on needing one.

Whitlock noticed the way that Cole's weird eyes glittered and involuntarily took a step back. "Now what?" Whitlock asked, startled.

"Now we walk."

• • •

With barely more than a breath of wind, the cold settled over them and seemed to weigh heavily on their movements. The Russians didn't shoot again, but he had made it clear that he was watching—and giving chase.

Cole hoped, at first, that it was some trick of the eye that made the Russians seem to be getting closer, like the way that, when you were hunting in the woods at dusk, a tree stump could seem to take on the shape of a bear. Imagination had gotten the better of more than one hunter. So he looked away from the distant silhouettes of the Russians. He gave it half an hour, timed on one of Vaccaro's wrist watches. Looked again. Definitely closer.

Vaccaro caught him looking. "You thinking what I'm thinking?"

"I reckon they're going to catch us before the day is out. Inna and Whitlock can't go no faster."

"Goddamn." Vaccaro looked again. "You

sure?"

"Well, maybe not catch us, but get in rifle range, which is the same thing."

"Let me guess, Hillbilly. You are planning on doing something about that."

Cole nodded. "It ain't much of a plan at the moment."

"Need some help?"

"I appreciate that, City Boy. But in the end it comes down to me and Barkov."

"God help Barkov."

"Them Russians don't believe in God," Cole pointed out. Cole was a believer, if not a regular church-goer. He appreciated a bit of fire and brimstone preaching to set one's mind right. "They put you in a Gulag if you do."

Cole thought he might have another couple of hours before something needed doing about Barkov, three at most. Maybe they could even stay out ahead of the Russians until dark.

As it turned out, they didn't have nearly that long. They had only been on the move for ten minutes when Inna stepped in a hole and twisted her ankle.

She sat on a rock, grimacing in pain, while Whitlock wrapped the ankle with his leather belt and a scarf. Vaska cut her a sapling to use as a crutch.

"Goddamn," Honaker said, sounding disgusted.

"I am so sorry," Inna said.

"Don't worry about it," Cole said. "It could have happened to any of us."

Their lead over the Russians shrank while they slowed down for Inna, who hobbled across the snowy frozen ground on her makeshift crutch, clearly in pain. It was only a matter of time before Barkov had them in rifle range.

They walked for another hour. Inna did not complain, but she grimaced with each step.

Vaska pointed ahead. "That is Finland."

All that they could see was a blur on the horizon where the open plain met forest, like land glimpsed at sea, but they would take the old Russian's word for it.

The thing was, they weren't going to make it. The border was still a long way off. The Russians were going to catch them before that border came into sight.

Cole thought it over. Time for a change in plans. Time to settle this business with Barkov once and for all.

Cole looked over at Vaccaro. "You ever see one of them western pictures?"

"Cole, you are such a hillbilly. I know for a fact that the first time you saw a western flick was movie night in the Army."

"The one I'm thinking of has a shootout on the street of the town between the sheriff and the outlaw."

"I'll bet you were rooting for the outlaw," Vaccaro said.

"The outlaw gets to wear a black hat in them movies. Who the hell wants to wear a white hat?"

"Why the sudden interest in westerns?"

"In the movie, the sheriff stands in the middle of the street with his gun on his hip, and he waits for the outlaw to come to him."

"This is all very interesting, Cole. I didn't take you for such a movie buff. Maybe you've got a movie projector in your back pocket and you are gonna surprise us all with movie night."

"No, there ain't gonna be no movie night, but sure as shit there is gonna be a shootout."

• • •

Barkov felt happy from his fur cap down to the tips of his felt-lined boots. The sun was out and he turned his face toward it, enjoying the faint warmth. The morning cold was dissipating, but the crisp air made you want to inhale great lungfuls of it. The Americans were almost within his grasp.

He had no illusions that re-capturing the escaped American would do him any good. There would be no medals. He might even find himself tossed into the Gulag. That was life in the Soviet Union for you—one's circumstances changed like the weather. One learned to take both nothing—

and everything—for granted.

The only blot on his good mood was the absence of the Mink. Stopping these Americans was a matter of personal pride. The sniper among them had killed his old friend.

He missed the Mink, who had been the closest thing he had to a friend. But in war, he had learned not to mourn for too long. Some people lived, some people died, some sooner than others.

When he caught up with that American sniper, Barkov planned to flay the skin off him with his whip. It was the least he could do for the Mink.

• • •

Although the sun was out, it offered far less warmth than a 40-watt light bulb. Ahead of Cole stretched the vast Russian plain, flat as a parade ground and wide as the sea. Sometime in the ancient past, glaciers had scraped this plain clean as neatly as a bowling alley built for giants. The few scattered boulders could have been the gutter balls. Now covered in snow, the plain would have made the perfect place to land a B-17 bomber—a whole squadron of them, in fact, and all at once.

There was absolutely no cover, and nowhere to hide. It was one hell of a place to be caught out in the open when a Russian sniper had you in his sights. Just the thought of it made Cole's spine tingle.

Cole saw how it would play out. Their group would still be laboring to get clear of this open place, when the Russians would arrive at the other end. Barkov was a deadly shot. In a place such as this, he could simply pick them off, one at a time.

A lot of what happened next depended on logistics. It was now a game of covering the maximum distance in the shortest amount of time. How far could they get before the Russians started shooting?

"Come on," he said. "We have got to haul ass. Whatever you got left in the tank, now is the time to pour it on."

"This is pointless," Honaker said. "We ought to get into those woods to the east of us. We are sitting ducks out here."

"Then what do you want to do?" Cole asked. "Hide all you want. All the Russians have to do is follow our tracks. No sir, I aim to end this, one way or another."

"What should we do?" Whitlock wanted to know. "Stand and fight?"

"Run," Cole said. "Or as close to running as you can get."

It was easier said than done. The snow tugged at their feet. They were exhausted and hungry. Inna had a painful twisted ankle. Whitlock put her arm across his shoulders and helped her along, just as he had done with Ramsey.

They hurried, gasping with the effort.

At the far end of the glacial bowling alley, the Russians came into sight.

"There they are!" Vaccaro said.

"Leave the packs," Cole said. "If that's Finland up ahead like Vaska says, we'll make the border before dark. No need for blankets or any extra gear."

Honaker opened his mouth as if to argue, but Whitlock was already shrugging off his pack. "What about the weapons?" he asked.

"Keep the guns and ammo," Cole said. "We ain't done with them yet."

They made better time without being loaded down. The Russians were still in sight, but they weren't gaining on them.

"Finland," Vaska said, pointing at a line of forest ahead. It was that close. Literally within sight. The Russians wouldn't pursue them into another country—especially one that was, nominally at least, an ally of the United States. With luck, there would also be a squad of U.S. troops just inside the boundary.

The problem was, they weren't going to make it without falling into rifle range. They were moving too slowly, even without their packs. The pursuing Russians moved just a little faster. Simple math. One way or another, they were going to have to take on the Russians before they reached the relative safety of Finland.

Cole stopped. "This is where I leave you," he said. "Me and Barkov have unfinished business."

"Cole, have you gone crazy?" Vaccaro asked, staring at him. "You can't take on those Russians by yourself."

"I ain't by myself." He hefted his rifle. "I got this. Now go on. I'll catch up if I can. I aim to trade lead with Barkov, so let's see how that works out."

CHAPTER 32

Cole walked out into the empty plain, backtracking through the snow. He scanned the landscape for cover, but there wasn't so much as a rock or a scrap of brush. Sunlight reflected off the snow. The brightness hurt his eyes. He squinted into the distance.

He had been half joking with Vaccaro about Western movies, but this is what it felt like. Like it was high noon on some dusty street. He'd be damned if he was the one wearing the white hat. Cole was black hat all the way.

Once he had put some distance between

himself and the others, he stopped. Shooting from a standing position was never easy, so he looped his arm through the sling just to help balance the weight of the rifle and steady his aim. He put the smooth comb to his cheek, fitting it just under his high cheekbones. The butt fit into the socket just where his arm met his shoulder. Looking through the rifle scope now, everything sprang closer. He could see the Russians coming through the snow.

Finger on the trigger, he waited.

• • •

Barkov squinted into the distance. The Americans were hurrying now, which made sense. Finland was within sight. He could see the difference in the terrain that delineated a national boundary. He turned to the men behind him and snarled, "Faster!"

As the group moved away, he saw a lone object outlined against the snow. He was fairly certain that it had not been there before. Perhaps a tree trunk? A stone marker? That made no sense. Whatever the object was, it gave the impression of rigidity, like a fencepost. Odd, out here in the middle of nowhere.

With his naked eye, he could barely make out anything in the plain ahead. He paused and put his rifle to his shoulder so that he could study the object through the scope.

The optics shrank the distance, although it was still quite far. He could see that the anomaly in the landscape was not a tree, or a fencepost, or a standing stone. It was a man.

Barkov blinked. Pressed his eye closer to the optical lens.

The man held a rifle and stared back at him through his own telescopic sight, like a distant mirror image.

Barkov snatched the rifle from his own eye, as if that would stop the other man from seeing too much of him. They were both too far apart to see real detail about the other.

He knew who it was. The American sniper. The one whom Ramsey had promised would be waiting for him.

A promise kept.

The man stood like a tree, a stump, a stone.

The other Russians sensed that Barkov had stopped and they halted, awaiting his orders.

For once, Barkov had none. It was only him and this American that mattered now. They might have been alone on the taiga.

"He wants me to fight a duel," Barkov said to no one in particular, although he half expected the Mink to answer. Then he remembered that his old companion was dead.

He put the rifle to his shoulder again, dimly aware of the remaining soldiers around him. Two stood, one behind the other, to his right, while Dmitri stood to his left. He knew Dmitri's name, but not those of the two other men. It was enough to call them *you* ... and *you*. That was a habit from the war, when men died so quickly there was no point in bothering to learn what they were called.

Barkov licked his lips and strained to see into the distance.

He considered his options. It was a difficult shot to make from that range using the standing or offhand position. A shooter wanted a gun anchored somehow—using anything from a window ledge to a fallen log was preferable to relying on the steadiness of one's own arms. Lying down was good. Even sitting down, with the rifle propped across one's knees. A marksman needed to connect himself and his rifle to the earth. Bone on stone.

Standing, it was hard to hold a rifle rock steady. At that range, the smallest motion meant that the bullet would miss.

Big and solid as he was, Barkov was more like a human boulder than a fencepost. He raised the rifle to his shoulder, acquired the target, let his breathing—

The sound of the American sniper's rifle echoed across the distance, seconds after the bullet ripped through the two men on Barkov's left.

He lowered his rifle to survey the damage.

Because they had been standing one behind the other, the bullet had punched through the head of the first one and then drilled into the throat of the second man.

The first man had died instantly, but the second was taking his time about it, clutching his throat as he lay in the snow, a big pool of blood spreading around him. Barkov observed the dead and dying man without any particular emotion.

You ... and *you*.

It would have been an impressive shot if it had been intentional. However, Barkov was sure that the American had aimed for him, and missed.

Feeling more confident now, he put the rifle back to his shoulder. He settled the reticule a few inches above the American's head—

This time, he actually *heard* the second shot whip past him on the left, just where Dmitri was standing. He thought that the shot must have killed Dmitri, but a fraction of a second previously, the boy had thrown himself face down in the snow, mittened hands covering his head as if that would offer some protection. That moment of cowardice—or good sense, call it what you will—had saved his life.

That left Barkov alone on the plain. He felt himself grow cold, although there also happened to be a tingling all through him that had nothing to do with the temperature. He recognized the feeling for what it was—fear.

Barkov felt afraid because it had occurred to him that the first shot had not been a miss. It had been very deliberate. Both shots had been fired quickly, at a great distance. The American was picking off Barkov's men. Leaving Barkov for last.

Not if he could help it. *He was Barkov the sniper!* He put the rifle to his shoulder, lined up the reticule again. The American stood there, daring him. It was a long shot, and Barkov was shooting offhand, which was the most difficult position.

He squeezed the trigger.

The rifle fired.

• • •

Cole saw the distant muzzle flash but didn't so much as flinch. He knew there was no way to dodge a bullet.

Instantaneously, Barkov's bullet zipped past his ear like a supersonic bumblebee—the sensation made his whole body thrum like a bow string. *That was close.* Close enough to make his insides feel like jelly.

He pushed every thought and worry from his mind. It had come down to just him and Barkov. He let himself slip deeper into his shooter's trance. His breathing became shallow, and his heart rate slowed. Shooting from the standing position was difficult, and normally his arms might tremble ever so slightly from the strain. Holding an eight-pound rifle steady enough to aim with any precision was harder than one might think. After a few minutes, your arms started to quiver no matter how strong you were. But now it was as if the cold had frozen him into place.

He kept the rifle steady and settled the crosshairs on Barkov. It was a long way off, but he had been lucky in the first two shots. He felt good about three out of three.

There was almost no wind, so Cole placed the crosshairs directly above Barkov's head to account for the drop of the bullet.

Hitting the head was too much to hope for—instead, he was trying for a body shot.

Everything launched into the air eventually fell back to earth, after all—baseballs, footballs, even bullets. They all fell at the same rate, thanks to gravity, but the speed of the object determined how far it traveled before falling to earth. To compensate for the pull of gravity, a marksman aimed above his target when taking a shot. The farther the target was, the higher you aimed.

Given time, Cole could have walked his bullets in. He did not have that option. He had one shot.

He had almost forgotten that his finger was

on the trigger. It nearly surprised him when the rifle fired.

There was a stab of flame, and the cool, still air actually rippled as the hot gases caused by the rapid burning of gunpowder geysered from the muzzle. Traveling at nearly 3,000 feet per second as it left the muzzle, the 152-grain bullet exited the barrel spinning like a drill bit. The still, clear air welcomed the bullet and wrapped itself around it, guiding the projectile like it was on rails. A full second later, the bullet completed its arc and punched through Barkov's rib cage.

● ● ●

One rib attempted to deflect the more than two thousand foot pounds of energy and was snapped in half for its trouble, resulting in splinters of bone joining the bullet as it churned through Barkov's liver. Barkov's body cavity was massive, big as a steamer trunk tipped on its side, and the bullet lost its way and wandered downward, nicking his stomach here, tearing out chunks of bladder and prostate there, before exiting just above the hipbone opposite where it had entered. Having lost its momentum, the bullet tumbled to rest in a snow drift just a few feet away.

Barkov was such a big man that the energy of the bullet did not knock him down, although it would have knocked down most men. He felt no pain at first. Just an odd sensation as if his insides were being stirred with a large metal spoon. He looked down to see where the bullet had gone in, and then reached down to feel for the hole where it had come out.

He even looked behind him and saw the gouge in the snow that the spent bullet had made. Some detached part of his mind thought, "Ah, so that is where it went."

His body was not so detached as his mind, however. The interior of his torso was now a raw stew of torn tissue, blood, bone, bile, and urine. Barkov's knees buckled. He dropped his rifle. He went down.

• • •

Through the scope, Cole watched the Russian collapse.

• • •

The impact put Barkov down. He knew too well that a bullet was a small thing, and yet despite its small mass the slug was moving at supersonic speed that increased its energy exponentially.

How many times had he watched a bullet wreak havoc on someone else?

Now, his own turn had come.

He got to one elbow and coughed up some blood. There was little pain, but only a numbness. Barkov tried to get up, but somehow could not will himself off his hands and knees. His body simply would not obey.

He heard footsteps on the snow behind him, and looked up to see Dmitri trotting past him. The boy paused long enough to snatch the *nagyka* whip from where it was tucked into Barkov's belt. The young fool was running straight for the American.

"Wait! You must help me!" Barkov shouted, but the youth did not stop. Barkov cursed him. "Traitor! Coward!"

Barkov thought that he had shouted the words, but then realized they had only been in his head. His lungs no longer had the volume for shouting.

He looked into the distance, but the American sniper had vanished, like a ghost.

Barkov's body, strong as it was, drifted into shock. He thought he heard shooting far away, but couldn't be sure. Mercifully, he lost consciousness.

• • •

Toward nightfall, Barkov came to his senses again. As he regained consciousness, he was surprised by the simple fact that he was still breathing. In Stalingrad, he had seen men miraculously survive terrible wounds. Maybe he would be one of those lucky ones. He ate some snow and felt better.

The day stretched on toward dusk. In the gathering gloom on the taiga, he caught a glimpse of something moving. Maybe it was that ingrate Dmitri returning to help him, after all. Barkov felt a glimmer of hope. Another shape flicked past in the gloom. Maybe it was another group of soldiers, coming to find him.

Barkov heard something in the snow to his right, and turned painfully toward the sound.

A large gray wolf stood there, head down, studying Barkov with its deep brown eyes. Measuring him.

Barkov cursed at the wolf, and tried to crawl away. His arms worked all right, but he felt like he was dragging a sack of broken crockery that had been dredged in warm lard—the sack being the rest of his body.

The wolf followed in the wake of Barkov's progress. Coming closer.

Panting from the effort, Barkov stopped trying to crawl. He reached for this whip, then remembered that it was no longer there. When the wolf was close enough, he shook a fist at it, driving the animal back.

"Son of a whore!"

The wolf retreated. But then another wolf appeared on its flank, and the first wolf advanced. Barkov couldn't keep an eye on both of them.

Barkov swung his fist again, but his strength was depleted. Propped up on one elbow, he flailed weakly at the wolf.

The two wolves moved closer, growling, jowls curled back from sharp white teeth. He raised his arm to protect himself.

The wolf darted forward and grabbed his arm. The second wolf went for the bloody wound near his hip.

This time, Barkov screamed.

CHAPTER 33

Whitlock and the others spent the rest of the day on the move. Having lost so much weight in the Gulag camp, he couldn't seem to get warm and his teeth chattered constantly, giving him a headache. For Inna, each step was a small agony, but like a good Russian, she did not complain. Honaker and Vaska plodded along silently. Vaccaro bitched enough for everyone else.

From time to time, they looked over their shoulders for Cole, but there was no sign of him. They had heard the rifle shots in the distance, and then nothing but the Russian wind and the squeak of snow under their boots. The silence revealed nothing about Cole's fate.

The sun was low and shadows stretched toward the horizon when they spotted the rescue party waiting for them at the Finnish border. Two Jeeps and what looked like six men. Through his rifle scope, Vaccaro saw that they were clearly Americans. They were all armed, weapons ready, as if they knew the Russians were just out of sight.

"I'll be damned," Vaccaro said, lowering his rifle. "There's a sight for sore eyes."

"I can't believe it," Whitlock said. "We made it!"

Inna made a happy sound.

They picked up the pace, all of them trotting now. Inna was limping as she ran, but she didn't let that stop her. After days spent crossing the taiga, having run out of food—having fought off wolves, for God's sake—it was hard not to be thrilled at the sight of the rescue party. Only Honaker lagged behind, bringing up the rear.

Nobody noticed when he stopped and leveled his rifle at their backs.

"Hold it right there," he said.

Something in the tone of voice stopped them in their tracks. They whirled around to see Honaker with his weapon aiming at them.

"Honaker, what the hell?" Vaccaro demanded.

"We can do this the easy way, or we can do

this the hard way," Honaker said, keeping the rifle pointed at them.

"Jesus, Honaker, we're almost there. What the hell are you doing? We made it!"

"Is that what you think? That you made it? Drop your rifle, Vaccaro. Put your hands on your head. All of you."

They had no choice. They did as they were told.

"What the hell is this about?" Vaccaro demanded. "What are you, some kind of Russian agent?"

The rifle didn't waver. The four of them weren't spread very far apart, so that Honaker covered them all easily with the weapon. "You don't get it, do you? Bring our boys home! It sounds good, but it's not that simple. Far from it. Nobody can let Whitlock here go back and tell the American public that the Russians are holding some of our men prisoner. The Russians are supposed to be our allies. How do you think that will make President Truman look?"

"Honaker, this is insane. Why did we go on this mission in the first place if we weren't supposed to bring anyone home?"

"You can thank Senator Whitlock for that. The old man has clout. There was no stopping him. It was strictly a back channel operation. He was going to send somebody to spring his precious grandson from the Gulag camp no matter what, so I went along as insurance, just in case we actually made it."

"Why did we cross all this territory? Why did you let us get this far?"

"You weren't supposed to. Hell, I even cut the oil lines in the C-47 that flew us here, but the damn thing made it on one engine. If it hadn't been for that goddamn Cole, you never would have made it this far. I could never seem to get the drop on him. That hillbilly has eyes in the back of his head. With any luck, Barkov is finishing him off right about now."

"Honaker, this is insane!"

"No, what's insane is the fact that you made it this far." Honaker turned the rifle on Inna. "If it hadn't been for this Russian bitch springing her lover boy in the first place, I doubt we would have made it out of the village."

Vaccaro shook his head, puzzled. "But what about you? If we didn't make it, you sure weren't going to."

"Some things are bigger than me or you, Vaccaro. It didn't really matter if I made it out or not, so long as nobody else did."

Whitlock spoke up. "I don't believe you, Honaker. I'll bet you had some kind of deal going with the Russians, you and whoever is behind this in the U.S. Government. You're a coward at heart. Anyone can see that. You were going to get out of this somehow. The lone survivor."

Honaker gave a wry smile and shrugged. "Do you really want to call the man pointing a rifle at you a coward? You might be right, though, about the escape clause. It wouldn't be so bad for me if it worked out that way. With any luck, that's just how it's going to play out, with me as the lone survivor."

Both Whitlock and Vaccaro had their eyes locked on the muzzle of the rifle, which looked big as a cannon and black as death. The rifle never moved. Honaker's gaze never left them.

Inna had started crying when Honaker made his explanation. She pulled off her mittens to wipe her eyes. Now she was wracked by big sobs, her arms crossed across her chest. She seemed to fold up on herself, squatting in the snow, all the resilience that she had shown over the last few hours evaporating.

Honaker said in a taunting voice, "Don't worry, honey. I'll make it fast. You won't feel a thing. Who do you want me to shoot first, you or your lover boy?"

Inna sobbed harder. Honaker gave a little laugh, as if he found it all amusing.

Whitlock spread his arms in a supplicating gesture. "Please. You can at least let her go. She's Russian, after all."

"No chance," Honaker said. "I'm real sorry about this." He put the rifle to his shoulder to aim it.

Whitlock said, "Honaker, if it's money you want—"

Inna was still on her knees, sobbing. Distracted by Whitlock, Honaker didn't see her right hand come up, quick and fast. She held the small pistol she had kept tucked in her boot. *Pop*. The noise of the gun was almost absurdly small. A slug smaller than a pencil eraser hit Honaker in the chest and he stared down in surprise at the bullet wound. The hold was no bigger than if he had been poked with a knitting needle. Didn't even hurt. He was too startled to react.

Inna stood and took a step toward him, keeping the pistol level. *Pop*. Another slug hit Honaker. She moved forward again. *Pop*. *Pop*.

The tiny soft-nosed slugs didn't have much energy, but they still tumbled through his chest cavity like rolling dice, flattening out as they went. He suddenly found it hard to breathe. Honaker dropped the rifle and clawed at his chest.

Inna kept coming at him. Honaker seemed to remember the pistol in the holster on his belt. The tiny slugs had torn him up, but hadn't killed him yet. He fumbled for the big .45 to put Inna down.

Inna was so close now that the muzzle of the tiny gun was practically touching him. Honaker kept his eyes on her as he went for his pistol. Inna fired her last shot. *Pop*. The slug hit him just above his right eyebrow. It made a tiny hole going in, like a fly had landed on his forehead. The mushrooming slug emerged out the back of his skull, spilling bits of brain across the snow like overcooked gray-green scrambled eggs.

Honaker's knees buckled and he went down like a rag doll. Just a few seconds had elapsed from Inna's first shot. It hadn't been enough time for anyone else to react.

"Sweet Jesus," Vaccaro said.

Inna stood there, gun down at her side, any trace of her crocodile tears gone. She looked deflated, but not all sorry.

Finally, Whitlock touched her shoulder. "Come on, Inna. You did the right thing. It was him or us. Now, let's get out of Russia. There's our ride home, just waiting for us."

They turned and started walking toward the Americans on the Finnish border. As they walked closer they could see that the soldiers still had their weapons raised, as if expecting trouble. Vaccaro glanced over his shoulder. Nobody there —if you didn't count Honaker's carcass.

"Those guys sure are edgy," he said. "I wonder —"

That's when the Americans opened fire.

• • •

Cole heard the shooting in the distance and

started running in that direction. It sounded as if his friends had run into serious trouble. The snow, up to his knees in places, weighed down every footstep. He willed his legs to move faster. Who was shooting? Why? Had another group of Russians somehow gotten ahead of them to cut off their escape? Maybe there was some kind of patrol at the border. None of it made any sense.

Just run, goddamnit, he ordered himself.

He trotted out of the valley where he had confronted Barkov and ran up a hill at the end, ignoring his ragged breathing as he dodged boulders and shrubs on the way up. At the top he looked down and saw the skirmish taking place.

Closer to him, he could see his companions taking shelter behind a rock. Two bodies lay in the snow, sprawled in a way that Cole was all too familiar with. *Dead*. He thought one of the bodies might be Vaska's. The other body, which lay a little ways off, was harder to identify.

He got down in a crouch so that he wasn't outlined against the sky. He put the rifle to his shoulder and looked through the scope. The others were caught out in the open, trying to use a rock and a half-assed bush for cover. Vaccaro was behind the rock, returning fire. Whitlock had found a rifle and was shooting back, but it was likely he couldn't shoot worth a damn, considering that he was a pilot, of all things. Inna crouched behind the bush, hands over her ears, trying to make herself as small as possible. Bullets plucked at the snow around them.

Vaccaro, Whitlock, and Inna. That meant the two dead men were Vaska and Honaker.

Cole moved the scope to focus on their attackers. Seven men—an eighth soldier lay face down in the snow. Probably Vaccaro's handiwork. The soldiers were clearly Americans, driving Jeeps with the big white star on the hood. Those were U.S. Army uniforms. *Our boys. So why the hell were they shooting at us?* Maybe they had somehow mistaken the rescue team for Russians, although that seemed unlikely.

He put the scope closer to his eye, straining to make out any detail. He was shocked that he recognized one of the attackers. Major Dickey. Dickey would sure as hell be expecting Senator Whitlock's grandson. He had been the one who recruited Cole, after all. He had set up the whole damn mission. Through the scope, Cole watched Dickey pop off a few shots from his sidearm. None of them had seen Cole up on the hill.

Cole's thoughts raced. What the hell was going on here? Unless Dickey was seriously blind, he would have recognized the other Americans. He was the one who had sent them out here. Yet he was here waiting for them. Waiting to ambush them.

It could only mean that he didn't want them to cross that border into Finland.

Cole was done thinking about it. There wasn't *any* good reason for Dickey to be leading this trigger happy welcoming committee. Cole wasn't going to sit up here on this hill and watch Vaccaro and the others get shot.

The crest of the hill made an ideal shooting position. He felt kind of exposed, but overall he couldn't have asked for a better vantage point. Cole lay down in the snow, splayed his legs out behind him, got his elbows settled deep into the snow, and put the rifle between a couple of rocks that gave him at least some protection. The sinking sun was at his back, so that was to his advantage.

As he settled into position, he realized that his heart was pounding. No wonder. First, the encounter with Barkov had poured about a pint of adrenalin into his system. Then the run up hill through the snow toward the sound of the shooting had left him winded. The crosshairs danced around more than he would have liked. *Got to cut out them cigarettes,* he thought.

He took a couple of deep breaths. Getting some oxygen back into his system. Cole felt his heart slowing. He had gotten so that he could almost will his heart muscle to beat more slowly, in the same way that you could clench or unclench a hand. His breathing smoothed out. This time, when he put the crosshairs on a soldier's head, they didn't dance at all.

It was just over two hundred yards. An easy shot. He pulled the trigger nice and smooth. The soldier went down.

Cole worked the bolt, picked another target. Fired.

Target. Fire. Target. Fire. Target. Fire.

Four down. Cole picked them off like birds on a wire. He tried not to think about the fact that he was shooting Americans. Right now, they were the enemy.

Their attackers couldn't figure out where the shots were coming from. Cole's attack had taken the wind out of their sails, that was for damn sure. Major Dickey started to get that panicked look that Cole had seen on more than a few faces in the last few months—usually German faces. Through the scope, Cole saw him say something to one of the shooters, who put down his rifle and got behind the wheel of one of the Jeeps, leaving the other Jeep. The two remaining men saw what was happening and climbed aboard. They got the Jeep turned around. Dickey and his boys weren't planning to stick around and get shot, now that the tables had turned.

Cole stopped shooting.

The Jeep tore off through the snow, hopping and skidding like a jack rabbit on the slick track. He tracked its progress up the unpaved, snow-covered path, and then the Jeep went around a bend and disappeared.

He watched the Jeep drive away, and then checked his rifle. He hadn't planned on a firefight and was down to his last couple of rounds. Not good. But the border was just ahead. Hopefully, no more shooting would be involved in reaching it.

He looked down again at Vaccaro, Whitlock, and Inna. They seemed to have made it through unscathed.

Was it his imagination, or did he hear the whine of a truck engine in the distance? He shrugged it off, thinking that it was just the Jeep making its getaway, or maybe the ringing in his ears. Cole started down the hill toward the others.

CHAPTER 34

Down below, what was left of the team watched Cole approach. His arrival wasn't exactly graceful. The slope was steep and the snow was slick. Once Cole got going, he half slid down, dodging boulders as he went, trying to keep the rifle out of the snow. Somehow, he got to the bottom without falling on his face—or on his ass, for that matter.

Over to the west, the sun sank lower through a layer of clouds that resembled the scales of a fish belly. Cole knew that the high, thin clouds promised good weather.

It was plain that Vaska and Honaker had seen their last sunset. Cole looked down at Vaska's body. The Russian had been a compact, sturdy man, and now he made a compact, sturdy corpse. Courtesy of the welcoming committee, a bullet had caught him through the neck, so Vaska wouldn't have suffered long. Looking down at the body, Cole felt a pang of regret. He had liked the old man. He reached down and pushed Vaska's eyelids closed.

He walked over to Honaker, whose body lay several yards away. There hadn't been any love lost between him and Honaker, but that didn't mean he was pleased to see him dead.

Cole looked more closely at Honaker's body. He had been shot multiple times by a small caliber weapon. He knew that Inna had a gun like that. He looked toward the others, puzzled.

"Somebody want to tell me what happened?"

"Honaker was some kind of double agent," Vaccaro said, shaking his head. He filled Cole in on what had happened.

When Vaccaro finished, Cole said: "You know what? I never liked that son of a bitch. You all right, Inna?"

"Yes." Her voice, sounding as if it had come from a long way off, was not convincing. Cole knew it was not an easy thing to take someone's life, even when he deserved it. Killing another human being for the first time, up close, sent your head down a slope even more slippery than the one Cole had just navigated. She seemed all right for now, though shaken. It would bother her later when she woke up in the depths of the night. Cole knew about that.

"You done the right thing," he said. "It was him or you, from the sounds of it."

"Shouldn't we bury them?" Whitlock asked.

Cole shook his head. He thought that Harry Whitlock was ever the Boy Scout, trying to do the decent thing. "There's no time," he said. "Vaska would understand. Honaker, well, to hell with him."

"What happened to Barkov?" Vaccaro wanted to know.

"I reckon that what's left of him is gonna get shit out by a wolf come tomorrow morning."

Inna gave a gasp of surprise and pointed toward the slope that Cole had just come down. A lone figure was slipping and sliding toward them. They could see it was a Russian soldier. He reached the bottom and starting running awkwardly toward them through the snow. He wasn't carrying any weapons.

"What the hell," Vaccaro said. "Looks like you didn't get them all, Cole. You're slipping."

Cole raised his rifle. "I can fix that."

"No!" Inna shouted. "I think I know him."

Cole kept the crosshairs on the Russian soldier's chest, just in case there was any funny business. The Russian raised his arms as he got closer. Through the scope, Cole could see that the soldier was still mostly a boy. The look of exhaustion on his young face was clear. He had some bruises across his cheekbones. This kid had taken a beating—more than one, from the looks of it. One thing for sure, he wasn't looking for a fight.

Cole lowered the rifle but kept it pointed in the Russian's direction. He kept his finger on the trigger. He hadn't lived this long by being trusting.

Cole didn't speak Russian, but he understood the first words out of the young soldier's mouth well enough.

"Inna Mikhaylovna!"

Cole, Whitlock, and Vaccaro looked at her in surprise. "You know him?" Whitlock asked.

Inna sighed. "This is Dmitri. He is the stupid boy I tricked into leaving his post at the Gulag gate."

"Then I reckon we owe him one." Cole lowered the rifle. He had a soft spot in his heart for idiots and fools. Not everybody was meant to be a soldier. Some were made to fight, against their nature. He thought of his boot camp buddy, Jimmy Turner, killed within minutes of landing at Omaha Beach on D-Day. Jimmy had been a lot like this young Russian, who wasn't cut out to be a soldier any more than Jimmy had been.

The Russian didn't have a gun, but he was carrying a kind of whip. He stepped forward and offered it to Inna, who shook her head emphatically, as if the thing were toxic. Whitlock took it from him.

"What is that?" Cole wanted to know.

"This was Barkov's. I hoped I would never see it again. If he has the whip, it means Barkov is dead."

"I reckon it's yours now."

They kept on toward the Finish border. Cole made Dmitri walk out in front, where he could keep an eye on him.

"How did you trick him?" Harry asked Inna. It wasn't much of a question, considering that Dmitri's puppy eyes told the whole story. It was clear that a gumdrop was sharper than the Russian.

"I made him think that I was going to sleep with him," Inna admitted, turning red. She had just crossed the taiga and shot a traitor, but confessing that she had flirted with Dmitri made her blush. "I got him to take off his clothes, and then I stole his key to the gate that you went through, and locked him in a room."

"Why, Miss Inna," Cole said. "You are full of surprises, ain't you?"

"Poor kid," Whitlock said. He laughed. "He never had a chance against you. He would've unlocked the whole damn Gulag for you."

Whitlock's laughter had just faded when they heard a new sound in the air.

Cole held up a hand. "Hush now, everybody."

They all listened, straining to hear. Then came the grind and grumble of vehicle engines.

Cole saw them first. Three Russian trucks, heading in their direction.

• • •

"Run!"

The Russians hadn't spotted them yet, but they had to get under cover. They had held off a squad of American assassins, but there was no way they could take on three truckloads of Russian troops. Desperately, Cole looked around. To their left was a patch of scraggly trees—not much cover, but at least it was something.

Dmitri stood there, looking kind of stunned. Like he wasn't sure if he wanted to wait around for the Russians or not. Cole grabbed him by the collar and shoved him in the direction of the trees. From what he had seen of the Russian army, he was sure the boy's execution would be swift, whether it was for desertion or consorting with the enemy or whatever else they decided was worth killing him over. There was no doubt they would shoot him.

Hidden among the trees, they watched the Russians arrive and swarm out of the trucks.

They began to search the area. They were doing a sloppy job of it, with everybody running every which way. Fortunately for the Americans, it was not ideal ground for following tracks. Thin blades of brown grass thrust up through the crusted snow, breaking up the outline of any tracks they had left.

"These guys don't look like experts," Vaccaro muttered. "Look at their uniforms. Still nice and clean. New recruits, maybe."

"Even a blind squirrel finds a nut now and then," Cole said. "We got to git."

Easier said than done. The trees reached toward where the Russians had left their trucks, but then what? It was basically a wide-open plain.

The Russian officers devoted most of their attention to the abandoned American Jeep. The existence of the border did not seem to inhibit them. There was no one around to enforce the boundary. There was a whole lot of nothing. The officers took their time poking through the Jeep. The soldiers took watches and weapons off the dead Americans.

Cole thought about it. There must be a Russian military base nearby. He guessed that the Russians had heard the shooting and sent a squad to investigate. It was hard to say if they were in cahoots with Major Dickey and Honaker, but if not, the shooting in their backyard would surely have gotten their attention.

Cole and the others were now stuck here, with a couple dozen Russians looking for them, and getting closer. It was only a matter of time before someone found their tracks and started toward the trees.

"Out of the frying pan, and into the fire," Cole said.

Vaccaro shifted his rifle to his shoulder. "We can take them by surprise, and at least get a few of them."

Cole touched his shoulder. "And then what? All they've got to do is turn those machine guns on us at that range and we're hamburger. No, I reckon I got a better idea." He turned to Inna. "Tell that kid to get his clothes off. Then I need you to put on his uniform."

Quickly, he explained what he had in mind. Inna nodded, turning even paler. It was risky.

She rattled off her instructions to Dmitri, who looked at her blankly until she hissed something that must have been the Russian equivalent of saying, "Now!"

Dmitri hopped to it. In half a minute he was shivering in the snow in nothing but his long underwear.

The uniform was big enough and baggy enough for Inna to tug on the trousers and coat over her own clothes. She topped it off with Dmitri's *ushanka* hat. The uniform wasn't going to pass a parade ground inspection, but it might be enough to give them all a second chance.

Inna nodded at them, then stood up straight and composed herself. She walked out of the woods and straight toward the nearest truck, struggling to disguise her limp. Cole had coached her to stay calm. Their lives depended on it.

One of the truck drivers had stayed behind, leaning against a truck and smoking a cigarette. He was a heavyset older guy who had the look of someone who was better with a wrench than a gun. Inna walked right up to him and bummed a cigarette. They chatted for a moment, and the truck driver laughed at something she said. Then she walked back and climbed behind the wheel of the truck.

Cole was impressed. "Damn, that girl has moxie."

"She broke me out of the Gulag, didn't she?" Whitlock pointed out.

Now, it was their turn to show some of that same moxie. They moved out of the woods toward the truck, forcing themselves to walk. Running would only attract attention. They had to cross a hundred feet of open ground. The truck driver Inna had spoken to was blocked from view by the angle of the truck, but they were clearly visible to the search party, if any of them cared to look.

Cole kept a nervous eye on the Russians, his rifle ready to fire. The Russians were still busy over at the Jeep. One of the officers must have found something; a knot of men was gathered around him, looking at what appeared to be a map.

Fifty feet to go. Someone shouted, and Cole's finger tensed on the trigger. But it was only one of the officers, pointing up the road that the escaping Jeep had taken. Maybe he wanted someone to go that way. The Russians kept their heads turned in that direction.

The truck started. The motor sounded rough, more like a tractor than a truck.

Cole held his breath as first Dmitri, then Whitlock and Vaccaro, climbed in the back. He took one last quick look around and got in. To his surprise, the interior looked much like every other army truck that he had ridden in: canvas top, wood sides, rough wood benches. Then again, it was an American vehicle, a Studebaker sent to Stalin to help them beat the Nazis. Cole shook his head. The U.S. government must have been run by fools to have given the Russians equipment that could be turned against it now that the shooting war was over.

Whitlock pounded twice on the back of the cab with his fist, alerting Inna that they were ready, and the truck lurched forward.

Cole realized that he had taken it for granted that Inna could drive a truck. He was impressed. What couldn't that woman do? The vehicle lurched and bounced along the track that had brought the Russians from their base. Once they were out of sight, Inna stopped the truck and Cole jumped down and got into the cab.

"You done good," he told her. "What did you tell that driver back there?"

"I said the radio was down and the captain wanted me to go back and get more men to help find the Americans."

"Huh. I guess that got a laugh out of him."

Inna grinned. "He cracked up when I told him the captain couldn't find his *zhopa* with both hands."

CHAPTER 35

With its deep ruts and rocks, the route they were following more closely resembled a roughly plowed field than a road. They bounced wildly. Whenever Inna tried to drive faster, the bucking truck wrenched the wheel out of her hands. She slowed to a crawl.

"Now what?" she asked.

"Keep going," he said. "Let's put some distance between us and that patrol."

They heard the whine of an airplane. A Russian fighter plane raced across the sky. The plane didn't seem to be interested in them. The pilot wouldn't be looking for a Russian truck. He would have his eyes open for anything that was clearly *not* Russian.

This was the first plane they had seen since jumping out of one over Vologda. It must be that here, near the border, there were air patrols. Cole doubted that they would get far on foot with a plane searching the landscape.

He was mulling that over when the truck went around a sharp bend in the road where it skirted an outcropping of boulders. Coming the other way was a Jeep—a genuine American Jeep —but this one was painted with Russian insignia. More goods from America to help them beat the Nazis.

The Jeep was blocking the narrow road. Inna had no choice but to stop the truck. Cole caught a glimpse of an officer who got out of the Jeep and approached. He had a purposeful stride, but he didn't have a weapon in his hand. Cole hunkered down in the footwell of the truck, keeping his rifle pointed above Inna's legs at the driver's side door.

The officer yammered something in Russian, and Inna yammered back. The exchange sounded calm enough, although it was hard to tell because everything in Russian seemed to be shouted. German sounded angry; Russian sounded loud. He heard the officer walking away and relaxed his finger on the trigger.

Then Inna grabbed the wheel and stared straight ahead. Cole chanced a peek over the dash and saw the officer get back in the Jeep. The vehicle struggled to turn around in the slick tire tracks and then started back the way it had come. The officer gave the truck a "follow me" wave that needed no translation. On the back of the Jeep a large machine gun was mounted, with a couple of soldiers up there with it, hanging on for dear life. They weren't aiming at the truck, but it would take them about ten seconds to swivel that gun around and turn the truck into scrap metal.

"What's going on?" Cole asked from the footwell.

"I told him that the radio wasn't working, so I was sent back to bring more men. He ordered me to follow him back to the base. He said he would get this truck loaded and then go with me personally."

"Damn. We don't need that kind of company right now. And we sure as hell don't need to drive into the Russian base."

"What should we do?" Inna wondered, hanging onto the steering wheel as the truck dipped into a rut and bounced back up.

"Ain't got no choice," Cole said, thinking about that machine gun up ahead. "We follow them and figure something out."

Inna leaned toward the windshield and

muttered something that sounded like a Russian curse. "You had better figure it out fast, Cole," she said. "I can see that base up ahead."

• • •

With the Jeep leading the way, no one challenged the truck. Cole was looking around, his eyes just above the metal dashboard. The guards opened the gate wide. It was a monstrous affair hammered together out of rough-cut lumber and barbed wire. It was more like a Gulag gate than the Gulag's had been. He wondered if it was to keep enemies out or to keep the soldiers in.

The base resembled a slushy barnyard. The open ground between the low metal barracks was a morass of muddy snow. Dirty smoke from metal chimneys stained the sky. Beyond the huts was an airfield with a few planes parked around. Over the truck exhaust he could smell some kind of sour food cooking, like maybe cabbage or potatoes. Even so, his stomach churned—it had been too long since Cole and the others had eaten anything besides a handful of jerky, a couple bites of rabbit, and some snow.

Up ahead, the officer jumped down from the Jeep and began barking orders. Soldiers started to scramble. His arrival was creating some confusion, which Cole thought could work in their favor.

"Cole? What should I do?"

"Don't stop here. Pull up next to that building over there, as close as you can."

Inna steered toward a larger Quonset hut-style building, made of corrugated metal. Tires and fuel cans were stacked up outside. This must be a shop to fix the trucks after they got beat to hell driving on what passed for a road.

The officer was so busy organizing the second wave of men for the search party that he didn't pay Inna's parking job any mind. Soldiers were falling in, still pulling on their uniforms and gear. Any minute now, they were going to head over to the truck and climb in. Trouble was, Vaccaro, Dmitri, and Whitlock were still back there.

"Slide out of the truck on my side, so that you're between the truck and the building," Cole said. "Out of sight, out of mind. I'll go first."

Cole got out and slung his rifle. The Springfield wasn't going to do him much good here. No way was he going to shoot his way out of a Russian military base. He unsheathed the big hunting knife, which would be the best way to deal with any curious Russians. They went around to the back of the truck and waved the others out.

"I think this truck has square wheels," Vaccaro said. He winced as his feet hit the ground. "That was a helluva ride. Kinda like being inside a popcorn machine."

"I hate to tell you this, but getting in here was the easy part," Cole said. "Take a look around, City Boy. There's no way to walk out of this place."

They hid among the stacks of tires and fuel cans in the maintenance area. That was all well and good until someone came looking for a spare tire. Dmitri was still in his long underwear, which would have been comical if they hadn't been surrounded by Russian soldiers. The kid's eyes darted from the Americans to the Russians, as if weighing his chances with one side or the other. Then he seemed to resign himself to staying where he was. The kid wasn't so dumb—the Russians might keep the Americans alive as bargaining chips of some kind, but Dmitri wasn't any sort of bargaining chip. He would get used for target practice.

The Russians would shoot Inna, too.

Dmitri looked at Cole. Inna, Vaccaro, and Whitlock looked at Cole. Cole wished there was somebody he could look at. He had gotten them this far. But he was out of ideas.

Just this morning, the day had seemed full of promise. The border with Finland was in sight. They had thought that their journey was just about over. Then Barkov had come into sight. Honaker had turned out to be some kind of communist traitor. No, the rest of the day hadn't gone so well.

Now, they had ended up even farther away from the border. They were surrounded by Russian troops. Vaska and Honaker were dead. A squad of Americans had attacked them for some unknown reason. The only good news was that that bastard Barkov was wolf chow.

Over by the gate, the Russian troops were just about organized. Any minute now, they were going to be heading over to the truck, to load up. He and the others wouldn't be able to stay hidden for long.

"Now what?" Vaccaro whispered, sounding desperate.

Cole gripped his rifle until his knuckles showed white, but meanwhile his mind was scratching and clawing like a cornered animal, trying to come up with something, anything. When it came to tight spots, he preferred the kind that you could shoot your way out of.

He looked around for some escape route. Ruled out hijacking a Jeep or truck. How far could they get trying to cross this landscape? On foot, that plane would spot them. The plane had looked like a fighter, which meant machine guns. Bombs.

Plane. He glanced again toward the airfield. Not so much activity down there. However, there were a handful of assorted planes grouped around the makeshift runway.

He had an idea. Glancing at Vaccaro, he said, "How's your back?"

"What?"

Cole thought about it. The problem was, the airfield was a couple hundred yards away. Everybody else on the base was in uniform. Cole and Vaccaro had on civilian clothes. Dmitri was in his long johns. They all stood out like moonshiners at a Bible meeting. What they needed was camouflage.

"Vaccaro, you grab one of those boxes over there," he said. "You too, Miss Inna."

"What is in it?" Inna asked.

"Don't matter. Grab it. Tell Dmitri to grab that other box. Me and Whitlock are gonna roll tires."

"What the hell, Cole," Vaccaro complained. "Are we supposed to do some work while we're here? Maybe straighten the place up for the Ruskies?"

"I told you there was no way we could just walk out of here, but maybe I was wrong. Whitlock, do you reckon you can fly one of them Russian planes?"

Whitlock grinned. "Does an angel have wings?"

Cole grabbed a tire. "All right, then. Let's get out of here."

CHAPTER 36

It was a universal fact of military hierarchy that nobody paid any attention to maintenance personnel on a base. It didn't matter if you were in the American, British, Russian, or German military, it was a given that these personnel were anonymous. The guy fixing the trucks and planes never got the glory. He didn't even carry a weapon. You didn't have to salute him. Officers you had to watch out for. Maintenance guys, on the other hand, could be safely ignored.

Perfect camouflage, to Cole's way of thinking. Cole was leading the way, rolling his tire through the slush toward the airfield. Inna, Vaccaro, and Dmitri followed, carrying their boxes. Then came Whitlock, rolling his tire.

All around them, soldiers ran by, scrambling toward the trucks. The whole damn base was mobilizing. Most of the Russian troops looked no older than Dmitri and they wore new uniforms. New recruits. They were too confused to even give Cole a second look. Like a typical officer, the Russian who had met them on the road seemed to have decided that there was no point in making do with one truckload of reinforcements, not when he could round up several truckloads of troops and make the whole operation seem more important. The entire base now resembled an ant nest that someone had poked a stick into.

They might have made it without any trouble if it hadn't been for Dmitri's long johns.

An officer went by and Cole kept his head down. At first, the officer didn't seem to notice Cole or the others. Then he slowed his pace and gave Cole a hard look, like the boss man on a road gang, before moving on. Cole tilted his head so that he could watch the officer out of the corner of his eye.

The officer stopped. Turned. Stared hard at the soldier wearing only long johns.

Setting his mouth in a grim line, he started toward Dmitri. He clearly seemed to be thinking that discipline had gotten too lax, even for the maintenance crew. He put his hand on the holster flap.

"Keep going," Cole muttered to Inna behind him.

He rolled his tire to one side, staying bent over it, still keeping his head down.

The officer approached, shouting something in Russian. He didn't sound happy. His hand was on his pistol, but he hadn't drawn it yet, which was a good thing—the Russians seemed to have a penchant for shooting soldiers over the smallest infraction.

Cole didn't let him get that far. He straightened up and turned into the officer to block his path. Dropped the box and got up close and personal. Now the officer seemed to sense that something was going on out of the ordinary. This time, he *did* start to draw the pistol.

Cole used his left hand to grab the Russian's wrist, preventing the gun from leaving the holster. With his right hand, he drew his hunting knife and plunged the blade into the Russian's throat. He hit him as hard as he had ever hit anything ever before. The blade sharpened on both sides at the tip so that it speared through the gristle and muscle. Cole put all his weight behind it, and the blade stopped only when the tip struck the vertebrae in the back of the Russian's neck. It was a horrible sensation, and Cole felt sickened as he wrenched the knife free.

The Russian wanted to shout, but couldn't. His voice box was destroyed. He sank to his knees, his hands at his throat, making wet gargling noises, dying.

"Go!" Cole shouted.

They dropped their tires and boxes, and ran the rest of the way to the airfield. In the confusion, none of the Soviet troops had noticed the attack on the officer. Not yet, anyhow. Cole figured they had a minute or two at most to catch a plane.

At that moment, Cole realized he hadn't thought something through, which was the fact that they would need a plane large enough to carry them all. There wasn't much to choose from. Cole saw a couple of smaller reconnaissance planes that appeared to be two-seaters, and three sleek fighters.

"This one!" Whitlock had anticipated the same problem, and was pointing at the largest plane on the airfield.

None of the other planes was big enough for them all, except for this airplane, which appeared to be some sort of cargo hauler. It probably flew in medical supplies, mail, and the commandant's weekly vodka ration.

On closer inspection of the plane, Cole's heart sank.

The plane looked flimsy, like it had been made out of old beer cans hammered flat and riveted together by the guy who'd been drinking the beer. Some of the finer work might have been done when the guy was hung over on Monday morning.

"I've never seen a plane that looked like it already crashed before it took off," Vaccaro said. "You sure about this?"

"It's this or back to the Gulag," Cole said. "Whitlock, you reckon you can fly this crate?"

"I can fly it," he said. "The question is, *will* it fly?" He ran to pull away the wheel chocks.

Cole cast a quick glance toward where the officer's body lay, leaking a pool of blood into the trampled snow. They didn't have long. "You all had best get in."

"What about you?"

"I'll be right back."

The others piled into the plane. When a cargo plane like this was on the ground, sitting on the third wheel in the tail, the floor was sharply sloped. Whitlock climbed toward the cockpit and the others scrambled to the rough seats that pulled down from the sides. The only windows were in the cockpit. The bare interior was cold and dark, and smelled heavily of oil and gasoline, with an underlying funk of spoiled potatoes.

It did indeed feel like being inside a beer can, with aluminum walls exactly that thin. A burst from a machine gun would cut the metal skin and everyone inside to shreds. The cargo plane didn't have any sort of guns itself. Totally defenseless.

Cole was running across the airstrip, his knife in one hand. The blade was still red with the Russian officer's blood. He reached the nearest fighter plane and jabbed the blade into the tires. Then he ran to the next plane. And the next. He didn't bother with the spotter planes. He was out of time.

Still, no one had taken any notice of what was going on at the airfield. He raced back toward their own plane and climbed in, pulling the hatch shut after him.

"Go!" he shouted.

Whitlock was flicking toggle switches and adjusting levers. "There's no time to do any kind of flight check, so we'll just have to pray that this crate flies," he shouted from the cockpit. "I hope to hell this thing is fueled up. I'll need to figure out what the fuel gauge even looks like."

Cole said, "Just get this thing in the air. There's no time to get fancy."

"I wouldn't call making sure that there's gas in the tank being fancy," Whitlock snapped. "It would be helpful if these goddamn instruments were in English. Or German, for that matter."

Cole raised an eyebrow. It was the first time he had heard Harry Whitlock swear.

"I reckon that's where Miss Inna can help us out."

They called Inna into the cramped cockpit,

and she walked Harry through the instrumentation and controls. What wasn't labeled, Harry guessed at. The entire procedure took about two minutes, which was thirty seconds more than they had. Looking out the cockpit window, Cole saw soldiers grouped around the officer's body. More soldiers moved toward the airfield, weapons at the ready. One tall fellow wearing a furry *ushanka* looked right at the plane and must have seen movement in the cockpit. He pointed.

Soldiers started running toward the airfield.

"Got to go," Cole said.

"Keep your fingers crossed."

Whitlock hit some switches, and the engines cranked to life. As soon as they were roaring, Whitlock taxied toward the runway. The soldiers in front of them scattered. So far, nobody was shooting at them. The Russians hadn't figured out what was going on.

"So far, so good," Cole said.

"You'd better go strap yourself in," Whitlock said. "You too, Inna. Things could get bumpy."

Cole and Inna didn't have to be told twice. They scrambled back and buckled themselves into the uncomfortable seats. Although he couldn't see out, the thin airplane walls made him feel like a sitting duck.

The plane gathered speed, bumping down the rough runway. The plane began to lift off.

That's when a burst of fire stitched holes in the aluminum skin. Cole guess it was what the Russians nicknamed a *Pe-pe-sha*, or PPSh-41 submachine gun. Ugly and deadly. He had spotted a few on the base. The plane was too loud to hear the chatter of the gun, but the new whistle of cold air through the holes was clear enough.

Then they were airborne, climbing into the Russian sky. Cole's ears ached and he tried to swallow to relieve the pressure, but his mouth was too dry. It took him another couple of tries before his ears popped. Whitlock climbed at a steep angle, trying to put a lot of air between the plane and the ground fire. The cargo plane was no sprinter, but it still managed to climb to ten thousand feet within half a minute.

When the plane finally leveled off, Cole unbuckled and made his way to the cockpit. The ground below was a glittering expanse of white, punctuated by hills and forests.

Cole wasn't normally a backslapper, but he clapped Whitlock on the shoulder. He shouted in Whitlock's ear to be heard over the engines.

"That is some damn fine flying."

"I probably shouldn't tell you this, but I'm surprised that we managed to get off the ground."

"You're right, you shouldn't tell me that. What's our plan?"

"To put this crate down somewhere in Finland, as soon as I spot an airfield." He tapped a gauge. "The good news is that we've got plenty of fuel."

There were nervous grins all around, everybody feeling good. They were finally getting the hell out of the Soviet Union.

Their relief was short lived.

"Oh, hell," Whitlock said, cursing for the second time in a span of ten minutes.

"What is it?"

"It looks like we've got company."

Tracers from a burst of gunfire raked the sky.

"We're sitting ducks up here," Whitlock shouted, sounding near panic. He craned his neck to look out the windows. "What the hell should I do?"

Cole pieced it together. They had disabled the planes on the ground, but he knew that one Russian fighter had already been in the air. They had seen it flying over the area, searching for whoever had fled the firefight that had got the Russians' attention. Someone on the ground must have radioed that plane. Now it was on their tail.

There was another burst of fire. Tracers ripped the sky again, but no bullets hit the plane.

"I don't understand it," Whitlock said. "They could blow us out of the sky."

"That was like a shot across the bow. They want us to land. They probably think they've got themselves a planeload of spies. Capturing us alive ought to get somebody promoted."

Cole thought about that. It was an option. They could turn around and head back to the airfield like the Russians wanted. There could be some kind of diplomatic wrangle. They might get home someday before the end of the century.

But not Inna. Not Dmitri. It would be the Gulag for them. Or a bullet.

Cole didn't plan on spending the next few years digging holes on some Gulag work crew for another version of Barkov.

The plane rocked as it hit a pocket of turbulent air. He gripped Whitlock's shoulder, steadying them both. "Got any ideas?" he asked.

"No. We sure as hell can't outrun a fighter," Whitlock said.

"Can't you do some fancy flying?"

"In this beat up old bird? Cole, it's like a goose trying to out-maneuver a hawk. We don't have a prayer against that other plane. It's a lot faster than we are, and we aren't even armed."

"Gotta try something."

Whitlock did. He forced the stick down, moving the plane into a steep dive. Wind whistled at the wings, threatening to rip them off. The whole plane bucked and shook. The Russian fighter raced past overhead and swung around in an arc to come at them again. Effortlessly. It was easy enough to imagine the Russian pilot with his gunsights on them, finger on the trigger, waiting for a radio message with orders to put another shot across the bow or just let loose with a killing burst through the fuselage so that he could get home in time for borscht and vodka.

The fighter pilot fired. The flurry of rounds punched holes the size of golf balls through the skin. Inna screamed. Vaccaro had been pale before; now he was the grayish color of dishwater.

The Russian pilot had not finished them off— yet. He was just showing them that he meant business. He wanted them to land the plane. He was making it clear that they were going down— one way or another.

Cole decided that he'd had enough. He wasn't going to wait around for them all to be shot out of the sky. And he sure as hell wasn't going to become a prisoner. That just wasn't his style.

He got down close to Whitlock's ear. "Listen up, Whitlock. You hold this plane real steady. I'm gonna try something."

He left the cockpit and made his way back to the cargo area. He reached for his rifle. Vaccaro, Inna, and Dmitri eyed him with a look that seemed to ask, *What's that crazy hillbilly up to now?* It was too loud to even attempt an explanation. Each breath turned to icy vapor. The plane rocked as frigid winds buffeted the fuselage. The wind coming through the bullet holes whistled like an angry teapot.

Truth be told, he wasn't sure that this was going to work. It was only a half-baked plan, but he had to try something.

He was glad that he hadn't wasted any more bullets than necessary on Barkov. He was down to his last two shells.

The question was, would it be enough?

Cole made his way as far back in the cargo area as he could. There wasn't any sort of bulkhead at the rear of the plane, just a seam where the two sides of the plane joined. It reminded Cole of how the stern of an aluminum canoe was riveted together.

He took out his knife and punched a hole through the skin, then sawed the knife blade in a rough circle. He soon had a hole the size of a dinner plate, about ten inches off the floor of the plane. Looking out the hole at the ground far below made his head swim. Nothing out there but air. He tried not to think about it.

Behind them, riding in the cargo plane's slipstream, was the Russian fighter. Head on, the fighter resembled something predatory, like maybe an oncoming falcon. Meanwhile, Cole and the others were riding in the pigeon. The fighter had a single propeller. Above the propeller was a windshield. Behind the glass, Cole could make out the silhouette of the pilot. If the pilot even noticed what Cole was up to, he must have been left scratching his head.

He lay down and rested his elbows on the floor of the plane. It was not comfortable, but he ignored the feel of the metal jarring up through the bone. Never mind that it was goddamn cold with the arctic air sucking at the hole in the airplane. He put the muzzle through the hole he had cut. Through the scope, the enemy fighter sprang much closer. The pilot's head went from being the size of a dime to being the size of a baseball.

The crosshairs settled on the target, then bounced away. Cole struggled to hold the rifle steady. The plane hit another pocket of rough air and shook all around him like a dog that had just come out of the rain.

All he needed was a patch of smooth air. He let the crosshairs drift over the target, finger taking up pressure on the trigger. At just the precise moment, the pad of his finger would take up the last bit of tension in the trigger.

Wait, he told himself. *Steady.*

The thing about this kind of shooting was you didn't want to think about it too much, at least not with the front part of his mind. He let his mind go kind of fuzzy. The crosshairs drifted while the finger stayed on the trigger. The back part of his mind would know when everything was lined up. His eyeballs and his trigger finger were connected in that back part of his mind.

Behind him, the Russian pilot fired another burst. The guns flared and crackled. A few rounds hit the fuselage and Inna screamed again. Vaccaro swore. Fortunately, most of the burst passed overhead.

The Russian was sending a message that he wanted them to put the plane down. *Now.* All he had to do was keep his finger on the trigger for a couple seconds longer, and they would be blown out of the sky.

Through the scope, he could practically see the pilot lining up the next burst. His crosshairs drifted to the pilot's head, just visible through the windshield.

Around him, the cargo plane quit bouncing.

Cole fired.

He wasn't sure just what he expected to happen next, which was why it came as a surprise.

The pilot opened up on them, firing nonstop. The burst clawed at the cargo plane until Whitlock, up in the cockpit, veered to the right so suddenly that Cole lost his grip on the rifle and slammed painfully against the fuselage. He crawled back to the hole he had made and acquired the target again. He couldn't believe that he had missed. Had he somehow miscalculated about firing on a moving plane, from a moving plane?

He had one bullet left.

By now the Russian pilot had stopped firing. The fighter simply flew on in a perfectly straight path, not bothering to follow the cargo plane on its new course. Cole worked the bolt, got lined up for another shot. The fighter flew blindly past them, headed to nowhere. As it went by, Cole caught a glimpse of a starburst of broken glass where his bullet had punched into the cockpit.

He hadn't missed. He realized that the final burst must have been the death reflex of the pilot's finger on the trigger.

Then the plane started to drift even farther to the left, off course. Soon after that, the nose dipped. The fighter plane started a long, steady slide toward the earth below.

All around them, the blue sky now stretched empty and limitless.

And he still had one bullet chambered in the Springfield rifle, so the possibilities were endless.

EPILOGUE

Two hours later they were somewhere above Finland when Whitlock spotted a runway carved into a forest. They decided to land, considering that a plane with Soviet markings would not get a warm welcome if they flew clear to Helsinki. Having narrowly dodged a Soviet fighter plane, they didn't want to take any chances with the Finnish air force.

After all that they had been through, it was an inauspicious arrival. A couple of Finnish guys came out and watched in curiosity as the cargo plane bumped down on the unpaved runway. The

Finns there spoke a smattering of Russian, so Inna asked to use the telephone.

Then, they settled in to wait.

The two Finns weren't exactly friendly, but once it became clear that the cargo plane was carrying Americans, rather than Russians, they were greeted more warmly. They were given food, coffee, blankets, and vodka.

"More reindeer stew," Vaccaro said. "I think I'm starting to like it. Now old Vaska, he would have loved it."

They slept soundly, warm for the first time in days, and well fed. The next morning, three vehicles appeared on the road into the airfield. This late in year, the road was snow-covered, so the vehicles all had chains on their tires. The lead vehicle was a 1938 Volvo sedan, ugly but tough, perfect for Finland's backroads.

Whitlock, Inna, and Vaccaro went out to meet the new arrivals. Dmitri stayed indoors by the wood stove. Cole hung back, his rifle held at the ready.

Four or five men got out of the other two vehicles. All of them were armed with submachine guns. They set up a loose perimeter, facing back toward the road.

Only then did Senator Whitlock emerge from the passenger door of the Volvo. He stood staring for a moment at his grandson, then stepped forward and hugged him. "My God," he said. "It's good to have you back, Harry."

"It's good to be back." Although emaciated and exhausted, Harry Whitlock had never looked better. He introduced Inna. "I think you already know Vaccaro and Cole."

The senator nodded. "Indeed, I do. I owe them a debt of gratitude. What about the others?"

Whitlock shook his head. "They didn't make it."

They went inside. Harry explained about the welcome party, commanded by Major Dickey, that had met them at the border.

The senator looked troubled. "That's why I brought those guards along, although I'm not expecting trouble."

"Honaker said something about the government not wanting us to come home. He said it would only cause complications."

"About that," the senator said. "I've made ... an arrangement with the president."

"The president?"

"Yes. This thing goes right to the top, and you can't get any higher than the Oval Office. The official story will be that you were wounded and that the Russians nursed you back to health. You weren't detained. You were hospitalized."

"But that's a lie!"

The senator held up a hand to fend off further protests. "These are complicated times, Harry.

We don't need another shooting war on our hands. You're home, and that's what matters."

"Major Dickey tried to assassinate us."

"Dickey." The senator practically spat out the name. "There are some concerns that there may be a rogue faction working in league with the Soviets." The senator paused. "Communists through and through. It sounds like Honaker was one of them, and Dickey too. If Dickey is smart, he won't show his face again. That's also why the president needs you to keep quiet about all this. We just fought a war. We need to appear unified. Can you do that, Harry? Can you keep quiet?"

"What about the others? We weren't the only Americans being held as pawns by the Russians."

"We can't save the world all at once, Harry. The best that I could do was to save you. One war ends and another begins. I'm getting old. We need young people like you to fight this new war. And win it."

Harry didn't look happy, but he nodded. "That was quite a speech, you know. You ought to be in politics."

The senator turned to the others. "What I just said to Harry goes for everyone here. We live to fight another day. Right now, we're heading back to Germany." His gaze settled on Cole. "Better make sure you bring along your rifle."

-The End-

ABOUT THE AUTHOR

David Healey lives in Maryland, where he worked as a journalist for more than twenty years. He is a member of the International Thriller Writers and a contributing editor for *The Big Thrill* magazine. Visit him online at www.davidhealeyauthor.com

Printed in Great Britain
by Amazon